Scoring
MR. ROMEO

USA TODAY BESTSELLING AUTHOR
A.M. MADDEN
JOANNE SCHWEHM

Table of Contents

CHAPTER 1

Luca

CONSTRUCTION PAPER CUTOUTS OF LETTERS and numbers lined the hallway. An array of children's artwork fluttered from all the activity. I couldn't remember the last time I was in a grammar school, nor could I recall it being that loud. The noise level finally lowered to a respectable lull, or I'd lost partial hearing.

Kids scurried through the halls to catch their rides home. Some that were covered in paint bobbed and weaved around me as I made my way to Cassie's classroom. The kindergarten teacher, who became one of my best friends, didn't know I'd be showing up.

Tonight we were going out for drinks and dinner. Our original plan was to meet at the bar, but since my afternoon meetings were canceled, I thought I'd surprise her. Little did I know the surprise would be on me.

A woman's voice shouted, "Michael Dillon!"

Not sure where it came from, I focused behind me when a little person and I collided. I let out an "oof," looked down and saw a dark-haired, wide-eyed little boy with paint on his hands staring up at me. Behind him stood a stunning blonde holding a wad of paper towels in one hand while the other covered her gaping mouth.

"Oh my God!" Her shocked gaze focused on my groin. "I'm so sorry." She stretched the arm holding the paper towels toward me, and it took a few seconds to realize she was going right for my dick.

Taken aback by her beauty, it didn't click why she appeared so mortified. At that exact moment, Cassie came out of her classroom, noticed my crotch, and burst into hysterics. Following her line of sight, I saw one green and one blue handprint on the top of my thighs.

Son of a bitch.

Before I could stop the woman, she began rubbing the fabric of my slacks with vigor and determination. Each pass of her hand caused the fucker between my legs to get a bit more excited. Stunned, I took a step back before she could feel my growing hard-on. Having her hand on me, so close to *me*, while standing in a grammar school was wrong on so many levels.

The two perfect handprints became a big blob of green and blue, framing each side of my zipper. "It's fine," I said, trying to sound convincing.

Her eyes cut to the little boy's. To ensure his hands weren't anywhere near her, she took his wrists and raised them in the air. "Honey, tell him you're sorry." The child's penitent expression ebbed my irritation.

"Really, no worries." I glared at Cassie who now had her hand clamped over her mouth. I was sure laughing wasn't in the "Adulting 101" handbook.

The blonde studied the exchange between me and Cassie. "I'm so very sorry. Please send me the dry cleaning bill. Miss Brooks has my address." Her tone indicated this was the last thing she needed today.

"I'm sorry. Are you mad, mister?" Big brown eyes met mine.

I squatted to get eye level with the little boy. "No, I'm not mad. Just be careful and be sure to listen to your mom. Okay, buddy?" He nodded, and I ruffled his hair before standing.

"I'm mortified." His mom peered back at Cassie with pure humiliation. "Excuse us, I better go clean him up before he takes another casualty." She walked away, steering him by his shoulders as not to get paint on her. Michael twisted his head, smiled, and waved his green hand at us.

I continued to watch them walk down the hall until they turned the corner. The woman's ass was perfect. Granted, she was the little boy's mother and most likely another man's wife, but there was no denying she was one of the most gorgeous women I'd ever seen. Compared to the other females who have been in and out of my life, she had more of a girl next door kind of vibe. Cassie rolled her lips between her teeth, her eyes drifted to my crotch, and the giggles escaped.

I checked the damage done and sighed. "I guess I need to make a pit stop and change."

"Oh, I don't know. You could be starting a new trend." The persistent laughing caused her eyes to water. She dabbed at them with her fingertips, her gaze lingering on my lower region. "Sorry, that's so funny."

"Okay, okay. Enough. Stop staring." Drawing attention to it made the situation worse for me.

"Why are you here, anyway?"

"I thought I'd pick you up. Bad idea." My eyes swept the hall where some minions still loitered with adults trying to corral them all. Most of the kids held their multi-colored hands up in the air on their way to the bathroom. "This place is a clothing hazard."

"It's finger painting day. I can't leave yet." She motioned toward the little artists. "As you can see, I need to help clean up."

"Okay. I'll meet you at the bar then." I gestured down and asked, "Do you have an apron or something I can use to cover this up?"

At my question, the hysterics began all over again, and all I could do was release another sigh.

Collagen-infused lips, bleached blonde hair, and tits the size of cantaloupes about to spring free from her low-cut blouse were inching closer and closer to me. A pointy, red-polished fingernail dragged over my left shoulder, to my wrist and back up before resting on my muscle that she seemed to be enamored with.

"My name's Izzy, what's yours?" She batted her eyelashes that no doubt were as fake as the rest of her.

"Luca." I turned to the bartender and asked him to close out my tab. Granted, I only had one drink while waiting for Cassie, but now I just wanted out of there.

"Mmm…" she groaned and licked her lips. "You have an accent. It's so sexy. Spanish?"

"Italian."

"Even better." Her voice sounded like a combination of Minnie Mouse and a porn star. "Are you here alone, Luca the Italian?"

Before I could answer I felt a petite hand replace Izzy's and tighten around the underside of my arm. "Hi, sweetie."

Ever since cupid shot his arrow into my friends' asses, I'd been flying solo. Well, sort of solo. My wingman had turned into a wing*woman* and the position was held by Cassie. It was when our mutual best friends fell in love with each other that our bond grew stronger.

Cassie was cool, and I loved hanging out with her. In all honesty, she was a much better wingperson than Kyle or Jude had been. Those two would constantly try to one-up each other, leaving me to pick up the pieces. Sometimes, that would work in my favor and I'd end up with a sexy woman for the night. Other times, I'd just end up with mascara stains on my shirt.

Cassie and I were the only single ones left in our group, aside from Desiree, but she was married to her job. Being an attorney seemed to be a twenty-four-hour gig. Whereas, Cassie had the best hours on the planet.

The one part she could play that Jude and Kyle couldn't was my girlfriend. She was the best at it, too. Since we had been spending so much time together, she knew when I needed an assist, so to speak. Of course, I provided the same courtesy to her. Although on occasion, I had sent a few guys away that she actually liked. That didn't mean they were right for her. It was an ongoing argument, but I didn't give a rat's ass. She was my friend, and I knew a snake when I saw one. Just as she knew a gold-digger or user when she laid eyes on one.

"Hi, hon." I leaned over and gave Cassie a quick peck on the lips before grabbing my jacket.

As always, she smiled wide and then introduced herself to whomever she didn't feel was appropriate for me. "I'm Cassie, Luca's girlfriend. And you are?"

"Izzy." The bottle blonde raked her eyes over Cassie's body before raising the corner of her lip into a half snarl that rivaled Elvis's. "Luca, if you ever get bored, here's my number."

"Excuse me, Dizzy was it? He's taken." Cassie was sweet, but she could be fierce when the situation called for it—apparently, this was one of those times.

"It's Izzy, and I don't see a ring on his finger."

Cassie's jovial expression turned livid, and I knew I needed to deflect... and quick. Before she could respond, I said, "Let's go babe, we're late for our reservation." I placed my hand on the small of her back, all the while she visibly fumed. "Nice to meet you, Izzy."

Our original plan was to have a few drinks before dinner. Thanks to Izzy, dinner would happen sooner rather than later. We left the bar and headed down the block to Gemma's restaurant. The cool spring air did nothing to calm my spunky friend.

Cassie mumbled for most of the short walk, until she spit out, "Seriously? The nerve!"

"I love you Cass, but she could have kicked your ass."

"Bite your tongue, Benedetto. Just because I'm small doesn't mean I can't go toe to toe with someone like that. Plus, she'd probably deflate with one good smack."

"Okay, Rocky, calm down." I pulled open the wooden door and prayed there was an old man hosting tonight. My date's gloves were still on, and I didn't need a gorgeous woman provoking her.

"By the way, I saw Sabrina on the way out of school. She feels awful and insisted she pay for your dry cleaning."

"Sabrina?"

"Mikey's mom. The Picasso who marked you." When she lifted her hand to cover her mouth at the memory, I glared at her. "Sorry."

"Tell her that's not necessary." *Sabrina.* Gorgeous name and it suited her.

The scents of tomato, garlic, and basil wafted through the air as we walked to our table. Sounds of flatware tapping on the plates caused those dining to amplify their voices.

"Anyway, sorry I was late. It took longer to clean up all the paint." I helped Cassie off with her jacket and hung it on the back of her chair before pulling it out for her. "Thank you."

"Actually, you showed up right on time," I teased. "One more minute and who knows what part of me she would've dug those talons into." Taking the seat across from her, I lifted my hand in the air summoning the waitress. "Would you like a drink? You look like you could use one."

"One? I could use a couple."

When the waitress came over and eyed me up and down, I glimpsed at Cassie who shot daggers at the poor thing. She had no idea she had just poked the hornet's nest... *just what I was afraid of.*

"Hi, my name is Cindy. I'll be serving you tonight." She never took her eyes off of me. "What can I get you?"

"Honey?" I prodded Cassie to reply. She requested a cosmo, I asked for a glass of wine, and Cindy retreated toward the bar.

"Am I fucking invisible tonight?" Her outburst caused me to laugh. "It's not funny, Luca. This happens all the time. I'm always the *friend* and never considered anything more by pushy women."

"But you *are* my friend."

"That's beside the point. She doesn't know that. Even you calling me honey didn't deter her from ogling you."

"I didn't notice."

"Of course, you didn't. What about Izzy? What type of woman does that in front of someone's girlfriend? Fake or not. It's women like her that make me want to stay home."

"Please don't say that. You need to get out more."

Paying no mind to what I said, she continued to rant. "That woman at the bar was appalling. You're very lucky to have me. God forbid you went to bed with her. She could've crushed you with her boobs."

I chuckled. "If I would've been *crushed,* it would've been because of your tardiness. However, I wouldn't have slept with her. But, thank you for the rescue all the same."

With pride, she nodded. "You're welcome."

The storm must have passed, because she now appeared cool as a cucumber. Cassie perused her menu before placing it down it in front of her. "Everything here looks so good. I'm surprised you like Italian restaurants." She sipped the glass of water in front of her.

"I'm Italian," I stated the obvious.

"Exactly. I thought Italians didn't eat at Italian restaurants because the sauce is never as good as their grandmother's?" Before I could answer, the waitress returned with her cocktail, my glass of wine, and a wink.

Cassie lifted hers up and muttered, "Bitch," before downing half of it.

"Hard day at the office, dear?" I winked, and she scowled. "Sorry, but you seem wound up. Was finger painting stressful?"

"Funny." She shrugged a shoulder. "Parent teacher conferences happened this week. Sometimes I wonder why people chose to procreate when they clearly didn't want to invest in their child's education."

Her passion for teaching was evident in everything she did. Cassie was a genuine person, and that quality was hard to come by.

"Sorry, Cass. Maybe tonight will be your lucky night." I waggled my brows and she rolled her eyes.

A few minutes later, the waitress was back. Cassie ordered the chicken parmesan, and I the ravioli with pesto sauce. Of course, I gave Cassie a bit of a smirk. She was right, no sauce was better than my nonna's. The only place I'd trust red sauce was at my uncle's restaurant.

"So, have you talked to Kyle? He and Vanessa barely come up for air." She ripped the end off a small loaf of bread the waitress had set down in the center of the table and dipped it into olive oil.

"No, not since Wednesday at the gym. He was going to Los Angeles with Vanessa to do a product launch party at some boutique on Rodeo Drive."

Cassie let out a whistle. "Nice. She called me, but I was in a meeting and couldn't answer. It's still hard to believe she's in a relationship... with Kyle of all people. Funny, out of three of you I figured you'd be the one to settle down first."

"Me? Why would you think that?" I took a sip of my wine and waited for her reply. This *had* to be good. I knew that the women in our group considered me the romantic one, which I was, but that didn't make me want to put a ring on anyone's finger anytime soon.

"Because you're..."

"Perfect?" My laugh caused Cassie to toss her white linen napkin at me.

"You know what? Forget it. Your ego doesn't need a boost from me. I've seen you in action, Benedetto."

"No really, boost it. I can't wait to hear this." I crossed my arms and pressed my back against the wooden slats of the chair.

"Well, you're handsome, kind, and from what I can tell, don't treat women poorly. Your dark brown eyes are swoon-worthy, and hair that looks so soft that any female, and I'm sure even some males, would want to run their fingers through it. Not to mention, the scruff that frames your jawline... well, some women would call that *lickable*."

"*Lickable*, huh? So what you're saying is I'm hot?"

"You know what? Never mind." She rolled her eyes. "Anyway, before I forget, a few of my students are playing a soccer game in the park not far from my apartment tomorrow and I told them I'd go and watch. Would you like to come?"

"Ahh, my sport. I was born to dribble a ball with my feet. Did you know I was a first-string soccer player? I held the record for most goals in my high school."

"Of course, you did. So, is that a yes?"

"Yes. Text me the details, and I'll meet you at your place and we can head over together."

"You don't need to do that."

"Yes, I do."

Cassie's phone chimed. Snatching it out of her coat pocket, she shook her head. "It's a text from Brae. She wants to know how our dinner is going." Her brows furrowed in confusion before staring up at me. "How does she know we're together?"

"I told Jude I was hanging out with you tonight."

"Ugh. Please don't do that. It only encourages her. You know she's on a matchmaking kick and thinks we're perfect together. Let me just tell her everything is fine."

Scoring
MR. ROMEO

Another chime and Cassie flipped her phone in my direction. "See what you did?"

A gif of some couple kissing appeared on her screen. "Who are they?"

"Are you even serious right now? That's Rachel and Ross from *Friends*."

I leaned in closer. "Okay, so?"

"So... because they were friends and became lovers, that's why." Her thumbs started flying over her screen. "There, that should settle it."

Once again she spun her phone toward me. I couldn't help but laugh when I saw a picture of Ross with someone else. "Ross is one lucky guy!"

"Eww! That's his sister, Monica. Jeez, do you live under a rock? Anyway, that should calm her tits since we're more like brother and sister."

Cassie couldn't have been more accurate with her statement. We were like family. She understood me and I her. My thoughts immediately conjured up the one night things got out of hand between us.

At yet another one of Brae's parties, she got everyone together for Valentine's Day. We saw right through her plan, knowing damn well she wanted to see us as a twosome. In our own rebellion, we never showed up and lied that we each had a hot date.

That night, to avoid all things hearts and flowers, Cassie and I took shelter at my place eating pizza, drinking beer, and watching a *Fast and Furious* marathon. Our plan to repel romance backfired after the alcohol went to our heads. One thing led to another, and before we knew what happened we were lip-locked and stripping.

It took all of sixty seconds of teeth clanking, noses

11

banging, elbows knocking before we burst out laughing, thus killing the moment along with any chance of us ever being more than friends.

I lifted my wine glass and said, "To Vin Diesel."

Her eyes lit up the moment she realized what I referred to. Mimicking me, she lifted her glass and said, "To our lack of chemistry."

"Salute."

Chapter 2

Luca

I F IT HAD BEEN CLOUDY, the air would have been too nippy to withstand a soccer game in the park. But, with the sun shining bright it was enough to bring New Yorkers out in droves to enjoy the crisp spring day.

When I arrived at my friend's apartment, however, she was dressed for the Arctic. In contrast to my jeans and a lightweight sweater, Cassie's jeans were tucked in her UGG boots, and a ski jacket with a fur-lined hood was zipped up to her chin. How she wasn't dripping with sweat baffled me.

"Expecting snow?" I asked as we headed to the park a few blocks away from her place.

"It's cold out."

"Yes, almost sixty is frigid." My comment earned me a smack on the arm. I pointed to an older woman on a bench with an afghan on her legs. "Maybe you should ask grandma to share her blanket."

Cassie threw me a sideways smirk. "Shut it."

A few minutes later, she led us to where two sets of

kids occupied opposite sides of a small youth soccer field practicing their shots on goal. Most of the adults who were there congregated at the center, leaving significant distance between them and us.

Cassie spread out a gingham blanket and plopped down in the center of it leaving little room for me. Some of the other spectators looked her way, smiling warmly and even offering a wave. She reciprocated, but made no motion to go over and greet them.

Where most of the men were busy watching the kids and chatting amongst themselves, some of the females made an obvious perusal in my direction. "Um… should we go over and say hello?" I asked, feeling like I was eye candy.

"No." Her quick response caused me to laugh, and she followed suit. "Sorry, if I go over there, I'll be bombarded with questions and comments that belong at a parent teacher conference and not a soccer game."

"Gotcha."

Cassie pulled the zipper on her jacket down and started to fidget a bit. "Getting warm?"

"Nope, just comfortable." God forbid she would have to admit I was right and she was overdressed. I figured by the end of the first half her jacket would be completely off.

A whistle blew and I watched the chaos on the field and wondered who was in charge of this mess. Some of the kids didn't even have the right socks on to cover their shin guards. It was the *Bad News Bears* on a soccer field. When the referee, who couldn't have been older than sixteen, blew his whistle, I asked, "Which team is your class?"

"The blue."

"Whoever is coaching them sucks."

She flung her gaze to my face. "They're five."

"So? That's the perfect age to get them ready for the big leagues. They have no clue what they're doing." I pointed to one little boy who sat on the grass while plucking dandelions. "He should be running laps for that."

"Oh my God!"

"What?" Her gape made me shake my head. "Americans. Please don't tell me they don't keep score and everyone gets a trophy." The expression on her face was all the answer I needed. "Figures."

Coaches arranged their teams in proper formation, preparing for the opening whistle. As soon as that shrill sound echoed, all ten players converged around the ball, immediately forgetting their positions.

Where the ball went, so did every member of both teams. At one point, even the goalkeepers came out of their areas trying to get part of that ball. My anxiety was getting the best of me. Neither coach, neither referee, nor any of the parents were attempting to teach these kids how to properly play the game.

When a boy in yellow picked up the ball and threw it to one of his teammates, I couldn't hold back any longer. "Oh, come on Ref! He's handling the ball!"

"Luca!" Cassie scolded me before smiling apologetically at the adults who were all staring my way. "You can't yell at the refs."

"Why the hell not? They suck!" I motioned toward the idiots who should have been instructing those kids. "Look, they aren't doing anything. What good are they? The kids are all over the place. Do they even have assigned positions? Were they taught the basics? Did they

15 ⚽ 🌼

practice before this game?" Seriously, my skin itched just watching this debacle. Then one of the kids in yellow kicked the ball out of bounds, picked it up, and threw it in. Once again, I threw my hands in the air and shouted, "Hey, that's Blue's ball!"

"Shh. You're going to get us kicked out of here."

"From a public park?" Cassie's eyes narrowed at me in response.

"Fine. However, let me go on record and say these coaches are doing a disservice to the kids." I folded my arms, huffing and mumbling Italian curse words under my breath for most of the first half. Every muscle in my body tensed from trying to restrain myself. I wanted to show those yahoos how to properly coach a soccer game.

Cassie's lips quirked to the side. "Noted." She shrugged off her jacket and set it beside her. When I pointed to it sitting on the blanket she snarled, "What? You're making me all hot and bothered."

"Yeah, I get that a lot." I laughed and earned my arm another smack.

It was almost halftime, and right when the whistle blew, Cassie's phone buzzed. She bent to retrieve it from her bag just as a soccer ball came careening in our direction. "Heads up!"

On my command, she buried her head into my chest giving the ball open air to hit me square between the eyes. Jesus Christ! It hit me so hard, my vision blurred. Through my haze, I saw Cassie clamp a hand over her mouth as she laughed her ass off.

"That's going to leave a mark." She leaned in closer and added, "I think I can see the word Wilson on your forehead." Her laughing resumed, and she doubled over in hysterics at my expense, swiping at the tears falling from her eyes.

"Fuck," I muttered. An instant headache took hold, spreading from temple to temple. "It's not funny." Rubbing my forehead failed to alleviate any of the throbbing pain.

A frantic woman holding a little boy's hand came running toward us. I couldn't believe my eyes when I saw it was Sabrina and Mikey. "Oh my God! We're so sorry. Are you okay? Do you want me to find an ice pack? Doctor?" When she realized it was me again, she gasped. "Oh no. You must think we're targeting you."

"It's not a big deal." I rubbed my head again with a forced smile.

"He'll be fine, Sabrina." Cassie chuckled through her response. "Hi, Mikey. That was a great kick."

Mikey hid behind his mom, peering at me with the same terrified expression as yesterday. His bottom lip trembled, prompting me to kneel, bringing us eye level. "Hey buddy, don't worry. I'm fine. Miss Brooks is right, you have an awesome kick."

A small smile played on his lips, otherwise he didn't acknowledge me. "Sweetie, say thank you." Sabrina mimicked my stance, squatting beside him. With her attention on Mikey, I took a moment to admire her. The woman was stunning.

Mother and son's physical traits couldn't be any more different, and the only thing they shared was a smattering of freckles over the bridge of their noses. Where Mikey was dark haired with big brown eyes, Sabrina was blonde with hazel eyes. The multi-colored flecks in them, combined with the definition of her cheekbones, her upturned nose, and full lips made her gorgeous.

"Thank you," Mikey said quietly. "And I'm really

sorry I hit you… and ruined your pants."

I turned my focus back to Mikey and shook my head at his apology. "Don't be sorry. They're just pants. And that kick… awesome. If I was the *net*, you would've scored a goal with that shot." He released a small giggle and shrugged.

"Mikey." His eyes focused on Cassie before she added, "Mr. Benedetto played soccer when he was younger."

"You can call me, Luca," I said, offering him my hand. With a smile he grabbed onto mine, and shook it.

"You did?"

"Yes. I grew up in Italy and played the game most of my life. I almost went pro, but even I didn't kick the ball that well when I was five. If you'd like, I can help you practice. I think you can be even better than I was."

"Really?" he asked, excitement altering his otherwise shy expression.

I winked at Sabrina, quickly adding, "If that's okay with your mom." As I did to her son, I offered my hand again with a smile. "It's great to meet you."

Cassie blurted out, "I'm so sorry, where are my manners? Sabrina, this is my friend, Luca Benedetto. Luca, Sabrina Callahan, Mikey's mom."

"Same here." A genuine returning smile spread across her face. Our eyes held before she broke the connection and pulled her hand from mine. "Thank you for the offer. Mikey loves this sport, but we wouldn't want to impose."

"No imposition… that *is* if you and his dad don't mind."

"I don't have a dad anymore," Mikey interrupted. A whistle blew, taking his attention back to the field. "Mom, I have to go." He took a few steps and stopped.

"Luca, will you watch the rest of my game?"

"Of course, buddy. I'll be right here."

An adorable smile lit up his face before he hustled back onto the field. And just like that, one little boy managed to steal my heart in an instant.

Chapter 3

Sabrina

AFTER MIKEY LEFT, LUCA AND I stood at the exact same time. While fidgeting nervously with the hem of my jacket, he offered Cassie a hand to help her stand as well. The first time I saw him I didn't have the time to appreciate his stature. At his full height he towered over Cassie, who was a few inches shorter than me.

When Mikey told Luca he didn't have a dad anymore, my heart clenched. I was so used to seeing pity in the eyes of those around us, but Luca was different. He didn't change his demeanor around my son. Instead, he watched my smiling little boy hustle out onto the field.

Becky, a friend of mine who had been eying Luca since she saw him from across the field, was right, the man was very handsome. With just the right amount of scruff, hair as dark as ink, and eyes as warm as melted chocolate, I imagined he had women swooning at every turn.

My eyes raked over him from head to toe, and when they landed on his face, I saw him staring back. "I hope I didn't overstep by offering Mikey my help." The tenor of his voice, mixed with the hint of a sexy accent, had me losing my train of thought. "Sabrina?" he prompted.

Oh hell. The way he rolled the R in my name rendered me stupid. So much so, I continued to stare as he raised his brows with an amused smile.

"Pardon?" I asked, feeling like an idiot.

"The practice. I hope mentioning it to Mikey was okay. I guess I should've asked you first."

"Oh, yes… I mean no, that was absolutely fine. As long as you're not some weirdo," I said with an awkward chuckle.

Waiting for reassurance from Cassie, instead she deadpanned, "He's an absolute wacko."

"Um…"

"Don't listen to her." He shot her a livid expression. "She hasn't taken her meds today."

"I'm just kidding. Luca's a wonderful guy and will get along great with Mikey since their maturity level isn't much different."

"Nice. Thank you for that," Luca fired back.

It was my turn to laugh at their adorable banter until Cassie batted her eyes at him and said, "You know I love you." Luca threw his arm around Cassie's shoulder and kissed the top of her head. My eyes darted between them taking in the scene in front of me. It was obvious they had a very strong bond, one I admired.

Luca turned and met my gaze. His arm still hung around Cassie's shoulders when he repeated, "Really, I meant it. I'd love to teach him some of my old tricks."

"Okay, great. Then we accept your offer. Um… I better get back to my friend. Enjoy the rest of the game." I walked away mid their goodbyes and hurried back to my chair.

The moment my ass hit the canvas, Becky blurted out, "Well, who is he?" She was also a single mom, except where I was more reticent, she lacked a filter. Her son, Jared, and Mikey were good friends and had much in common after Becky and her husband divorced last year. She liked to tell people it was due to *irreconcilable differences* with an asshole. Becky kept her eyes pinned on Luca, she licked her lips and sighed. "He's gorgeous."

"That's Miss Brooks' boyfriend. The poor guy got it good from Mikey. Yesterday he was at the school and Mikey barreled into him with his hands covered in paint, and… well… let's say he left his imprints framing Luca's manhood in an embarrassing way. Khaki pants, blue and green paint." I cringed as hard at the memory as I had when it happened.

"Wait—I just got a visual. Let me enjoy this."

"Shut up. It was mortifying. And for Mikey's second attack, today Luca got a ball square between the eyes."

"I'd like his balls square between my—"

"Becky!" I scanned the area, grateful that none of the parents appeared to have heard her.

"What?"

"That's your son's teacher's boyfriend."

"You know that for a fact?" She swung her gaze their way and tsk'd. "They're not touching. Maybe they're just friends."

I followed her eye line. Luca watched the game intently while Cassie fiddled with her phone. "Doubtful, she said she loved him."

"So? Love is bullshit, I should know." Luca turned his head in our direction, and if there was any doubt we were talking about him Becky's flirty little wave squashed it.

"Damn, that man is hot as fuck. My God, look at that face."

"Stop staring at him. It doesn't matter, he's taken. And stop distracting me, we're here to watch our kids play," I snipped, turning my attention back to the game.

"I'd rather watch him," Becky muttered, and I really couldn't blame her.

By closing my eyes, I could still picture his face along with his body perfectly. Not to mention, his deep voice with an accent that made everything he said sound romantic. The visual caused me to sigh, not going unnoticed by Becky. Ignoring her, I squinted and pretended to be concentrating on the field.

Crap, it'd been a long time since a man had stolen my focus.

The rest of the game went much like the first half: no goals, no progress made, and no sense of order. When the final whistle blew, like rockets, both teams shot over to the mom in charge of their snacks.

Noticing the way Cassie and Luca were together, an irrational jealousy took hold as I watched them laughing in a carefree manner. I couldn't remember the last time I laughed like that, and then my jealousy turned to sadness.

"Mom, can you hold these?" Mikey asked, with a juice box and a small package of Oreos in hand. "Tommy's mom brought the good stuff today."

"Sure, honey." He dropped *the good stuff* in my lap and sprinted toward Luca without another word.

"Mikey!" I called after him, not deterring him in the slightest. Once he got there, he flailed his arms in full-out animation as Luca squatted listening, laughing, and smiling. For some unknown reason, the easy connection between them warmed my heart.

"Becky, I gotta go. Thanks for the loan of the chair," I said as I grabbed my bag off the back of it. "I'll call you," I added before trotting over to them. Feeling like I was intruding on their reunion, I stepped right up to my son. "Michael Dillon Callahan, you know the rules. You don't run away without telling me where you're going and asking if it's okay."

"Sorry, Mommy. I just really, really, wanted to tell Luca that my coach said I played good today." My sweet boy... *starving for male attention.*

"You did play well," Luca agreed. "But your mom's right, you shouldn't run away from her like that."

"Sorry," he repeated, not looking the least bit sorry.

We moved into a wonderful community this past July. So many of the fathers tried to fill the void in Mikey's life, but never had my son warmed up to any of them like he already seemed to with Luca.

"Can I eat these now?" He snatched the cookies from my hand. "Luca, you want a cookie?"

I *snatched* them back before his tiny fingers could tear into them. "You haven't had lunch yet. So, just one."

"Aw, man. Ooh, can Luca eat lunch with us?" He focused on Cassie. "Miss Brooks, you can come too, if you want. Mom makes mac and cheese for me on game day. I can show you my new hermit crab! He never comes out of his shell. Mom thinks he's dead, but I bet he'll come out for you, Luca!"

Luca chuckled while I stood dumbfounded at my son's audacity. "Mikey, I'm sure Miss Brooks and Luca already have plans."

Mikey's five-year-old lack of a filter blurted out, "Do you?"

"We do." Luca met my gaze before admitting, "We're

going to grab pizza."

"I love pizza!" *Oh Lord.* "Mom, can we go too? Puh-leeeze?" He pressed his palms together in mock prayer.

"Mikey…" I stopped and offered Luca an apologetic smile.

His response was a genuine smile before he said, "We'd love to have you *both* join us."

Cassie nodded at Luca with a gleam in her eye. "Yes, Sabrina, why don't you join us."

"Mom? Can we?"

Between Mikey's pleading eyes, Cassie's nod, and Luca waiting for my answer, how could I say no? "Fine. But first you're coming to the bathroom with me so we can get you cleaned up and changed out of your stinky uniform."

"Yes!" His little arm shot up in triumph and without warning, he catapulted toward Luca who caught him mid-air.

All I could do was watch in shock. Cassie met my surprised expression with one of her own. She patted my arm and without words conveyed just what she was thinking. This would be good for my son, and I should indulge him.

Of course, I would, yet, I wondered what had gotten into him? He never acted that way, and the only explanation was a tall Italian man named Luca.

A young man at the counter peered up when we walked in. After confirming there were just four in our party, he showed us to a nice, red and white cloth covered table. Luca pulled out Cassie's chair and then mine, which Mikey decided to sit on. Luca laughed and proceeded to pull out the chair next to my son.

"Can Luca sit next to me, Mom? You can sit over there next to Miss Brooks." His little finger pointed to the empty seat next to Cassie.

Luca turned toward me for guidance, something he'd done more than once since meeting us. "Honey, I'm sure Luca wants to sit next to Miss Brooks."

My not-so-shy son piped in, "Do you?" His pleading eyes locked on Luca.

Cassie interjected, "He can sit next to you. Boys have cooties."

Luca gasped and placed his hand over his heart. "That's a lie, right Mikey?"

"Yeah. Girls are the ones with cooties," he said, bouncing in his seat. "Okay, Mom. You sit over there."

Once again Luca pulled out my chair. "Third time's a charm?" His deep voice was laced with humor. *God, he smelled good.*

"Looks that way, thank you."

The patrons' conversations in the restaurant competed with the Italian music playing over the speakers. Most of the tables were occupied, and a few men behind the counter worked furiously at keeping up with demand. An older gentleman tossed his dough in the air with finesse, capturing my son's attention.

Mikey clutched his stomach as if he hadn't eaten in weeks. "I'm so hungry. Mom, can I have my own cheese pizza?"

"I think an entire pizza would be a lot for you."

"Aw, man. Can I have half a pizza?"

"Let's take one slice at a time, okay?"

"Kay," he said with a pout.

We perused the menu. When the waitress came over, Cassie and I ordered a veggie pizza to share. At the mention of vegetables, my adorable son opened his mouth, stuck his pointer finger in it, and began to gag. "Luca, do you like vegetables?"

"I do, but not on pizza." Luca agreed with a grimace.

"See, Mom. It's gross."

I ordered a slice of plain cheese pizza for Mikey before Luca ordered a large meat lovers with extra sausage, and then thanked her in Italian.

"That sounds so good. Doesn't it, Mommy?"

Who was this child sitting across from me? The only meat he ate was in the form of a nugget, deep fried and breaded. Rather than get into that discussion, I nodded. "Yummy."

Before the waitress stepped away, she placed some crayons on the table for Mikey to color his placemat that served as a coloring book.

"What did you say to that lady?" my son asked Luca.

"I thanked her."

"Want to color with me?" He grabbed the blue one, his favorite color, and handed it to Luca.

Without hesitation, Luca took the crayon and started coloring with my son.

My heart squeezed with emotion at something so simple, yet it spoke volumes. Not only on what type of person he was, but the fact my son took an immediate liking to him. There was nothing I loved more than seeing him happy, though at the same time his trusting manner scared me.

"Magnifico." Mikey looked up confused and Luca

translated, "Magnificent."

"Your accent is faint." I said out loud what I was thinking.

"Thanks to my dialect coach… and Yale." His eyes lifted to mine and held. "It comes out every now and again."

"He also slips into Italian whenever he's emotional." When the hand he used to color stopped moving, Cassie leaned closer to inspect their work across the table. "Mikey, you better teach Luca how to color. He has trouble staying inside the lines."

Luca furrowed his brow and he ignored Cassie's jibe. His tongue poked out from the corner of his mouth, just like my son did when he concentrated.

Mikey regarded his teacher. "Miss Brooks, he's doing a great job."

"Yeah, Miss Brooks. I'm doing a great job." Luca and Mikey shared a smile and continued with their artwork.

Before long, our meals were delivered. At the exact same time, Cassie and I pulled out a small bottle of hand sanitizer. "Hands please," we said in unison. Both Luca and Mikey looked at each other before complying. Without hesitation, Cassie squeezed a drop on each of Mikey's palms.

In a daze, I focused on Luca's strong, big, masculine hands. Luca cleared his throat, waiting expectantly. "Oh, sorry." Rather than squirting the liquid myself, I handed him the bottle. *Jesus, Sabrina, get a grip already.*

Once we were all sanitized, Cassie dished out a slice of veggie pizza for her and one for me. "Mikey, do you want to try some?" I asked holding my plate up.

His little nose scrunched up and he shook his head. "No way." I tilted my head until he amended, "I mean, no thank you," which earned him a smile.

He picked up his slice, but he appeared to be in awe of the pie in front of Luca. "Would you like a piece, buddy?"

"Yes, please! It looks soooo good."

Luca served Mikey, engaging him in a deep in conversation about the history of pizza. I couldn't help the smile on my lips at the way their conversation bounced from food to Italy to soccer and back to food in a matter of five minutes.

While the guys were oblivious to our company, I leaned closer and whispered to Cassie, "My son has never eaten a piece of sausage in his life. Not to mention pepperoni."

"I know… even when we have a pizza party in class he has plain cheese. Luca has a way about him, though."

"You're a lucky lady. He seems like a great guy."

I was confused by her instant moan. "We aren't dating."

Assuming we still couldn't be heard over their chatter, I misread her groan and said, "I'm sorry. Maybe with time…"

She placed a hand on my arm to stop me. "No, no, we're just really good friends. He's like a brother to me."

At her last statement, Luca's eyes met mine, and he smiled. My stomach flipped at the possibility he had heard everything we said. "Oh… um… that's great." Nothing else came to mind as an acceptable response. Except for maybe—yay?

As quickly as the thought popped into my mind that he was single, it flew right out. I had no business worrying about Luca's relationship status, or mine for that matter. That little boy across the table was all I needed to worry about. After the year we had, and all the years stretched ahead of us, anything that had to do with me and my love life would have to wait.

My priority was Mikey.

Chapter 4

Luca

MOST WEREN'T FANS OF MONDAY mornings, I however, loved them. It made for a perfect segue from having too much time on my hands, especially now that my two friends were attached. Throwing myself into my work helped clear many of the cobwebs that could plague my mind, and most of them had to do with how different everything became after Jude's wedding.

I talked a good game when it came to my friends, and all that went with being an eligible bachelor in New York City. Truth be told, I was envious of what they found, and often wondered if that kind of connection was in the cards for me.

There shouldn't have been any reason for me to feel love wasn't something I'd someday find. My parents have been married for many years, as have my grandparents. Divorce wasn't a word we Benedettos were familiar with, so the obvious belief that I'd also have a wife and kids in my life wasn't farfetched. Yet, I couldn't relate to what my two best friends were lucky enough to find.

I, Luca Benedetto, had never been in love.

Being in the states for twelve years, one would think at one point someone would have piqued my interest. Whether at school or even while living in the city, all the women I'd encountered should have increased my odds. Sabrina was the first woman who intrigued me.

My mother still claimed my soul mate resided in Italy, and not America. I had hoped by now my parents would have moved on from their argument for me to move back to Italy. Just as recent as my weekly phone call to them yesterday, my mother carried on by laying on the guilt that they weren't getting any younger, and she'd like to see her sons settle down before she died.

Luca, there's a lovely young lady that just moved to Milan. I met her at mass. You should come home and meet her. She's very nice.

Nice, her keyword for she wouldn't win the *Miss Italy* title anytime soon. My mother went on and on, in Italian, telling me more about this mystery woman.

I listened diligently and then replied, *No, thank you.*

I wasn't the only one they pressured. My older brother, Dante, got the brunt of our mother's complaining. He was the first to come to America, and I followed two years later. Our baby sister, Gianna, stayed behind in Milan and was coddled and spoiled.

A knock on my door forced my attention to Jude, who stood holding an envelope while grinning. "Got a minute?"

"For you, I have two. Come in."

He walked to the chair facing my desk and sat, making himself comfortable. "Good weekend?"

"Uneventful," I said with a shrug. "How was yours?" The salacious grin on his face spoke volumes. "I don't want to know," I interjected, preventing whatever was about to fly out of his mouth. Pointing to the envelope he held, I raised a brow and asked, "What's that?"

"Well, it's the reason I'm here. We both know you don't like to be disturbed on a Monday morning, but this is important."

My thoughts immediately flew to Waldon, the prick client that had it in for me since Jude disappeared last year on that stupid social experiment where he met Brae. Because of Kyle's prank, Jude was gone for six weeks, leaving me to run this place as he frolicked in the Caribbean while falling in love.

"If that asshole is still griping about his portfolio not performing, tell him I have proof of otherwise. I made that jackass almost nine million in the last year alone."

A sideways smirk spread over Jude's face. "Actually, it was nine and a half, but it's not about Waldon. He won't be bothering you anymore."

Part of me felt a thrill that maybe he took his complaining rich ass elsewhere, but then in spite of all the heartburn he gave me, I'd be losing a nice size bonus every year. Optimism turned to anger at that possibility, and I scraped a frustrated hand through my hair ready to release a pent-up rant. "Fuck that shit. Wherever he moved to, I can guarantee that it wasn't me who..."

"Benedetto, calm down." Jude opened the flap of the envelope, removing the contents inside. "He didn't leave Soren Enterprises. What I meant was he is no longer your problem, but is now that of my executive director's."

My mouth gaped while I blinked a few times trying to understand what the fuck was happening. "I'm the executive director. Am I being transferred or something? If so, I'd prefer to go to L.A., and not Chicago."

"No, not transferred but promoted." Jude sat

watching my expression, waiting for me to process what he had said. After a few long moments passed and my mouth still hadn't uttered a word, he laughed and handed me the paper he held. "Congratulations, I am promoting you to executive vice president of Soren Enterprises." I took the paper with a shaky hand, and scanned it quickly, but couldn't focus on any specifics other than my new title.

"I don't know what to say." My eyes cut to Jude's face as he smiled over how flustered I appeared to be.

"Thank you would be a great start."

"Thank you. But you know what I mean. I wasn't expecting this. I just got promoted not more than a year ago."

"Right, and you also played the role of president while I was gone those six weeks, of which were very profitable regardless of my absence. That is just one of the reasons I want to do this. The other, you always have my back, and that means a lot. Really, I should be thanking you."

I studied the paper again, this time paying attention to the salary increase, and stock options that now came with my new title. Other benefits such as travel amenities and vacation time were also laid out in full detail. "Wow, this is amazing, second in command, huh? Are you planning to disappear again?"

"No, but now I can without feeling guilty. I want to surprise Brae with a trip to Hawaii for her birthday in June, and like the last time I won't be taking any calls or communicating with the outside world." At my surprised expression, he added, "Except you."

"Gotcha. So, you're giving me two months to get comfortable wearing your shoes?"

"Pretty much."

I shook my head, and he laughed. "You know I'm kidding. This company is what it is today because I had you by my side. Since day one, you've had the same knack I had, and I trust you implicitly."

"Thank you." I stood and offered my hand for him to shake. "I'll do you proud, my brother."

"You always do," Jude said, holding our handshake for a few more seconds. "Just promise me one thing."

"Anything."

He stood and shoved his hands in his pockets. "When Brae calls you later, please remember she is the love of my life and you shouldn't hold her antics against her. She means well. Otherwise, I'll have to hurt you, and a worker's comp claim isn't something I want to file."

"Noted," I said, dreading why the hell Mrs. Soren was going to call me later. Just before Jude stepped through the door, I added, "Hey, a hint at least?"

"Her name begins with a C, and she'll be joining us for dinner tonight to celebrate." With that, he walked out leaving me wanting to call Cassie to warn her.

Cassie and I arrived at the Sorens' apartment building at the same time. I knew Brae would be elated thinking we came together. The woman was relentless in her quest to see us as a couple and was lucky we both loved her.

I knocked on their door and when Jude opened it and saw us standing there, he gave me a cocky smirk. "Please, not you too." I handed him the bottle of wine I brought and stepped aside for Cassie to walk in first. "Our simultaneous arrival is a coincidence."

"Hey, Jude. How are you?" Cassie rolled up and gave

him a kiss on the cheek before walking in to hug Brae, who was wiping her hand on a small towel.

"Hi!" If Brae was a bottle of champagne her bubbly personality would cause the cork to explode with force. After she released Cassie, she threw her arms around me and whispered in my ear. "You both are so adorable. I told you." I let out a sigh and shook my head just as a ding rang out from the kitchen. She released me and said, "That would be dinner. I'll be back. Have a seat at the table."

Cassie and I sat on one side, leaving room for the Sorens on the other.

"Brae cooked?" The uncertain tone in Cassie's voice made me laugh.

Jude shook his head. "No, just reheating. You know she's lucky if she doesn't burn peanut butter and jelly sandwiches."

I poured myself and Cassie a glass of water from the pitcher on the table, shaking my head at my friend who clearly had lost his mind. "You don't cook peanut butter and jelly sandwiches."

He nodded. "I know."

"Hey, I heard that." Brae appeared with a tray of four plates. Jude being the kind husband stood and took it from her, so she could hand us each our dinner.

"Is Bobby Flay in your kitchen?" I bobbed my head to the left and right trying to spot the chef.

"No," she sat down and placed a napkin on her lap. "But this Chicken French, from Le Gourmet Kitchen around the corner, is to die for. I hope you like it."

Jude chuckled. "Aside from the dry cleaners, that restaurant is my biggest weekly expense." Brae snarled at him, but his peck on her cheek placated her. He poured us all a glass of wine and held his glass in the air. "Thank you both for coming here to celebrate the promotion of my new Executive Vice President. Congratulations, Luca."

We all gently tapped our glasses together. When I turned toward Cassie, she beamed, "Congratulations. I didn't know you got a promotion today, that's fantastic!"

I was a bit confused because even though I never had the chance to call her, I figured when Brae invited her she would have told her. "Why did you think you were coming to dinner?"

She cut her eyes to Brae who gawked at us as though she just discovered electricity. "Oh, no way. I know what you're thinking, missy, and we are going to nip this in the bud right now." Jude set his fork down and gave Cassie warning eyes. "Nope, you can get that look off your face, Jude. Your wife is one of my best friends, but enough is enough."

"But, Cass," Brae smiled sweetly at her. "You two are so cute together, why not?"

My best move was to keep my mouth shut and keep eating. Cassie, however, didn't feel the same way. "Because, although Luca is a wonderful man…"

I leaned over. "Thank you."

"You're welcome." She refocused on Brae, lifting a brow to emphasize her point. "He *is not* the man for me. We are friends that's it—if you must know, we did make-out once and there weren't any sparks. Remember when Jude kissed you on stage when you first met and your body got all fluttery?"

"You got fluttery?" Pride shone all over Jude's face.

Brae rolled her eyes at her husband while Cassie continued, "Well, when I kissed Luca I didn't feel anything remotely close to a flutter."

"Gee, thanks."

Jude let out a laugh, and now Cassie was the one rolling her eyes. "Oh, shut it. And why aren't you agreeing with me?"

I cleared my throat, "Everything she said is true. There wasn't an *a-ha moment* or anything remotely close to it. We're just good friends, that's it."

"Brae." Cassie had a tenderness to her voice that I imagined she perfected in her classroom. "It was like kissing my brother or a cousin. Not that I go around getting naked and kissing my family, but do you understand?"

"Wait—" Brae thrusted her hand palm up. "You guys were naked?"

Cassie brushed it off. "That's not the point. The point is, not everyone needs or should be a couple."

"I know. I just want all my friends happy, that's all."

Jude kissed his wife on the cheek. "Sparky, they *are* happy. Let it go." She nodded and the conversation was dropped.

Dinner was fantastic, and we all agreed to hang out at our favorite bar, Dispatch, on Friday night. Cassie and I shared a cab home, and when we arrived at her apartment building, I walked her to the door to make sure she got in safely before heading to my place.

"I'll talk to you soon, be sure to lock the door when you get into your apartment."

She kissed my cheek, "Yes, sir. Text me when you get home so I know you're safe."

"Yes, ma'am."

Cassie was a great woman, and it was a shame we

didn't have that fluttery feeling, as she called it, because she'd make the perfect girlfriend. But, she was turning into one of my best friends… and to me that was better.

Chapter 5

Luca

FRIDAY COULDN'T COME SOON ENOUGH. Thanks to my new job title, my workload was a bit heavier than normal. Mostly due to all the meetings I needed to attend. Jude handled the majority on his own, and even though I walked six weeks in his shoes when he was away, it was different now. I was the one in charge of several projects.

It was a good thing we were going out tonight because I needed to relax. Kyle and Vanessa were back in town from California. I missed my pal, and it had been way too long since we hung out.

Before going to the bar, I went home to change out of my suit and tie and into a pair of jeans and T-shirt. I grabbed my leather jacket and hopped into my car rather than taking a cab. Even though traffic was a bitch, and horns were blaring, this was my quiet time.

Dispatch started offering valet parking on Friday and Saturday nights, for which I was thankful. When the young man greeted me at the curb with a massive grin on his face, I handed him the key and a fifty dollar bill. "Park her somewhere nice and there's another one of these in it for you later." He nodded and slowly pulled away. I watched until my black car turned the corner and the taillights were out of sight.

Kyle had sent me a text letting me know they had a table in the back of the bar and left of the dancefloor. The place was packed with the usual Friday crowd. Couples, singles, and business people winding down filled the room. I waved to a few familiar faces and headed toward my friends.

"There he is." Kyle got up and gave me a bro-hug. "It's good to see you."

I kissed the girls on the cheek European style, shook Jude's hand, and took a seat next to Cassie. "Where's Desiree?"

"Right here. Sorry, I'm late. I had a meeting that ran over." A waiter came by and took our drink orders. "So, how is everyone?" Desiree focused on Vanessa, "You look gorgeous. You're so tan."

Vanessa let out a sigh, "I absolutely love California. Even though we were there for work, we were able to enjoy the sun."

"My girl is a sun whore." Kyle laughed. "I've created a west coast monster."

Vanessa shrugged. "It's true. Even though it's just California, experiencing life out there makes me feel worldlier."

"Speaking of," Desiree chimed in. "I have an announcement to make."

"What's up, Des? Is everything okay?" Cassie asked with concern in her voice.

"Yes, actually, it's more than okay. I got a promotion." All three of the girls squealed. "I know! I'm so excited."

I threw my arm around her shoulders. "That's great,

congratulations."

"Thank you, and I hear congrats are in order for you as well." The waiter dropped off our drinks, and I clinked my glass to Desiree's. "So, what is the promotion?"

All eyes focused on Desiree waiting for her to tell us details. "The firm acquired a new client and I've been assigned as his counsel... in London."

Did she say London? When I dared to glance at the other ladies, they all stared at her with wide teary eyes.

"London?" Brae's voice cracked. "You're moving to England?"

"Not permanently, but yes. I'm not sure how long I'll be there, but this lines me up to become partner. Believe me, I wish I could have talked it over with all of you, but time was of the essence and I couldn't pass it up."

"That's great, Des, I'm happy for you." Again, I lifted my glass to tap hers. Cassie glared at me from the corner of her eye. "What?"

"She's leaving." Cassie blinked her eyes a few times. "I'm happy for you, Des. I really am, but we're going to miss you."

Vanessa's lips curled down, "When do you leave? What about your apartment here?"

"I leave next week. My company is subletting my place because everything is happening quickly. The time difference isn't that bad, and we can FaceTime. Not to mention our group chats that Brae loves." Everyone at the table groaned. We all hated that damn app.

"Nessa and I will be out to visit you in the fall." Kyle focused on Vanessa's face with a smile. "It was going to be a surprise, but I have a trade show to go to in London and planned on scratching off another location on my girl's bucket list."

"Really?" she part squealed, part yelled. His nod caused her to grab his face to initiate a very inappropriate kiss for a public place.

"Um…" While the two kept making out, Jude raised his glass. "Congratulations. This calls for champagne, right Sparky?" Brae wiped a few tears and nodded.

"I'll go get it." I got up to go to the bar and Cassie hopped up and followed me.

"I'll help you."

The two of us stood at the bar, ordered champagne and seven glasses. "Are you okay, Cass?"

She shrugged her shoulder, "I guess. Des was my only single friend left."

"Um…"

"You know what I mean."

I did. I knew exactly what she meant since both of my friends were now attached and busy with their significant others. "You'll always have me. If you don't mind watching sports and action movies."

Out of the corner of my eye, I spotted her—Sabrina. She was laughing with another woman who I recognized from the park. Cassie was talking, but I wasn't paying attention, not until I heard, "So, all you'll need to do is ride a unicorn down Fifth Avenue while wearing a feather boa."

"What?"

Cassie let out a laugh. "Jeez, where did you go?" She followed my line of sight to see what, or in my case, who distracted me. "Ahh, Sabrina. I wondered why you didn't ask me about her yesterday."

"I'll ask now. What's her story? Where's Mikey's dad?"

The sadness on Cassie's face wasn't something I'd seen before. "He passed away last year."

I whispered, "Shit." My first thought was divorce. Dealing with a divorcée was much different than a widow. At least when a couple divorced, the bond was broken by one or both of them. A death, the bond was still there even if the other person physically wasn't.

"Why don't you go talk to her?"

The bartender set our order on the bar. "Maybe later, we need to get back to our friends."

While my eyes were still trained on Sabrina, she turned my way catching my stare. A small smile tugged at her lips. Her friend on the other hand, arched her back and stuck her chest out causing Sabrina to blush. I nodded once in acknowledgment before taking the tray of glasses off the bar.

Back at the table, the girls were huddled together while Kyle and Jude stared at them. Cassie let out a sigh before placing the bottle down.

After I set the tray down, I began to fill the glasses with bubbly. Since the girls were still in deep conversation over Desiree's move, a rap of my knuckles on the table got their attention. Jude and Kyle passed each of the ladies a glass. "A toast." Before I could continue, Cassie took over.

"To you." She angled her body toward Desiree. "Even though we may not seem very happy, we are thrilled. There is nothing we want more than for you to… " She stopped when a small sniffle turned into a full-blown wail.

Brae took over, adding, "Follow your dreams?" Cassie wiped her face with the back of her hand and nodded. With our glasses still suspended in the air, Brae continued. "Let's make sure we set a schedule to speak often." She paused, and Jude brought the champagne to his lips thinking his wife was done. "Jude!" Brae scolded him. "I'm not finished."

"Sorry, Sparky."

With a huff, she continued. "Anyway. Yoga won't be the same, nor will our brunches. We're going to miss you so...so... so... " She stopped and dragged in a deep breath with a sob. These women were dropping like flies.

"For the love of Christ." Vanessa released an exasperated moan and took over. "Des, have fun, meet hot guys, have loads of sex, take London by the balls, and make that city your bitch. Cheers."

Just in case, Kyle, Jude and I waited a pause before drinking. Only when we saw the four girls taking a sip did we follow suit. The champagne was long gone well before the sobbing ceased.

Sabrina

"**G**O TALK TO HIM." BECKY nudged me with her elbow. "It's fate. That's what this is."

"It most certainly isn't fate. It's coincidence." I turned and watched Luca and his friends. The guys were deep in conversation, while the women cried. The entire scene didn't pair well with the champagne.

"Sabrina, seriously. Look at the man." We both continued to stare in his direction, and my entire face heated when he caught me. "See, his eyes have been on you all night. Go." Again she nudged me almost causing my drink to spill out of my martini glass.

"No, he's busy. Plus, if he wanted to talk to me, he knows where I am."

Becky's lips quirked to the side, and we both swiveled our stools to face the bar. "Fine, but you don't get out much. You shouldn't waste this evening."

"I'm not wasting it, I'm with you."

"Right, and Mikey is staying over at your parents' house, so let loose will you?" She snapped her fingers in the air summoning the bartender. "Two lemon-drop shots please."

He nodded and went to make her order. "I hope those are both for you." I smiled knowing full well what her intentions were.

The bartender set them down and winked at Becky. "Let me know if you need anything else, beautiful."

She batted her eyelashes. "Oh, you know I will, handsome."

I laughed at her obvious flirting. "You're crazy."

"Nope, I just know how to have fun. Raise your glass." I did as she asked. "To the men who kiss like Romeo and fuck like a porn star." A few men beside us turned and grinned at her. She lifted her glass as a confirmation. "Am I right, gentlemen?"

"Focus, Becky." We downed the shot and I swear every taste bud in my mouth contracted. Music started playing just as a loud voice came over the sound system announcing the dance floor was open. To my left, a few women huddled in a circle dancing as if they didn't have a care in the world.

Becky leaned over and yelled a bit louder than necessary into my ear. "You should go ask him to dance."

I shook my head. "No, why don't you go ask him." With my back still facing Luca's direction, she craned her head to look behind us. "His friends are hot as fuck, too. Damn. Oooh, only one of the two has a wedding band." She made a move to get off of the stool only to sit right back down. "Nope, he's also taken."

The music changed to a slower song. Luca's friends occupied a portion of the dancefloor. His one friend held on to his wife as if she were going to escape. Another couple could have starred in the movie, *Dirty Dancing*. Hell, they were grinding like nobody's business, and I blushed at the sight of them.

Then, the other woman from their group started dancing with some guy, leaving Luca and Cassie at the table. A few seconds later, they joined the rest of the crew. The two of them were adorable. While the other couples were in a tight embrace, Luca held her in a proper ballroom frame. Every few beats, he'd twirl her and they'd both laugh. It made me wonder why they weren't a couple.

I had known Cassie for a while. We moved to the city from a small town in Upstate New York last summer. It was important for me to meet with Mikey's potential teachers before he started Kindergarten. I could tell from the first day I met her that she'd be the perfect teacher for my son, and I was right.

Rather than continue to gawk at them, I turned my attention back to my cocktail that I had been nursing for the better part of an hour. The shot Becky just forced me to do accomplished what my watered-down drink hadn't. I rarely drank, not ever wanting to be out of control in case Mikey needed me. So, when I did partake, the effects were immediate. Alcohol made me giddy, silly, and impulsive.

"Care to dance?" A baritone voice caused the fine hairs on the back of my neck—and other parts of my body—to stand at attention. His warm breath tickled the soft spot behind my ear. The luxurious scent of his cologne wrapped around me like a warm cocoon. When I tilted my head, his face was so close to mine, his lips almost landed on my cheek.

That impulsive instinct kicked in. God, I wanted to kiss those gorgeous full lips. Instead, I nodded shyly. "Sure," came out of my mouth in a weird breathy sound that I'd never made before. I passed my bag to Becky, and said, "I'll be back soon."

"And... I'll be waiting," she replied with an exaggerated wink.

Luca offered his hand and escorted me to the dance floor. The song wasn't one I recognized, but Luca took control. Even though he held me similar to the way he did Cassie, being so close to him had my heart thrumming inside my chest.

"I've never seen you here before." Luca's deep brown eyes stared into mine.

"Do you remember everyone who comes here?"

A model-worthy smile showcased his straight white teeth. *Maybe he was a model.* "No, but I'd remember you." I was about to tease him for using such a cheesy line until he said, "That's not a line either. My friends and I come here a lot and if you were here, I would've noticed."

"You would have?" I asked surprised. Our bodies continued to sway in perfect rhythm to the music.

"Without a doubt in my mind." The sincerity in his voice caused my breath to catch.

I looked away to break the spell he had over me. "This is my first time here. My friend, Becky, dragged me out tonight."

"Where's Mikey?"

"With my parents." He smiled, and his wide hand that splayed across the small of my back pulled me toward him.

"He's a great kid." He waited a few moments and then added, "And his mom is beautiful."

"Thank you." My eyes cut to his handsome face. Again, he held my gaze. His parted lips seemed like an open invitation for mine. The desire to kiss him continued to overwhelm me. If I just lifted up on my toes, the few inches that separated us would no longer be an issue.

My eyes were still pinned to his lips when he spoke. "Hey, would you like to…" When he paused, my heart skipped a beat. If he was about to ask if I wanted to get out of there, I had a feeling my mouth would blurt out yes before my brain stopped it.

"Like to?" I prompted, when more words hadn't come.

"Um… I'd love to take you and Mikey out for breakfast tomorrow." A pang of disappointment hit until that stunning smile of his spread over his lips. At the sight of it, I forgot he had even spoken at all. "Does he have another soccer game?"

"Oh… um, no. He's spending the weekend with his grandparents. I'm solo tomorrow."

His large hand shifted to the side and settled closer to my hip. "Well, then, how about I pick you up around ten? There's this great place near the Seaport we can go to. It's supposed to be a nice day."

"I'd really like that, Luca." I couldn't help but grin at seeing the joy on his face.

Sure, the man was beautiful, but combined with his personality he could no doubt break hearts without intending to. A twinge of fear pinched my subconscious. Just by staring into his warm chocolate eyes, in that moment I could see that happening to me.

Chapter 6

Sabrina

WHEN THE MUSIC ENDED, LUCA released me before taking my hand and leading me back to the bar. There was something super sexy in the way he took control while remaining an absolute gentleman at the same time.

It had been over a year since I'd been intimate. Dillon's deployment schedule and life getting in the way, we weren't as sexually active as I would've liked. Regardless, I hadn't met a man who I wanted to spend time with, nonetheless date.

Yet, there I was with Luca, and in the short time we'd spent together I could already imagine all sorts of situations with him… some even lewd. Of course, that was my libido talking.

The other part of me, specifically my heart, just craved the company of a man. Someone to spend time with, laugh with, enjoy being with. There was a time I had that with Dillon, but somewhere along the way we lost ourselves. The reasons to why became clearer after his death, once it was too late.

While Luca and I were dancing, the warmth of his large hand wrapped around mine, the hard muscle of his upper arm under my left palm, and his overall presence just made me feel safe. Why that would be something I felt when I barely knew him, I truly had no idea.

One thing I knew for sure, I liked him. The flutters, the giddiness, and the nerves that came with the thought that I had a date with Luca Benedetto were all emotions that were long overdue for me.

Breaking through that awkward phase when two strangers went out wouldn't be an issue, and neither would breaking the news that I had a son. I could count the number of dates I'd been on since Dillon died on one hand. The number of second dates I had after they found out I was a mom could be counted on one finger.

"Hey, guys!" The joy on Becky's face as we approached spoke volumes. Before I could make the introduction, Becky thrusted her hand toward Luca and said, "I'm Becky, Sabrina's bestie, and you're gorgeous."

A deep chuckle erupted before he accepted her hand and said, "It's nice to meet you, Sabrina's bestie with impeccable taste."

"Holy hell, you have an accent."

"No, *you* do," he teased with a wink. Becky's eyes widened, and her hand continued to pump Luca's well past the acceptable amount of time a normal handshake should last. All this occurred while she waggled her eyebrows at me.

Oh Lord.

When she finally released Luca, a fake pout altered her features. "Although I would love to get to know Luca, my Uber is here. I must relieve the babysitter. Not everyone is lucky enough to have parents on standby."

The pout turned into a grin when her eyes dropped to where Luca still held my hand, something I was also very aware of. As I reached for my bag on the bar, I tried to hide my disappointment. "I guess I'll see you tomorrow then?"

I was surprised to see what I felt mirrored on his face. "You need to leave too? I can get you home if you want to stay longer."

"Of course she'd love to stay." Becky kissed my cheek, patted Luca on the shoulder, and with a simple wave left me standing there without giving me a choice.

He took my jacket off the back of the barstool and led me toward his friends. The nerves I felt earlier paled in comparison to what was happening inside my stomach now. With each step my heart rate spiked, and I was grateful Cassie was there to play as a buffer.

Each of their faces were just as stunning as the next. All seven of them could pose for a magazine or walk a runway, Luca included.

"Hi, Sabrina." Cassie stood up. "So glad you're joining us."

"Hi, Cassie. It's good to see you." I gave her a quick hug. Luca pulled an unused chair from the table next to ours and held it out for me. I forced a swallow and sat down. The other women regarded me with fascination, and my nerves tripled.

"Sabrina," Luca said with a smile. "These are my friends." He started pointing to each one as he said their names. "That's Jude and he's married to the beauty sitting next to him, Brae." She gave me an enthusiastic wave. "Then that clown is Kyle, his girlfriend, Vanessa, that's Desiree who just got a promotion and is moving to London, and you know Cassie."

I prayed I'd remember their names. "Hi everyone, thank you for letting me join you." Focusing on Desiree, I said, "Congratulations on your promotion. London is lovely."

"Thank you. You've been there?"

"Yes, my husband was deployed in Europe when we were first married, and we traveled to various countries."

The elation vanished. No one said a word. *Shit.* Once I yanked my foot out of my mouth, I blurted out, "I'm not married. He's dead now." My stupid comment was met with wide-eyed silent stares. Brae, the married one, grabbed onto her husband's arm with her mouth hanging open.

For the love, Sabrina!

"I mean, I didn't kill him," I added with a nervous giggle. "He passed away a little over a year ago." During the three or one hundred seconds of silence, since I really couldn't tell how much time had passed, I chanted—*stop talking, stop talking,* over and over in my head.

Luckily, Luca chimed in. "Um… Sabrina has the cutest little boy. Cassie is his teacher. Actually, that's how we met. First, he got finger paint all over my pants, and then at the park he kicked a soccer ball and hit me square between the eyes." He draped his arm across the back of my chair. It felt comforting, although I was still appalled at my rambling.

"It was hilarious. The first encounter you could see the *imprint* of Mikey's hands framing his family jewels, and then encounter number two, you could see the *imprint* from the ball on Luca's forehead. His eyes crossed at impact." Cassie started laughing, and everyone followed suit.

"That ball was aimed for *your* head, so you're welcome.

The kid has quite a kick," Luca explained.

As his friends all ribbed him over being schooled by a five-year old, I thanked God the tension was broken. Internally, I still felt like a fool. These people didn't know me or my story, just Becky and my family did. The conversation compelled me to want to explain everything to Luca.

Luca

SABRINA'S NERVOUSNESS WHILE HANGING OUT at Dispatch was obvious. But when it continued even after we left, and during the drive to her apartment, I tried to help her relax.

In the short time I'd known her, I already recognized when she was caught up in her own thoughts. As quickly as she drifted off, she could come back into the moment from a simple comment or question.

By telling her tales of my college days with Jude and Kyle, by the time we pulled up to her place the shield she hid behind was nowhere to be found. Her carefree laughter echoed in the car, the sound of it warming me in a way I wasn't familiar with.

Double parking in front of her building, I turned to her and said, "So, I'll see you tomorrow morning then?" She fiddled with the strap of her bag, her lips parting and poised to speak, yet no words came out. "Are you okay?"

"Yeah. Um… would you like to come in for some coffee, or something?" The invite contradicted the tension on her face. I didn't want her to feel obligated in any way, and before I could decline she added, "I'd like to chat a bit."

"Sure. Let me find a spot." She nodded before I circled the block in search of an available parking space. A few minutes later, I found one a block or so away. As I trotted over to her side of the car to open her door, she was already standing on the curb waiting for me.

"This is a great area," I said as we walked the short distance to her apartment.

"We like it here. Mikey has made some awesome friends in the building. My work is close by, as is his school."

"What do you do, Sabrina?"

"I'm a hairdresser. I rent space in Becky's salon. She's been such a help in letting me set my own hours," she said with a smile. "You have great hair, by the way. The day we met I had to fight the urge to touch it."

I laughed at her candor, bending a bit to bring my head closer. "Feel free."

She stopped walking and met my amused smile with one of her own. Without hesitation, I watched her reach up and run her fingers through my hair. The feel of her touch sent a jolt through me. "Just as I imagined, like silk."

Between her touch and the way her eyes held mine, ignited a fire within me. Our chests rose and fell in sync. Sabrina was just as affected as I was. When she lowered her hand, I immediately missed the physical contact.

"I can't take all the credit. Kyle makes a kick-ass shampoo that I've been using for years."

"Kyle makes it?"

I nodded at the shock in her tone before taking her hand in mine. "Yes, he's a chemist. He creates fragrances and hair products for men and women. He's a genius when it comes to that stuff, but a fuck-up with everything else in his life… except for Vanessa. He managed to get that right."

She smiled. "They seem like a great couple."

"They are a great team. Vanessa works with him now. She's got quite the knack."

"I'll tell Becky. She might want to carry his product line in her salon."

"He can set her up with inventory."

"By the way, I enjoyed hanging out with your friends. They seem like great people."

"Two are mine, as I mentioned they are my best friends since our days at Yale. The girls I inherited." A sweet giggle erupted as I continued. "Jude met Brae because of Kyle's practical joke, signing him up for a dating experiment."

"Nooo," she said on a gasp.

"Yes," I mimicked her tone. "Jude wanted to kill him. He had to spend six weeks on a remote beach getting to know Brae. He left me in charge of his company as they frolicked in the Caribbean while falling in love."

"Oh my God, that's so romantic." Her free hand covered her heart.

The light breeze lifted the glossy strands of her trendy haircut, revealing the smooth skin of her neck. She wore little makeup, which was such a refreshing change to most of the women I met. She truly was beautiful. A natural beauty was hard to come by in this city.

Remembering her statement, I responded, "Yeah, especially for the man who didn't have a romantic bone in his body."

"And the others? How did you meet them?"

"The four girls were all friends. Once Jude and Brae got together, and Kyle and Vanessa started their thing, we became a dysfunctional family of sorts. Cassie and I were left to fend for ourselves while Desiree worked her ass off as an attorney. And the rest you know."

"You guys complement each other perfectly."

I chuckled at her observation. "Not sure about that, but even when we want to kill each other, we still have each other's backs. I'd do anything for those guys."

"There's no doubt in my mind. I know we just met, but I can tell you're a genuine person."

Her words warmed me in an unexpected way. I hadn't realized I continued to stare until she dropped her gaze and blushed. The combination of her attractiveness and shy demeanor made Sabrina very desirable to me. Add in the fact she was a mother, and no woman I'd been with had ever been sexier. If we didn't start walking soon, I was going to toss her over my shoulder, carry her into her bedroom, and our cup of coffee would turn into breakfast.

She lived on the second floor of a walk-up. Once we reached her door, she unlocked it, gave me a smile that would melt ice on the coldest winter day, and headed inside.

I followed in as she flipped on some lights before tossing her bag onto a side table. The apartment was small, but neat. You walked directly into a living room with a small kitchen to the right. Mikey's toys were organized on bookcases that lined the wall of windows.

Motioning toward them, I asked, "He likes trucks, I see?"

"Loves them. Actually, anything with wheels. His room is decorated in a race car theme. He's either going to be a mechanic, or a Nascar driver. Here, let me take your jacket." I removed it, handing it to her. Sabrina then motioned toward a navy couch that faced a modest television. "Make yourself comfortable. I'll make us some coffee."

She retreated into the kitchen, the sound of cabinets opening and water running filtered out to where I sat on the couch. A click sounded before a voice recording of Mikey said, "Mahmmm! You packed the wrong hat. I wanted my Ranger one. I can't watch the game with Pop Pop wearing the wrong hat." The message abruptly ended, and Sabrina's heavy sigh caused me to chuckle.

The dynamics between mother and son were so real, honest. I knew when we met their bond was strong, and now knowing what they endured made it even more profound.

In the apartment, Mikey and Sabrina's personalities shown through and meshed in the perfect balance. Wooden furniture held smiling photos of the pair, a few of them with others who must have been important in their lives. A picture of a tropical sunset hung on one wall; beside it two smaller framed crayoned drawings of the same scenery.

One photo propped on an end table was of a uniformed man holding Mikey as a toddler while Sabrina stood behind them smiling. Intrigued, I lifted it and stared at the family. Questions such as how long had they been married, where had they met, why didn't they have other children—all floated in my mind.

Sabrina walked in holding a tray with two steaming mugs of coffee, a container of creamer, and sweeteners. "I don't know how you take it," she said, stopping when she saw the photo in my hand.

"Mikey looks a lot like his father."

"Spitting image. If I hadn't delivered him, I'd doubt he was mine. Same stubborn streak, too." A small smile played on her lips when she sat beside me, placing the tray on the coffee table. "That was Mikey's second birthday. Dillon had just gotten back that day from being deployed in the Middle East, surprising us all."

"He was a Marine?" I asked the obvious.

"Yes. He followed in his father's and his grandfather's footsteps." She lifted the cream in a silent question.

"Yes, just a drop please. No sugar." As she prepped my coffee, I placed the photo back on the table and took the mug from her hand. "Is that how he died?"

"No. He was killed in a car accident." My shocked expression forced a short nod. "I know. Ironic, right? Every time he left me, I had to prepare for the worst and hope he came back. Once he did, and we were ready to move past his career choice into a safer more stable one, the unthinkable happened."

I stretched a hand toward hers and gave it a gentle squeeze. "I'm so sorry, Sabrina."

She shrugged with a small smile. "Thank you. Things happen for a reason, I guess." The tone in her voice was off, strained. I didn't want to push her into telling me more, and prepared to change the subject when she added, "I do love being back in New York City. So, there's that."

"Back?"

"I'm originally from Manhattan. Dillon and I moved upstate to his hometown before we married. His entire family lives there, small town, very Mayberry like. He felt it'd be a better place to raise a family."

"That must have been hard on you, leaving your family."

"That was very hard. But, with time I made friends, and his family welcomed me like one of their own."

"Do you still visit often?"

"No." She sipped her coffee and remained silent.

Assuming their relationship was strained after their son died, I offered my two cents. "People grieve differently."

"Does that include denial? That's not rhetorical."

"I guess. They haven't been able to accept he's gone?"

"Or that he was a lying cheat." I spit my coffee out at her nonchalant comment. "Sorry," she said with a smirk, grabbing a napkin to help me clean up the embarrassing dribble on my chin. "I have to refrain from showing my real feelings so much around Mikey. When he isn't here, my bitterness shines through."

The lines on her face revealed what she must have gone through. I wasn't going to steer this conversation, and waited to see if she'd continue or not.

Sabrina needed to get something off her chest, and her next comment made that clear. "His mistress showed up at the funeral. Such a display, making her grand entrance in her black dress with tears streaming down her face while sporting a nice baby bump. One for the memory books. I guess him not wanting more children only meant not wanting them with me."

A vortex of anger toward him, and sadness for her and Mikey consumed me. It took a few long moments for me to speak. "How did you know who she was?"

"She was very forthcoming with her information. Of course, I didn't believe her. This was my honorable husband she claimed loved her. When I told her as much, she showed me pictures that spanned back two years. I know that because in one of the pictures, Dillon's most recent tattoo wasn't on his arm."

The more she revealed, the angrier I became. I set my mug down and regarded his picture. The respect I felt, for the man I assumed he was, vanished in a blink of an eye. How could he do that to such a genuine woman and his son?

"How ironic that at my husband's funeral my mourning both began and ended that day." Her gaze focused on the picture for a few seconds. "She had a boy. That's all I know. Have no clue what his name is, or who's helping her. I don't want to know. I made my in-laws swear they'd never tell Mikey, otherwise I'd share what a *wonderful* man his father was. My mother-in-law hated my ultimatum, arguing Mikey should know he has a sibling. Dillon could do no wrong in her eyes, and somehow him cheating was my fault."

"Are you serious?"

"Completely," she said with a shrug. "Whatever, it's her issue, not mine. One day I'll tell Mikey, but not until he's much older and can understand the situation. Not a day sooner."

She noticed me staring at the simple gold band on her finger. "You're still wearing it?"

"Oh no, this isn't my wedding band. I bought this at a department store. His is sitting in a drawer waiting to be sold someday. I'll use it to buy Mikey his first car or something. I wear this because it's easier to deflect the questions I tend to get." After another sip of her coffee she placed it on the table and dragged in a deep breath. "Pathetic, right?"

"Yes, *he* was pathetic. Look at all you should be proud of. You relocated with your young son to a different city, picked yourself up, and moved on." I reached over and held her face, forcing her to stare back into my eyes. "That's far from pathetic."

"I'm really sorry. I didn't mean to dump all of that on you. After my outburst at the bar, I owed it to you. Besides my parents and Becky, I've never told anyone. But, you're very easy to talk to… don't you feel lucky?"

"Very."

Our eyes connected and the air between us crackled. Whether it was from a sexual attraction or plain desire, all culminated into the same result… I wanted her. With each second that passed, I wanted to kiss her. With each second I waited, it appeared she wanted me to. But with kissing her came uncertainty. Was she ready for this? Was she ready for more?

No longer caring, the need to feel her full lips against mine won the battle. I pulled her closer, framed her face, and fused our lips together in a gentle kiss. The taste of coffee melded between us. Her lips were warm and just as soft as I knew they'd be. I felt her hands move to grip my wrists tightly. I heard a soft mewl when I pulled away.

The kiss didn't last long, and that was purposeful on my part. If I continued kissing her I worried it would be a mistake, and even more so that she'd let me for the wrong reasons. There was too much I didn't know about Sabrina, and kissing her intensified my curiosity tenfold.

Yes, she was a widow, a mother, and a woman hurting over the loss of her husband. And not because he was dead, but because he betrayed her in a despicable way. Still, I hardly knew her, and she knew even less of me.

Only an inch separated our mouths, but the cool air that replaced her warm lips had me going back for more. Wanting to feel them again, the second time I pressed harder. She parted just enough to convey she also wanted more.

My conscience nagged, forcing me to again break the connection and end the temptation. Her breath hitched when I added more distance, as if I removed her source of oxygen.

"I better go," I whispered. The uncertainty in her eyes killed me. "Sabrina, I don't want to... I *need* to."

Chapter 7

Sabrina

EVEN HOURS LATER, I COULD still feel his lips moving against mine. Each time I closed my eyes, he appeared before me. Specifically, the expression on his face when I told the awful story about my husband's affair. It was a humiliating tale, but for some reason talking to him about it was easy.

Laying in bed and thinking of Luca, was a sure-fire way to have sleep evade me. It was also the way to make me ache in places that hadn't been touched by a man in over a year. On its own volition, my hand snuck its way under my sheet and rested on the apex of my thighs. I knew it wouldn't take much to alleviate the pressure.

The lace fabric of my thong tickled my middle finger as I gently grazed it. Keeping my eyes closed, I pretended my finger was Luca's. I imagined his strong arm resting on my stomach, his cologne engulfing me as he brought his lips, then tongue, to my oversensitive skin. For a moment, I hesitated when the palm of my hand moved past my stretchmarks. Dillon hated them and always wanted me to try different things to cover them up. Even when I wore his favorite bikini, that used to turn him on, it did the opposite.

My back arched when I slipped my finger under my panties and over my hot skin. I was wet, slick, and the longer I thought about him the more turned on my body became. I wanted him and needed him to touch me, to make me feel like a wanted woman again, just as he had when we kissed.

A frustrated moan escaped, my insides coiled like a snake ready to strike. Strike it did when I rolled my clit under the pad of my finger. In a hushed voice I whispered his name and my climax took hold. Sated, I brought my finger out from under the sheet, waited a beat for my legs to feel normal and not like Jell-O, and walked into the bathroom. I stared into the mirror as I washed my hands.

For the first time in a long time, I felt hopeful that maybe I found a great guy. *Was it too soon to feel that way?* I wasn't sure. With Dillon it was a slow build of attraction and not an instant spark like I felt with Luca.

I crawled back into bed, pulled the comforter underneath my chin, closed my eyes, and drifted off to a nice peaceful sleep knowing I'd be seeing Luca in the morning.

The sun peeked through the sides of my window coverings. Normally when Mikey spent the weekend at my folks, I'd sleep in and catch up on all the hours I missed during the week, but today I was invigorated knowing I had a date.

After I showered, styled my hair, put on a minimal amount of makeup, I went to get dressed. My bed resembled a dressing room at Bloomingdales. Three different pair of jeans, four different tops, and a couple of different pairs of shoes were all strategically placed as if I was preparing for the runway. I couldn't help but laugh at myself. *For Christ's sake, we were going to breakfast, not a night club.* Deciding on my favorite pair of light washed boyfriend jeans, a blue V-neck sweater, and my favorite wedges, I was ready.

The buzzer on my intercom sounded. Nerves laced with adrenaline coursed through my body. I cleared my throat, pressed the white button on the speaker. "Yes?"

"Good morning, it's Luca." Like that sexy accent could belong to someone else?

"Come on up." I checked my face in the small mirror next to my door. Quickly running my hands over my hair to calm any stray fly-away strands, I then grabbed a light-colored lipstick out of my bag and swiped it over my lips.

Three knocks sounded on my door. When I pulled it open, I wasn't fully prepared for who stood before me. Holding a bouquet of pastel-colored flowers was the sexiest man I'd ever laid eyes on. I took a moment to rake my eyes over his body from head to toe. His dark denim jeans, accentuated the length of his legs ended at a pair of casual black loafers, a maroon crew neck sweater was covered by a black leather jacket. If it wasn't for the gold chain peeking out of his neckline, and the silhouette of a cross under his sweater, he'd look sinful. "Come on in."

He handed me the flowers and gave me a swift kiss on the cheek. "These are for you."

"Thank you." I brought my nose to the blooms and inhaled. When was the last time I received flowers from a man? "They're lovely. Gerbera daisies are one of my favorite flowers. They remind me of when I was a little girl, and my grandfather would leave one for me on my swing set." The memory hit me full force. I used to sit and pluck petal by petal, reciting the childhood limerick, *he loves me, he loves me not.* Even knowing they were my favorite, Dillon never gave me Gerbera daisies, which hadn't occurred to me until now.

A proud smile graced his handsome face. "I'm glad you like them."

"I love them. Let me put these in water and then we can leave."

The air was crisp, the sun was shining making for a perfect New York morning. As we approached where his car was parked, it looked even sleeker in the daylight. It was then I noticed the make and model—a Jaguar F-Type. My eyes went wide thinking Mikey had something similar in his collection of Matchbox cars. Of course, being the gentleman he was, he opened my door and waited for me to slide in before closing it behind me.

The black, supple leather seat formed around my body. Just as I thought last night, this was the perfect car for a single man—two seats, pristine interior, no crumbs on the carpet, or an errant French fry left behind from a kid's meal. It even smelled clean and masculine, like Luca. And not like a pair of soccer cleats that had been worn in the rain and forgotten under the back seat.

Luca slid into the driver's side, and I couldn't take my eyes off of him. "What?" He smiled at me and pushed the start button on center console. Listening to his car rumble to life was exhilarating—*I really needed to get out more.*

"Mikey would love this car."

"It's my pride and joy. I'll need to take him for a ride one day." Luca pulled away from the curb and we were off to the Seaport. Although a two-seater Jaguar was not child friendly, the way he wanted to include my son warmed my heart.

"Or, you can save yourself from being harassed and just let him sit in it," I suggested to avoid the hassle of a booster seat messing up his leather. "He's at a very obsessive age right now."

A chuckle filled the small area, "That's fine. I'd be the same way if I was his age. Hell, I'm the same way now on some days, thus explaining the impractical sports car in New York City."

Our conversation was easy during our drive. It wasn't long before we pulled into the lot, left the keys with the parking attendant, and walked to the restaurant.

The narrow path the hostess led us through in the crowded restaurant ended with a table in the corner. The warmth of Luca's knuckles on my skin as he helped me remove my jacket elicited goosebumps to emerge. After he pulled out my chair and we sat, I ordered a cup of coffee and Luca ordered an espresso.

We each took a few minutes to study the menu. Deciding on something simple, I set my menu down and admired the man sitting across from me. The waiter came back and with him the aroma of rich coffee wafted around us. He placed a large mug of my morning drug before me and a small demitasse cup in front of Luca. We placed our orders, pancakes for me and Nutella French toast for him.

Once our server took the menus from us and retreated, I said, "Thank you for taking me out this morning."

He reached across the small square table to rest his hand on top of mine. "Thank you for coming." With our gazes tethered, the fluttering I felt whenever he looked me directly in the eyes began. Along with it, came the chagrin I felt telling him about my husband's infidelity. Sensing something was off, he squeezed my hand. "Sabrina, what's wrong?"

I hesitated a bit before admitting, "After all I dumped on you last night, I wasn't sure you'd still want to go out with me."

That was the god's honest truth. Having a woman tell another man her husband had been cheating on her didn't bode well. Did he wonder why? What would make Dillon want or feel the need to be with someone else? Didn't I satisfy him? Wasn't I pretty enough? Loving enough? These were all the things I thought of—how could he not?

"Sabrina, why would you think that? If anything, I commend you for your honesty." He flipped my hand so that our fingers linked together. "I enjoy spending time with you. I know we just met, but I feel like we've known each other for a while. It's strange." I felt the same and smiled at his admitting that to me. "Plus, Mikey is a great kid and I can't wait to start teaching him some soccer moves. By the time I'm done with him, he'll be the captain of his team."

Once again, I respected the genuine fondness he had for my son. "He's so excited about it. You know, he didn't stop talking about you last week after lunch. He even called my parents and told them about a cool guy he met at his soccer game that was going to be his private coach. My father has bad knees and can't help him with sports." I omitted the part where my mom grilled me on who this man was. My parents knew what Dillon had done; there was no way not to tell them since I didn't show much sadness after his funeral. Yes, I was sad he wouldn't be around to see our son grow into a man, but my heart no longer held love for him, just gratitude for our little boy.

"Does he have a game next week?" he asked, his fingers tightened between mine. It was obvious Luca was a very affectionate person, something I wasn't used to. Each time he squeezed, an electric current ran right through me.

Remembering what he had asked, I nodded. "Yes, but it's later in the day on Saturday."

"Perfect, we can go to the park in the morning and get ready. Then have an early lunch before he needs to play. If that's okay."

I smiled wide at his suggestion, even more so because he wanted to see me next week. "Yes, he'd love that." My gaze drifted to the view outside. "It's beautiful here." The restaurant Luca picked was in the heart of the Seaport. From where we sat, the view was of the Brooklyn Bridge and various sized boats leaving white-capped slices in the dark blue water of the East River.

"It's a tourist trap," he said, staring out the window as well. "But it reminds me of a little place in Venice that I enjoyed, less the Brooklyn Bridge, of course."

"I've never been to Italy. Sadly, that was one country we didn't visit while stationed overseas."

"You should go one day. I go back once a year, although my parents don't think that's frequent enough."

"That's a dream of mine. Mikey would love it— especially all the gelato."

"We can go to a place in Little Italy that makes the best Nutella gelato."

"See, Nutella gelato makes sense... Nutella French toast, not so much."

"You have no idea what you're missing. It's my

favorite. You may want to be forewarned, I'm a Nutella junkie."

Before he could go on, the waiter appeared with our breakfast. My three-stack of pancakes seemed boring compared to his culinary masterpiece. Luca twisted his plate so the fresh berries were at the top and the powdered sugar dusted bread was in front of him.

With the side of his fork, he cut into it. Soft chocolate oozed from the slice he speared and offered to me across the table. My nose crinkled with uncertainty. "Trust me."

Tentatively, I leaned forward, opened my mouth, and watched Luca eyes focus on my lips as they dragged the piece off the fork. The nutty confection assaulted my taste buds. I wasn't expecting it to taste so delicious. My soft moan followed by my tongue poking out to lick my lips proved as much.

"It's good, right?"

"Yes, very. I'm regretting my decision." Out of nowhere, he swapped our meals. "What are you doing? You said it was your favorite."

His brown eyes met mine. "I'd rather watch you enjoy them. Plus, I make it for myself all the time."

"You cook?" As we eased into conversation, I nonchalantly gave him one of the halves. He cocked a brow. "I can share, too. So, cooking?"

"Yes, my mother wouldn't have it any other way. She taught all of her kids how to make a meal."

"I love to cook. Though, I don't often enough, because of Mikey's unsophisticated palate. How many siblings do you have?"

"Two. An older brother and younger sister."

"Ahh… middle child. Do they also live in New York?"

He shook his head as he chewed. "No, my brother lives in Chicago, but he's barely there. My parents and sister live in Milan. I do have an uncle who owns a restaurant uptown. We rarely see each other because he's always working. How about you? Siblings?"

"Yes, I have a younger brother. Michael lives with his girlfriend in Denver."

"That's nice, you named your son after your brother?"

"Yes, much to Dillon's dismay. But, Michael and I were always very close. He wanted to move back after Dillon passed away to help with Mikey. I told him no, and he needs to live his own life. I'd never expect anyone to alter their goals because of what happened here. He does come to visit. Actually, he was just here last month."

"That must have been fun."

I nodded over my last bite. "That was delicious. Thank you for sharing."

"I'll turn you into a Nutella addict one way or another." He finished the rest of his half and dove into the pancakes. "You sure you don't want some?"

"Are you kidding? I couldn't eat another bite, but thank you."

"Do you have plans for the rest of the day?"

"Yes, my first client comes in at two."

"Okay, until then, we can take a walk and enjoy the spring weather. Then I'll drive you to work. Do you have an appointment after your two o'clock?"

"Yes, but I should be done by four-thirty."

"I'll drop you off and be there when you're done. We'll have dinner together." It wasn't a question. I wasn't used to a man taking control, but because it was Luca I liked it.

"Are you asking me out tonight? You're assuming I'm not busy?" I teased.

His brows furrowed, "My apologies, would you like to have dinner with me this evening?" He paused a beat. "That is, if you're available."

I could feel the corners of my lips turn up. "I'm teasing you. I am available, and I'd love to. But no need to pick me up at the salon. You can pick me up at my apartment."

"Sounds good. Now, how about that walk?"

Chapter 8

Luca

I SPENT THE REST OF THE day planning my night with Sabrina, something romantic and unexpected. When the perfect activity presented itself, it didn't take long to make the necessary arrangements.

While getting ready, an unpredictable excitement took hold. It wasn't like I hadn't dated before, but what I realized while shaving was I hadn't really set out to date. How strange was that? Of all the times I took a woman out, whether it was dinner or just drinks, I never once considered it more than just that.

It had to be Sabrina. There was something about her company that just felt comfortable, and I meant it when I said it felt like we'd known each other for years. The more time I spent with her, the more I wanted to. Considering we were together all morning, and I pushed to see her tonight, that most definitely wasn't a normal occurrence for me.

I made it to Sabrina's apartment on time. She insisted I call her when I arrived, so I didn't have to bother finding a parking spot. As I waited in front of her building while leaning against my car, my phone buzzed with a text.

> **Kyle:** Where are you?

> **Me:** Why?

> **Kyle:** I bought a new dress and need your opinion...

He added an eye rolling emoji, before the dancing dots appeared again.

> We're all going out to dinner. Want to come?

> **Me:** No.

> **Kyle:** Why not? Have a date with your hand?

I debated lying, then thought better of it.

> **Me:** No, fuckhead. I'm going out with Sabrina.

I expected dots, but got an actual phone call instead. "What?"

"Bring her."

"I don't want to."

"Why not?"

"Because."

"Are you planning to get lucky tonight? Shouldn't you take it slow? She's a mom, you know."

"I'm hanging up."

"Wait!" I released an audible sigh and waited. "It's been awhile, do you need pointers?" I ended the call before getting a laughing emoji from the jackass.

A few minutes later, Sabrina appeared in black slacks and an off-white jacket. I watched her walk toward me, sporting a smile that I couldn't stop. "Hi," she said shyly when I pushed off my car.

"You look amazing." With a hand on her elbow, I chastely kissed both her cheeks before opening her door.

Before she got in, she placed a hand on my arm and said, "Thank you, Luca."

A smile tugged on my lips. "For?"

She gave a gentle shrug, "It's been a long time since someone… a man treated me like a lady."

"Sweetheart, you ain't seen nothing yet." I winked and closed her door. It infuriated me that she hadn't been treated well in the past. That was all about to change—starting with tonight.

I pulled out onto the road heading to our destination. "So, where are we going?" she asked, twisting in her seat to watch me as I drove.

"Dinner."

"That's specific." When I cut my eyes her way, her full lips quirked to the side in a smirk. "Is where we're going a surprise?"

"You don't like surprises?"

"I used to… not anymore." I slowed the car for a red light and turned to face her. Her expression seemed cynical, my thoughts moving to the truth she shared regarding her husband's infidelity. Before I could change the subject, she asked, "Do you like surprises?"

"Yes, with the right person surprises can be… orgasmic."

"Orgasmic, huh?" A devious expression lit up her hazel eyes. "I'm due for orgasmic."

Well, fuck. A sudden pull had me leaning toward her. She mimicked my motion, and just before our lips touched a horn sounded causing her to jump.

"New Yorkers," I mumbled, driving through the

intersection annoyed at not getting a kiss. "If we were in Italy, the guy behind us would've cheered for us to continue."

The melodic sound of her laughter filled the car, and the vibration under my palm as it rested on the gearshift calmed me. Even though the heady feeling that I could fall for this woman... *really* fall for this woman, should have had the opposite effect of relaxing me.

Every once in a while, I'd glimpse at her. Her hazel eyes sparkled as she looked straight ahead. "Would you like to listen to some music?"

She smiled as we approached another red light. "Sure, whatever you like is fine. I'm usually listening to Disney music or some new kid's album. Which really wasn't new music. It was music from when I was a kid now sung by kids." I couldn't help but chuckle, "Sorry, I'm rambling."

"I like listening to you ramble."

"Do you have a sexy comeback for everything?" In the dim light, I could see her face flush right before she turned toward the window.

"You think I'm sexy?"

Her head slowly turned toward me, "No." She bit the corner of her lip.

"I didn't think so." I winked and turned the radio on just as the light turned green. Gesturing toward the touchscreen console, I said, "Go ahead, pick something."

With trepidation, she reached forward and touched one of the preset stations. The first song she landed on was, *Pour Some Sugar on Me.* Another stab at the small screen changed the tune to, *Come on Baby Light My Fire.* It didn't take long to mimic her previous action, changing the station once again, to land on, *I Want Your Sex.* She groaned, and mumbled, "Oh my God."

I started laughing, "How about this." My thumb changed the mode to my iPhone. "I rarely listen to the radio since my taste in music varies, I prefer my playlists."

Ed Sheeran's, *Thinking Out Loud*, filtered through the speakers. She sighed, "I love this song."

"Me, too."

The rest of the drive was filled with my favorite tunes and easy conversation. When I pulled into the parking lot next to the pier, her eyes widened like the sun. "We're going on that yacht?" The inflection in her voice solidified that she'd love this surprise.

Pride filled with relief washed over me knowing I made the right choice. "We are." I exited the car, walked around to her side to open her door. Without hesitation, she took my outstretched hand, linked our fingers together as if this was our tenth date rather than our second, if you counted this morning. The chilly night air caused her to shiver. I released her hand to drape my arm across her shoulders. "It's warmer inside."

"Mmm, I'm cozy now," she said, staring up at me.

Once we checked our jackets, we were led into the dining room. Some diners were already sitting at their tables, each set with a red rose in the center. But when we reached ours, Sabrina let out a small gasp. "Oh, Luca." Stepping in front of the maitre d', I pulled out her chair. Sabrina's eyes focused on the colorful Gerbera daisies in the small square vase on the center of the table. "How?" She reached out and stroked a few of the petals with the tips of her fingers. "Everyone else has roses."

"Roses aren't special enough for you. Plus, they're not your favorite." Her eyes shimmered. The pretty hazel orbs blurred by unshed tears. I reached into my jacket pocket, pulled out a monogrammed handkerchief, and handed it to her.

Her lips twisted into a smile as she dabbed the corner of her eyes. "Thank you. I'm sorry, it's just…"

Repeating the words she had said before, I finished her sentence. "It's been a long time since someone treated you like a lady."

She nodded. "You're a wonderful man, Luca. How is it you're single?"

It should have taken me longer to come up with a reply, but there was only one that came to mind. "Because we just met." That was the absolute truth. This woman stirred things in me that went beyond me wanting nothing more than sex. Thoughts of her body wrapped up in my arms, her lips touching mine—simple things made my pulse quicken. But, the day I sank deep inside of her, fusing us as one, no doubt would make my soul want to soar.

Her lips made a small "O" as she expelled a breath and stared at me. "You know what's funny?"

I cocked a brow. "What?"

"I think you really mean that." On my nod, she looked down at the mascara stained cloth in her hand. "I'm so sorry, I'll have this cleaned and return it to you."

"Keep it. I have a dozen of them, compliments of my nonna."

She smiled and ran her thumb over the stitching. "What does the S stand for?"

"Salvatore."

"Luca Salvatore Benedetto." Hearing my name roll off her tongue made me want her to repeat it. "Can't say that's Irish." She laughed.

I knew Callahan was Irish, but that was her married

name. "What's your maiden name?"

A coy smile grew across her face. "Ricci."

"You're kidding, right?"

"Nope, my father is half Italian, half Greek. My mom is from Switzerland…" Her fingers fiddled with the ends of her hair. "Hence the blonde. I'm a spitting image of my mother."

"She must be gorgeous."

"Thank you. I suppose you could say I'm a mutt."

"That's the last thing I'd call you." *Sabrina Ricci.* That sounded so much better than Callahan. Maybe I'd use that when I introduced her to my mother. That thought stopped me dead in my tracks. When did I ever *want* to introduce any woman to my mother?

I know… *never.*

"So, how is it that you're Italian and your son never had pepperoni or sausage before? I think I had sausage before strained vegetables."

"My son is the pickiest eater on the planet. The only time he has red sauce is on a pizza." All I could do was stare at her in disbelief. "I know what you're thinking. Believe me, it makes my father cringe when we go there and Mikey has pasta with butter. That's why I was so stunned when he was more than happy to eat what you were having last week."

"And you said you've never been to Italy?"

"No, sadly. My father keeps talking about going back to see his great-aunts and uncles, but we haven't made it there yet."

We studied the short menu, there were only a couple of options to choose from. Once the waiter was back, we placed our order along with a bottle of Cabernet.

A small dance floor was strategically placed between the tables and a long bar that stretched along the back of the boat. We had been so comfortable with our conversation, I hadn't even noticed we started moving. When soft dinner music started to play, I stood. "Dance with me."

The jazz instrumental song that played, filled the room with a seductive aura. I circled her waist with my arms, resting my hands on the curve of her ass. Because of our difference in height, she placed her hands on my chest. I could feel the warmth of her touch through the fabric of my shirt.

Our hips pressed together, leaving no space between us. With each sway, the friction between our bodies became a distraction, as did the look in her eyes. I didn't want to move too quickly with her, especially because of the hurt she carried. It was buried well beneath the surface, but with the subtle comments she had made caused shards of her past to surface. Sharp enough to reopen wounds and cut into her happiness.

"This was a lovely surprise."

"I have many more surprises for you." My words were absolutely true. There were so many things I wanted to do, and while living in New York never had anyone I wanted to do them with. For the first time since moving here, I could picture that person clear as day. Seeing the sights, taking drives, laying on a beach, or even making out at the back of a darkened theater were vivid in my mind, and Sabrina was who I saw doing it all with me.

I watched her watch me, wondering what else she was thinking. Asking her could ruin the moment we shared, but ignoring could as well. If I had to guess, she spent the last year of her life, or longer, ignoring her own needs. How could I have been the first man to come along and pay her the attention she deserved?

This woman needed to be properly romanced.

And I was just the man to do that.

Chapter 9

Sabrina

THERE WAS NOTHING SEXIER THAN a confident man. The way Luca led me to the dance floor, pulled me into his arms, and began leading us with slow deliberate movements was a major turn on. Looking into his eyes while we did so, awakened parts of me I thought were asleep for good.

No other man had my body reacting with a single touch, not even my late husband. At first I thought it was nerves. But, the thing was, I wasn't nervous. If anything, I was the complete opposite.

His deep brown eyes focused on me. "What are you thinking about?" He tucked my hair behind my ear eliciting a surge of boldness laced with anticipation inside of me. There was a level of instant comfort being in his presence. Granted, the longer my hands stayed pressed against his muscular chest, the quicker my resolve was going to fade. Part of me wanted to stay on this dance floor forever, but the other part of me, the part that hadn't been with a man in over a year, wanted to go home.

"That I wish we were alone." I moistened my lips. "Did you have any plans for us after dinner?"

"Yes, to please you." His lips curled up at the corners, heat pooled in his eyes, and he leaned down to bring his mouth as close to my ear without touching it. "Why? What did you have in mind?"

A surge of desire shot through me, settling right between my legs. "I'd like to go back to my place."

Dinner was great, the company was even better, but walking into my apartment with Luca right behind me was the perfect way to end our date. I had never been the aggressor in a relationship before. He was the epitome of a man. Every movement, touch, smile, wink, set my female parts on fire. Even the way his Adam's apple bobbed when he sipped his espresso turned me on.

I set my bag and keys on the small table by the door and hung my jacket on the coat rack. "May I take your coat?" *In other words, please stay.* He shrugged it off, and I hung it next to mine. "Would you like something to drink?"

"No, thank you." He inched closer to me. "I do want to kiss you, though."

"I want that, too."

In a slow and deliberate move, he slid his fingers into my hair. The heels of his hands rested on my cheekbones. Soft, strong lips met mine, and on a moan, I parted my lips. I could feel his smile when the tip of his tongue slid into my mouth. He tasted of coffee and all man. It was like an aphrodisiac spurring me to want more, to taste more, to savor more.

Our mouths became eager, our kiss more fervent, and

it took every ounce of strength I had not to tear off his clothes. God… had a woman ever orgasmed solely from a kiss? On their own volition, my hips pressed into his, finding the friction they craved. His hardened length on my stomach caused me to shift to the side, seeking what my body wanted.

How easy it would be for me to wrap my legs around his slim waist, to put him exactly where I needed him. Luca broke our kiss, and I immediately felt the loss. His breathing labored, "We need to slow down."

I wanted to ask, *Why?* But my brain knew he was right, so all I did was nod.

"Want to sit down? We can watch a movie or something."

"That sounds fine, and if you don't mind, can I please have a glass of ice water?" I nodded. "But first, I'm going to use your bathroom."

I pointed to the hallway. "It's the first door on the right."

It may have been chilly outside, but my apartment felt like the tropics. I grabbed two glasses and opened the freezer to get some ice. If I had time, I would have stuck my head inside to cool off. Instead, I filled our glasses and headed back to the sofa.

Luca walked out, his eyes never leaving mine. "Did you find something to watch?"

Hell, I hadn't even thought about that yet. "No, but here." I handed him his glass of water. Rather than take a sip, he set it down on the table. Mine, on the other hand, was already half empty.

When I stretched my arm past him to reach for the remote, he stopped me. Placing his hands on my shoulders, he positioned me so my back was facing him.

My muscles danced for joy when they felt his strong thumbs press into them. His fingers worked magic on every tense muscle he touched. "Mmmm…"

"Feel good?"

My head lolled forward. "Yes, it feels great."

Puffs of warm breath caressed my neck, his hands no longer on my shoulders, but in front of me. His fingers rested on the buttons of my blouse. "May I?"

"Please." I could feel my nipples harden against the sheer fabric of my bra, waiting, needing, and wanting him to touch them.

What felt like an eternity, but only mere seconds later, my blouse pooled at my waist. His soft lips met my shoulder in a kiss as he unfastened the clasp of my bra. The restrictive elastic loosened, but he didn't remove it. I lost all sense of myself when his hands gently urged me forward. Before I knew it, I was face down, stretched out on the sofa, with my cheek flat against the cushion.

"I'll be right back." I didn't know where he was going, but when he returned, he straddled my upper thighs. The sound of a plastic cap opening and closing caught my attention. Without delay, his hands were sliding up and down my back. "I borrowed the lotion that was on your vanity. I hope you don't mind."

I shook my head, falling deeper and deeper into euphoria. His strong hands continued to knead my tired muscles. Knot after knot was untied by the use of the correct amount of pressure. The way he caressed my skin was how I imagined a musician strummed his guitar or played the piano—methodical, deliberate, and with purpose.

Not an inch was missed from the top of my neck to the waistband of my pants, which I cursed having on at the moment. With smooth, long strokes, his hands moved up and down my spine, to the base of my neck and all the way to my wrists. He'd give my skin a little pinch as he made his way back to my shoulders. His fingers lingered a bit longer when he reached the side of my breasts. It wouldn't take much for me to lift myself up to give him access to palm and caress the front of me.

Each time Luca moved his hands toward my head, I could feel his arousal against my ass. I closed my eyes trying to picture it, but I knew whatever image I conjured up in my brain wouldn't do it justice. What I did know, was it felt long, thick and hard—perfect.

"That feels so good, Luca."

"Good. Turn over." At my hesitation, he repeated it. He raised up on his knees, giving me room to flip onto my back. It'd been so very long since a man had seen me naked, an eternity since it was a man other than Dillon. My insides trembled at the thought, but the desire that coursed hot and thick through my veins won the battle.

I slowly turned over, holding the lace of my bra to my breasts until I was flat on my back. Luca's eyes darkened, his black pupils practically eating up the chocolate irises. He didn't speak in words; it was through his expression that I could read his thoughts. His fingertips began at my forehead and slowly slid down my face tickling my skin along the way. I closed my eyes, feeling his firm touch travel over my jaw and down my neck. They reached the swell of my breasts and stopped.

When I opened my eyes, he lifted his gaze to meet mine. "You're stunning." He removed my bra, and continued the path over each exposed breast, down my belly, and around my sides. His fingers gripped my back just as he bent his head and placed the softest kisses on the faint marks left from my pregnancy. I flinched when his warm lips hit each one. The more I did, the more he kissed them. Lifting his head, he held my stare for a pause. "Stunning, Sabrina. Every inch of you."

His words did little to hide my embarrassment. I slid my hands over the marks.

"Hey." He waited for my eyes to come back to his.

"I hate them."

"You should be proud of them. Plus, I find them sexy. It shows what a strong woman you are."

God, this man.

His expression softened when he saw the tears shimmering in my eyes. No more words were spoken. Luca spent what felt like an eternity worshipping the marks on my body with his lips and his touch.

Luca

PERFECTION.

How could she doubt she was anything but perfection?

The way her warm, firm skin felt beneath my hands, my lips, spurred a deep-rooted desire to boil within me. It wasn't lust that I'd felt many times in my life. It was something else. A hunger would be the closest way I could describe it.

I wanted to devour her.

Repositioning myself as I was before she turned over, I straddled her hips and bent to kiss her mouth. I started slow, enjoying the contours of her lips, the smooth silk of her tongue. I kissed her like I needed to draw breath from her body into mine. She responded, arching her back and digging her fingers into my hair.

Fuck, I was hard as stone from just kissing her and feared I'd never recover if I didn't get relief soon. But this wasn't about me, it was about Sabrina.

She mewled in disappointment when I broke the kiss. The distress turned into a moan when my lips continued sucking, licking, nipping her smooth skin from her neck to her breast. Her nipple begged to be touched. I ran a fingertip over the hardened nub a few times before latching on and drawing it into my mouth.

"Luca," she said on a breathy sigh.

"Do you want me to stop?" I asked in between open-mouthed kisses over her breasts.

"No."

Those two letters provided the green light I needed. When I moved to her other breast, my fingers found the button of her slacks and then the zipper. I slid my hands between the fabric and her skin, pushing them down and away without breaking the connection I had on her breasts.

Once they were around her knees, I straightened and stood to remove them. She lay on the couch, naked except for her black thong.

"Don't move."

A nervous giggle erupted before she shook her head. "I won't."

I leaned over and plucked an ice cube from the glass before settling between her legs.

"What's that for?" she asked, her eyes wide and curious. "Although, I could use some ice. I feel like I'm on fire. But then again, you know that. I'm sure my skin feels clammy and sweaty. Oh God. Am I clammy and sweaty?" She skimmed her hands over her stomach and cringed. "Luca, I'm nervous. I'm…"

"Stop talking, Sabrina."

The moment I put the ice on her, she jumped. Once I began using it to paint her belly button, her stretch marks, and the edge of her thong, she moaned with pleasure. Her panting and my breathing were the only sounds in the room.

I left the cube on her as I removed her thong, revealing the smooth skin of her pussy. I took the Lord's name in Italian right before swearing.

"I don't know what you said, but I loved how it sounded."

"I said, Jesus Christ, you're fucking stunning." She trembled when I used the back of my hand to skim over her. "So beautiful," I added, my voice filled with reverence and awe.

I could see her chest rising and falling with every breath she took while I stared at her body. By the time I repositioned between her legs, the ice left a tiny puddle in her navel.

Ready with a fresh piece of ice, I popped it into my mouth, rolled it around my tongue, and then latched onto her clit. She bucked at the assault, forcing me to hold her hips while I licked and sucked her until the cube melted in my mouth. I stopped long enough to repeat the process, three times. By then, she gripped my head in a silent command to continue until she came.

Once she calmed and relaxed, I lifted my head to meet her gaze. "Luca, let me…"

"No," I cut her off. "Not tonight." Desire blazed in her eyes, her taut legs were now languid at my sides. Exhausted, sated, and satisfied… for the moment. I wasn't done with her yet. Truth be told, I wasn't sure I'd ever be done.

Chapter 10

Luca

SOMETIME BETWEEN THE TIME I went down on Sabrina and the end of the movie we started watching, she fell asleep. Except for a throw I draped over her, she stretched naked beside me. The only thing I had removed were my shoes. Having her bare while I wasn't worsened the predicament between my legs. I honestly couldn't remember the last time I was this aroused.

Everything from the silkiness of her hair, to the floral scent that screamed Sabrina, was perfection. Watching her come was the sexiest thing I'd ever seen. Being with her brought out a different side of me. Of course, I had always made sure my lovers were completely satisfied, but this was the first time my satisfaction had nothing to do with me and everything to do with the woman I was with.

It was late, and rather than wake her or move her to her bed, I clicked off the TV, kissed the top of her head, and closed my eyes. In a hushed breath, I whispered, "Good night, sweetheart."

I spent the night with her nestled in my arms, not sure

of when I had fallen asleep. Unaware of what woke me, I blinked my eyes open and saw sunlight dance off the prettiest blonde hair. *Sabrina.* Her body shifted, and not wanting her to land on the floor in front of the sofa, I instinctively strengthened my hold on her.

Her hands started moving up and down my forearms. If I didn't get up soon, we were going to have a problem. "Sabrina?"

She moaned. "Mmm…" I stifled a laugh. Finally realizing where she was, she sat up practically clocking me in the face. "Oh, my God. What time is it? What happened?"

Her eyes widened as she realized her nakedness. In a swift move she snatched the blanket off the couch and draped it around her in a makeshift dress.

"I need to go shower and get Mikey." Her brows furrowed when she noticed I was still in last night's clothes. "You slept in your clothes? That couldn't have been comfortable."

I sat up rubbing my eyes with the heels of my hands. "I'd never been more comfortable." I checked the clock on the cable box. "It's only nine a.m. What time do you need to pick him up?"

"Ten. I've never been late to get him." Panic laced her words and her eyes did little to hide her discomfort.

I stood and pulled her into my arms. "Sweetheart, you won't be late. You go take a shower and I'll make coffee." She nodded before I leaned down and brought my lips to hers. It wasn't an open-mouthed kiss, after all, it was morning, but I needed her to know I wanted to be exactly where I was.

She smiled, her breathing calmed, and she looked up at me with those gorgeous eyes of hers. "Last night was incredible. I just feel badly that you didn't get a good night's rest. I'm sure your weekends are the only time you sleep in."

"To be honest, I'm usually done working out by now, so don't worry about my beauty rest."

Sabrina shimmied out of the room never releasing the grip on the throw. When I heard the bathroom door click closed, I cursed myself for not using it first. Rather than make coffee, I grabbed her apartment keys from the table and hustled to the corner coffee shop.

After using their facilities and getting us coffee, muffins, and the biggest sugar cookie with sprinkles for Mikey, I went back to her place. The sound of her hairdryer ceased, and she walked out just as pretty as the day I first laid eyes on her.

She noticed the cups of coffee and bag on the table. "You went out?"

"Yes, you went into the bathroom before I had a chance to use it. Plus, I didn't want to rummage through your kitchen for coffee." I shrugged. "Nor, did we have time to make breakfast. You need to eat."

I pulled the muffins out of the bag and set them each on a napkin. "I wasn't sure what you liked, so I got a variety and a cookie for Mikey. But, I'll leave that in the bag until you say it's okay for him to have it.

"Thank you, he'll be thrilled when he gets home. I'll give it to him after lunch." She sat at the table and checked the time. "I'm sorry, but I really need to head out. Please take a muffin for yourself."

"Would you and Mikey like to meet me for lunch?"

She worried the corner of her bottom lip. "Sunday is movie day. It's been a thing we've been doing since… well, since he's been going to my parents every other weekend. It lessened the guilt having not been with him the entire day before. It's sort of *our* time."

"Sounds like a great day." She nodded and suddenly the air felt a bit thick. For the first time I wasn't sure what I should do, and by the uncertainty on her face, neither did she. "Have fun today, I'll get out of your hair so you can get going." I walked up to her and circled her slim waist with my arms. "I had a wonderful time last night."

Her eyes sparkled recalling our evening. "I had the best time I've had in a long time." She lifted up on the balls of her feet, wrapped her arms around my neck and hugged me. My hands splayed across her back as I pulled her into me. "Thank you, Luca."

When I released my hold, I looked down at her. "I'll call you later." I kissed the top of her head and picked up my cup of coffee.

She nodded and walked me toward the door. "I'm sorry about today."

"No worries. Tell Mikey I'll see him next Saturday."

"I will." She pulled the door open. "Thanks for breakfast." I planted another swift kiss to her lips and left.

When I got home, I brushed my teeth, changed into my gym clothes, and headed to a place where I could clear my head. Everything with Sabrina was going at Mach 1 speed, and I needed to decide how to play things with her.

The sound of weights clanging, heavy feet hitting the treadmill, music, and grunts from people exerting themselves welcomed me as I walked into the gym. After I put my things in my locker, I grabbed my gloves, and went to start my workout routine.

To my surprise, Kyle was still there. "Hey, Benedetto.

I didn't think you were going to make it." Sweat dripped off of him as he continued to row on the machine.

"Just running late this morning is all. Where's Soren?"

Kyle released the pulley, grabbed a small white towel, and dried his neck and face. "He took off about thirty minutes ago. He was calm until he saw the stock ticker scrolling across the bottom of the TV." He tilted his head to the one television that had CNBC on. "I swear, he's the only one in here that actually pays attention to what they're watching and not just use it as a distraction. Anyway, the last thing he said was, 'They're vulnerable.' He smiled and told me he'd catch me later."

I knew Jude wanted to start acquiring businesses. He must have found one that was ripe for the picking. "I'll check in with him later and find out the scoop."

Rather than head to the free weights, I headed to the kickboxing area. Kyle followed behind me. "Care to tell me why you're boxing this morning? It's usually when you're sexually frustrated." I ignored him and fastened my gloves, tightening the second Velcro strap with my teeth. Kyle slid on a pair of punching mitts and stood across from me.

"I'm not frustrated." *Right jab.* "We had a great time last night." *Left jab.* "She's not like any other woman I've ever met." *Left uppercut.* The sound of my glove smacking Kyle's mitt spurred me on. "Her kid is great." *Right hook.* "I feel like I've known her for months rather than days." *Left hook.* "She's smart and beautiful." *Right uppercut.* "I slept with her in my arms last night, and we never even had sex. I think I'm falling for this woman." *Left uppercut.*

I hadn't noticed Kyle had lowered his hands until my gloved fist landed on his jaw and he landed on the ground. "Holy shit! Are you okay? Why did you lower your hands?" I yanked off my gloves and knelt next to him. A few other gym goers stood along the side of the mat waiting for movement.

Kyle slowly rolled to his back. "Seriously, what the fuck, Benedetto?"

I could feel my eyes widen. "Me? You lowered your hands, you idiot."

Once everyone saw that Kyle was fine, they went back to what they were doing. I pulled him up noticed a bruise started to form on his face. "You say something like that and not expect me to react?"

"You're an idiot."

"You said that already." He rubbed his jaw with his hand and winced. "Vanessa's going to kill you for hurting me."

I let out a chuckle. "Really, that's what you're going with? I'm sure she's wanted to punch you herself a time or two. But seriously, I didn't mean to hit you. Are you sure you're okay?"

"Yeah, I'm fine."

"Come on, let's get out of here. I'll buy you breakfast. At least that's soft food." I started laughing.

"You're a dick."

"Yeah, a dick who knocked you on your ass."

Our usual waitress showed sympathy for Kyle before bringing us our meals and him an ice pack. "There you go, sweetie. Put that on your jaw and it won't swell."

Kyle smiled, well, it was more of a grimace. "Thank you." The older woman glared at me before walking away. "See, you even got on *her* bad side."

I shook my head. "Whatever."

"Okay, so tell me about your date last night other than the fact you didn't get any action."

There was no way I was going to divulge that just because *I* didn't get any action, as he so eloquently phrased it, didn't mean I wasn't satisfied. The look she had on her face when she came would be ingrained in my head until the next time I saw it.

"We went to dinner, talked, and went back to her place. Her son, Mikey, was at her parents' house. She's special. And her little boy, he's a cool little dude. Do you know he never had pepperoni on pizza until we went to lunch last week?" I cut a triangle shaped bite of my pancakes and put it in my mouth. "Or sausage, and I found out he has Italian blood in him. That's like sacrilegious. To be honest, I was a little bummed he wasn't home."

I took a sip of my orange juice and noticed Kyle had an eyebrow cocked. "Do you hear yourself?"

"What? He's a great kid. I'm actually teaching him how to play soccer since his coaches aren't worth the ball they play with."

"You mean the ball that hit you in the head when you weren't paying attention?" He let out a chuckle and winced.

I waved the syrup-covered fork at him using it to point at his chin. "That's karma right there, buddy. Keep laughing and you'll make it worse for yourself." He grimaced and gingerly chewed his French toast. "But really, wait until you meet Mikey; you'll see for yourself. Even Cassie has a soft spot for him."

"Sucks he doesn't have a father."

The thought of that asshole cheating on Sabrina made my blood boil. "Yes, it's a shame. A little boy needs a male figure in his life."

"I'm going to ask you again, do you hear yourself? You've told me more about Mikey than you have Sabrina."

"You've met Sabrina. All I'm saying is the kid is great, and she's a great mother. I don't know Kyle, it feels fast, but I really have feelings for her. She's kind, strong, level-headed… and for someone who's been through what she has, she has every right to be mad at the world, but she's not."

"Don't forget beautiful."

Hearing Kyle call her that annoyed me, but it wasn't a lie. "Yes, she's stunning, but that has nothing to do with it. I've been with enough beautiful women to know that's just the surface. With her it's more."

He nodded. I knew he understood because Vanessa was absolutely gorgeous, yet it was her personality and attitude he was drawn to. Appearances became secondary when the person you wanted to be with was prettier on the inside.

"When are you going to see her again?"

"Next weekend. Mikey has a soccer game in the afternoon, but I'm coaching him in the morning. Someone needs to show the kid how the game is played."

"Wow, you sound like a dad."

A dad? "No, I'm just a friend who's helping a little boy learn the best sport on the planet."

"I thought you were teaching him soccer, not hockey."

"Very funny."

"Just be careful. Don't get in too deep. A mother's bond with her kid—especially a single mom's, is tight."

All I could do was nod in acknowledgment. Yes, he was right. Their bond was undeniable, as was their love. "I'm not planning to interfere in their lives."

I just want to be included in it.

Chapter 11

Sabrina

THE DIMNESS IN MY ROOM meant it was either super early, or it was cloudy out. I checked my phone and was happy to see it was barely six a.m., which afforded me at least an hour or so more of sleep that I desperately needed.

It'd been a busy week with Spring Break coming. The salon was jammed with New Yorkers wanting their hair cut, colored, and styled for the trips they were about to embark on. By Wednesday, I craved the weekend for several reasons.

Today, my schedule was free of clients. We had Mikey's game and were supposed to be spending the day with Luca. My thoughts drifted to the man who seemed to be on my mind more and more with each day that passed.

But due to the weather, I wasn't sure if we'd see him as we hoped. Luca's plan to help Mikey practice before his game hung in the balance. Rain in the forecast meant it could be canceled. I was thankful I hadn't mentioned Luca to my son. There were two things you never did with a five-year-old. First, you never promised anything, and second, you never revealed plans until the day of.

It was hard not to share with Mikey what we would be doing on Saturday, especially since he'd bring Luca up all the time. The protective mother in me worried my son seemed to latch onto a man who, for all intents and purposes, was a stranger to him.

No one had influenced Mikey since Dillon's death, except for maybe my brother. But even with Michael, I felt as if my son was cognizant that his uncle lived far away and getting too attached wouldn't work out well for him. As far as his grandfathers, well, they were just that. They doted, loved and spoiled him—exactly what they were supposed to do.

Luca and I spoke a few times since Saturday night, always after Mikey was in bed. He also sent me texts throughout the week to ask how my day was going. Even though I hadn't seen him in person, the imagery he provided after our romantic evening had me reliving every delicious moment.

What felt like a minute later, Mikey came barreling into my room whining over the rain that pelted our windows. I felt bad for the kid; he looked so forward to his soccer games. Because of the weather, I convinced him to watch cartoons in my bed so I get a bit more rest. Getting up so early on a rainy Saturday meant a long-ass day for me.

"Mom?" he asked, shaking me with a small hand on my shoulder.

I propped up on an elbow and kissed the top of his messy head of hair. "What's up, baby?"

His puckered brow indicated he debated on what to say. When his big brown eyes focused on mine, he asked in a tiny voice, "Do you miss Dad?"

"Of course I do," I responded with no hesitation.

"You never really talk about him."

My heart instantly squeezed in my chest from a shot of regret. "Well, I think about him all the time. Sometimes, it's hard to talk about him." *Boy, wasn't that the truth.*

There wasn't one memory I held that hadn't been tainted. When I remembered the day he proposed, visions of him with *her* superseded the joy I experienced from being engaged. When I remembered the day I surprised Dillon with the news he was going to be a father, the child *she* had made me bitter and angry.

I wrapped an arm around my son and pulled him closer. "Baby, did you have another dream about Daddy?" It happened often, sometimes Mikey would wake up crying and calling for Dillon. Other times, he'd wanted to sleep in my bed because that was where his dad used to sleep.

"No. I just get sad a lot," he said after a long pause.

"It's okay to be sad."

He twisted in my arms to stare up at my face. "Do you think if Daddy didn't die we'd still be living in our old house?"

"Yes, baby."

"Then that makes me sad because I wouldn't be friends with Jared or Scottie. They are my best buddies, and then Luca, too. Do you think Daddy is upset in heaven because I have new friends now?"

The irises of his eyes shimmered in the dimly lit room. "No…" I paused to swallow the lump that had lodged in my throat. "No, baby. I think Daddy is watching you with your new friends, and he's smiling that you're happy." I pulled his head closer to kiss his forehead before tucking him under my arm.

We both stared at SpongeBob, each lost in our own thoughts. Thinking the conversation was over, he surprised me and said, "Yeah, Mom. I think you're right. And you know what else?"

"What, baby?"

"I hope I'm always friends with Jared, Scottie, and Luca, so I can tell them all the fun things I used to do with Dad."

A slow tear escaped from my eye. I swiped it away and nodded in agreement. "Me, too, baby. But remember, you'll always meet new friends in life. Like when you get older and you go to college or even start a job. Friends are like stars in the sky. You can never have too many, and even if you meet new ones, the old ones will still twinkle in your life."

"Right. But my friends now are like the Big Dipper. They'll always be there."

I hope so.

I stared at my son, a mini-me of his father. So much sorrow had happened in his short life. By the same token, he had so much life yet to live. I wouldn't be able to protect him from heartbreak, but I could damn well try.

The episode ended with my son giggling at that stupid sponge's antics. And just like that, he was back to being a carefree five-year-old boy.

"Hey, who wants a Mickey Mouse pancake?"

His head twisted with a huge smile. "With whipped cream?" I couldn't help but smile at his request. Dillon never put syrup on his pancakes, and he passed his weird preference for whipped cream onto our son.

"Absolutely with whipped cream." I ruffled his hair

before slipping out of bed. Making my way to the kitchen, I started up the coffee pot and pulled out the mix for the pancakes. My cell chimed with an incoming text where it was plugged in on the counter.

Luca: I'll come by at ten to pick you guys up.

Wondering if the rain had stopped, I walked to the window carrying my cell in my hand. A steady downpour continued, and I quickly texted back.

Me: I'm sorry. I was going to text you in a bit.
The game is canceled.

The dancing dots appeared, and his response came quickly.

Luca: We'll just have to figure out something else to do. See you soon. Okay?

I couldn't believe he still planned to spend the day with us. The battle of confusion, between wanting him to or not, percolated within me.

The woman I was wanted nothing less than to spend the whole day with Luca. Remembering how I felt with his arms around me as we danced, his lips on mine, the intimate act he gifted me with, had the need to see him today swelling like a balloon being inflated. But the mother in me feared it was too soon.

My conversation with my son left me feeling raw, inadequate. It was obvious Mikey was searching for that man to replace his father. If things didn't work out with Luca, and there were plenty of reasons to believe they wouldn't, how could I set Mikey up for more loss in his young life?

Bottom line, he made me happy, he made Mikey happy, and it wasn't like he was proposing marriage. The man wanted to hang out, do something fun. How could

I find fault with that?

I hesitated enough for him to send another text.

Luca: Sabrina?

Me: Okay.

I walked out of my room, dressed in jeans, a long sleeve gray T-shirt, and my Converse sneakers. Mikey sat at the table, half of his pancake still buried under a mountain of whipped cream.

"Hey, mister. If you don't finish your breakfast, you won't be ready to go."

Remnants of Mickey's chocolate chip eyes were smeared across his bottom lip when he asked, "Go where?"

"It's a surprise. But since it takes you *for… ever* to finish one pancake, you'll just have to stay in today and, oh, I don't know, practice your spelling words?"

He shoved the last few bites of Mickey's ear into his mouth. While still chewing, he said, "Done!"

"Good boy. Go clean up, wash your face, and brush your teeth. Meet me in your room."

He shot out of his chair and bolted toward the bathroom. I waited until the very last minute to tell him, glancing at the clock on the microwave to confirm as such. Down the hall I heard evidence of him brushing his teeth, and then he ran into his room.

"Mom! What should I wear?"

Not knowing exactly what Luca had planned, I figured we couldn't go wrong dressing for the weather. "Put on a pair of jeans and one of your favorite sweatshirts." I smiled at the sound of his drawers opening and closing. "Mikey, don't forget clean underwear and socks."

"I know, Mom!" came at me without hesitation.

In less time it took for him to eat half a pancake, my adorable son stood in front of me... with one blue sock and one red one. "Sweetie?" I pointed at his feet.

"Oh." He laughed and ran back into his room.

The buzzer on my door sounded. I knew it was Luca, so I hit the unlock button and cracked open my apartment door. It didn't take long for him to be standing in my doorway. He pushed it open and scanned the room. When he realized it was just us, he planted a swift kiss on my lips. "Good morning, beautiful. Where's the ball of energy?"

"Putting on matching socks... and good morning."

He closed the door behind him and lowered his voice to a whisper. "I thought we could go to an indoor soccer field and then how does an indoor waterpark sound?"

"Mikey would love that, but let's not tell him until we're sure that's what we're doing. He was so disappointed his game was canceled." I studied the gorgeous man in front of me for a moment. "Are you sure you don't have other things you want to do today?"

"This is what I want to do today. Go grab your bathing suit, and Mikey's." No sooner did Luca finish his request, when Mikey came barreling out of his room.

"Okay, I match!" He wiggled his toes with pride before noticing we weren't alone. "Luca! You're here." In a flash he was across my small living room and catapulted himself into Luca's arms.

"Hey, buddy." Luca gestured toward my bedroom with his head, and I went to go grab our swimwear.

Being that it was April, I wasn't prepared to don a

bathing suit. I knew I couldn't skirt out of this since Mikey would be in the water, which meant, so would I. A bikini wouldn't be appropriate for today, so I decided on a one-piece. It wasn't overly conservative, yet it had enough material that covered what needed to be.

Once I had my suit and Mikey's packed, along with a hairbrush, comb and a small can of hairspray, I was ready to go.

When I walked into the living room, Mikey was sitting on the couch with Luca telling him all about his week at school. "You should have seen it. I was the fastest one in my class. No one caught me for tag. It was the coolest thing. Then, Miss Brooks taught us how to make these cool beach balls out of... um..." He turned to me for assistance. "Mommy, what was it called?"

"Papier mâché."

"Yeah, that's it." Luca's eyes went wide as did his smile at Mikey's enthusiasm. "It's really flour and water. Did you know it makes this cool paste and then you rub it on newspaper? We covered a balloon with it. Miss Brooks said it didn't matter if the balloon popped or deflated because it would still be a ball. Then we painted it. Miss Brooks is the coolest. Wait, I'll show it to you." He finally stopped to take a breath and jumped off the couch.

Luca released a hearty chuckle.

"What did you feed him this morning?"

Before I could answer, Mikey was back holding the rainbow-colored ball. He handed it to Luca who let out a whistle. "Wow, buddy, this is fantastic. You did such a great job. It's exactly like a beach ball."

"Thank you. Miss Brooks said we all did a great job. You can keep it." My heart lodged in my throat. Mikey looked at me with wide eyes. "Mommy, is it okay if I give it to Luca?"

When I noticed the way Luca's eyes focused on Mikey before moving to me, there was only one answer to give. "Honey, if you'd like him to have it, then that's up to you."

He spun back around and faced Luca. "Would you like to keep it?"

Luca smiled. "Of course, but on one condition." Mikey's nose crinkled from confusion. "An artist always signs his work."

Once again, my son bounced off of the couch and returned with a marker. Luca held the ball as my son etched his name onto the yellow stripe. His little tongue poked out of the side, which made me smile.

I almost had to excuse myself when Luca pulled him into a hug to thank him. "This is the best gift I've ever gotten. Thank you. Now, how about we head out of here and have some fun." Mikey nodded. "Grab a jacket because it's chilly outside."

Chapter 12

Luca

AFTER MIKEY CHANGED FROM JEANS to track pants, made a last minute bathroom visit, said goodbye to his hermit crab, and put the papier mâché ball in a plastic bag we were on our way… or so I thought. Then Mikey ran back into the apartment to grab his favorite hat, and we were finally on our way.

Sabrina and I walked down the stairs with Mikey between us, chattering away about the gross lunch his friend Jared brought to school yesterday.

"Egg salad. Yuck. It stunk up the whole classroom. Eggs are so gross. Do you like eggs, Luca?"

"I do."

"Hmm. Maybe I should try them again one day. Grandma made me scrambled eggs once, and they weren't too yucky." I peered at his mother over his head, smiling as she rolled her eyes. My hand itched to hold hers, but now wasn't the time or place.

When we got to the lobby, Sabrina lifted the hood of Mikey's raincoat. "Aw, Mom, it's hardly raining out." He pushed the kelly green nylon off his head and pointed to the Yankee cap. "That's what this is for." Again Sabrina rolled her eyes, but chose to pick her battles.

"Why don't you guys wait here while I get the car?"

Sabrina met my eye, and raised her brows in question. "Maybe we're better off taking my car?"

"No need. Wait here. I'll be a few."

"We can walk with you," Mikey volunteered. He pointed toward the glass door. "See, it's stopping." He looked to his mom, clapping his little hands together and begging, "Puh-leeeze?"

Sabrina flipped the hood up on her jacket with a sigh. "Okay."

Mikey ran out the door with Sabrina and I close behind. "Where are we going, Luca?" he asked, bouncing on his sneakered feet. We started walking toward the corner as a light drizzle fell.

"Well, first we're going to practice your soccer skills. There's an indoor field I reserved for us."

"Awesome! I need to stay on top of my game since we aren't playing today." He stopped walking long enough to kick an imaginary ball through the air. I couldn't help but laugh at the determination on his face.

"Stay on top of your game? Where did you learn that?" Sabrina asked, trying to hide her smile but failing.

"Scottie," he said with an obvious raise of one hand. Turning his attention to me, he further explained, "Scottie's dad is our coach."

"Ah, gotcha." *The man sucked at coaching.* "Well, today I'll help you learn some moves that you can impress Scottie's dad with. How's that, buddy?"

"I can't wait! I'm the only one on the team who has a best friend that actually played soccer in Italy." He went on to explain his conversation with his friends about the best countries in the world who play the best soccer. "Jared said Brazil people are the best, but I said, no way. Italy people are. Right, Luca?"

"I don't think so, buddy. But I believe we're tied for second in most World Cup wins."

"Well, that's just as good as first. Right? There's like a million countries they beat." I nodded a lot, listening intently, but my true focus was on Sabrina. She seemed very quiet, and I wondered what was on her mind.

After a few minutes, I led them to a blue rented SUV parked halfway down the block. When I raised the key fob to unlock the doors with a beep, Sabrina twisted her head with a look of shock on her face.

"Is this your car? Cool!"

"No buddy, I'm renting it." I opened the back door for him. He jumped inside, sat on the booster seat, and pulled the webbed belt down to buckle himself in.

"It's so clean," he added, his eyes taking in the pristine interior. "Mom, our car is messy."

"And whose fault is that?" she countered with a raised brow.

I shut the back door and waited a pause before opening the front door for Sabrina. "Are you okay?"

Her gorgeous hazel eyes widened as her bottom lip trembled with emotion. "Luca, I can't believe you did this."

One of my shoulders raised in a casual way. "It's no big deal."

She shook her head, contradicting my words. "It *is* a big deal."

We stood staring at each other. The need to reach out,

dig my fingers into her hair, and draw her mouth to mine was strong. But the need to keep it platonic for Mikey's sake won out.

A solid knock on the window broke our moment. "Are we going?" We heard a muffled impatient voice ask with hands raised palms up.

"Sorry, buddy." I opened the door for his mother, and whispered, "To be continued."

After practice, we started to head to the water park. Of course, Mikey was asking a thousand questions when he heard we weren't going home yet. The excitement on his face was reminiscent of seeing Santa Claus.

"That was the coolest place, Luca. I've never played on fake grass before. You're really good, too." I looked into my rearview mirror when he got quiet. His brows furrowed as I caught his reflection.

"What's wrong, buddy?"

Sabrina twisted in her seat, craning her head to see her son. "Are you okay?"

Mikey started and stopped his question a couple of times and then blurted it out. "I'm just wondering, well, I mean, Luca taught me how to head the ball today, which was really awesome, but I'm wondering why he didn't when he was at my game?"

I let out a chuckle and Sabrina covered her mouth. Apparently, she knew laughing just encouraged children, whereas I'd rather laugh with them. "Well, usually during a game, a header is strategic... and planned. Your kick surprised me. But, believe me, that won't happen again." Mikey rewarded me with a smile.

"Oh, next time I'll tell you it's coming." He paused for a second. "But, I won't tell the other players because then they'll know what my strat… my strat…"

I filled in the blank. "Strategy?"

"Yeah, that. I won't yell my strat… gee out loud."

"Good plan." I turned into the parking lot of our next destination.

As soon as the car slowed, Mikey started to squirm in his booster seat to get a glimpse of where we were. When the sign for Splash Wave Water Park came into view, a shriek that could almost shatter crystal came from the back seat.

"Michael Dillon, use your inside voice, please." Sabrina's voice was calm, meanwhile my ears were still ringing.

"Sorry, Mommy." He paused for a second. "And Luca."

"That's okay, but you need to follow rules today. I know you're excited," Sabrina said, "but it's a very busy place, and you can't horse around in there. Got it?"

"Got it."

I grabbed my duffle along with Sabrina's and we all headed in. Mikey's eyes widened to the size of inner tubes when he caught sight of the slides, wave pool, and lazy river. I bought our tickets, and once we had our wristbands fastened we were off to have some fun.

The scent of chlorine filled the humid air. Kids and adults raced down slides laughing and having a great time. Yeah, this was a fantastic idea. If I could have reached around and patted my own back, I would have.

Sabrina took her bag from me, "We'll go change in the locker room and meet you back here, is that okay?"

Even she seemed excited to take a trip down one of the slides. Whereas I was excited to see her in a bathing suit. I motioned toward a seating area with tables. "I'll be over there."

She nodded. "Sounds great."

"Mom, can't I go to the men's locker room with Luca? I don't want to be with the girls." He let go of his mom's hands and crossed his little arms in front of his chest. Sabrina let out an exasperated breath. I had a feeling she'd dealt with this more times than not, so I kept my mouth closed.

"Honey, it's a family locker room. There will be boys in there."

"Then can't Luca come with us?"

Our eyes met, and as much as I wanted to go with them, I took the burden off of Sabrina. "Buddy..." I squatted to get to his eye level. "It'll go faster if I go to the men's locker room. We don't want to waste time, do we?" He shook his head. "I didn't think so." I kissed the top of his head and smiled at his mother who was staring at me with the same look she had earlier.

"Okay, then it's settled." Sabrina took Mikey's hand. "See you soon, Luca."

I changed into my swim trunks, tossed on a tank top and my sport slides, stuffed my bag into a locker, and headed out to the deck area to find us a table.

When they started walking toward me, my breath hitched in my throat. The one-piece black suit she wore was not sexy or revealing in any way, but holy hell you could still tell her body was spectacular—and I knew for a fact it was. However, some of the other men there couldn't keep their eyes off of her either.

It was going to be a long day.

Mikey caught sight of me and ran right to where I was waiting. "I've never been to a water park before. This is gonna be so awesome!"

"That's the plan, buddy."

Sabrina approached with a wide smile. "Mikey, stay here with Luca. I'm going to grab a few more towels." Like a magnet for my eyes, I pinned my line of sight to the seductive sway of her butt as she walked away.

"Luca."

I looked back at her son, and he waited for me to pay attention. Based on his mannerism, he must have had called my name more than once. "Yeah?"

"Can we do that?" He pointed to the giant spiral slide at the far end of the park.

Not wanting to promise him in case he wasn't allowed, I said, "That might be for grown-ups only. We'll see." For some reason, the words reminded me of my mother. I had to swallow a chuckle at how "parenty" I sounded.

Two weeks ago, family outings weren't on my radar. How quickly things could change. Being with Mikey and Sabrina felt natural. It didn't hurt that he was a great kid and that his mom was quickly becoming someone special to me.

Speaking of, the way Sabrina's hips swayed as she made her way back to us made me thankful I decided to wear board shorts rather than my usual European cut suit. She set the towels down and smiled at her son who was ready to pop out of his water shoes.

"What do you say, Mikey? Are you ready?" He nodded enthusiastically. "Then what are we waiting for?" Sabrina said as she smiled brightly at her son. "Do I need to remind you of the rules?"

"No, Mom. I know. No running and stay where you can see me. If we get separated, I need to go to a lifeguard. You told me all of this in the locker room. I'm not a baby." He pouted. "Right, Luca?"

"Oh no way, buddy, you're not involving me in this. Your mom has good rules. You should listen to her no matter how old you are."

Mikey shrugged. "Okay, if you say so. Can we go now?"

The three of us started out on the more tame water slides where Mikey could ride alone. After climbing up and down the stairs and ladders numerous times, we decided to float in the lazy river.

We climbed into the inner tube, and Sabrina and I sat side by side. Mikey took the flat surface between us. I was close enough to stretch my arm out behind her. The tip of Sabrina's ponytail tickled my skin. Her face was makeup free, the freckles across the bridge of her nose making her appear younger than her age.

The way the wet nylon clung to every curve, dip and crevice of her body, made me wish we were done floating and somewhere alone.

"This was a wonderful idea."

I shot my eyes down to Mikey beside me. He was busy kicking his legs trying to get his toes to touch the water. While he was occupied, I lifted my hand and started playing with her ponytail. A small smile tugged on the corners of her full lips. "I'm glad you're both having fun."

When my fingers drifted to trace lazy patterns on the back of her neck, her smile changed to something else. I'd been dying to touch her all day, and as long as we were in this tube floating aimlessly, I would continue to.

But Mikey had other plans. As we approached the

debarking area, he twisted toward his mother. "Can we see if I'm big enough for the big slide now?"

Sabrina's gaze cut to the monstrosity he referred to. "Um…that one is way too big for your mom."

"Please? Luca can take me." He turned toward me. "Right, Luca? You're not afraid of it."

"Hey, I'm not afraid either. It's just…" Sabrina stopped and turned to me with a pleading look on her face.

"If you're big enough, *I'll* go with you."

She mouthed a silent thank you before telling her son that would be his last slide for the day. And based on his not arguing, must have meant he was exhausted.

A romp down the jumbo slide turned into two. The sheer joy spread on her son's face once we emerged from the pool had Sabrina agreeing to "one more time." It was close enough to the dinner hour that we decided to have something to eat at the park. Sabrina felt once Mikey hit his booster seat he would be out for the count.

I ordered us a pizza to share, and ice cream for dessert. By the time we changed out of our swimsuits, walked out to the car, and hit the parkway, Mikey was out cold. Sabrina turned in her seat to stare back at her son. "You wiped him out," she said with humor in her voice.

"I could say the same. He sure has stamina." I looked over at her with a smile. "I know he had fun. Did you?"

A nod began before I finished asking my question. "I did. Thank you, Luca. For the soccer lesson, the water park… for everything."

"It was my pleasure." I took her hand in mine and rested them on the center console. Her fingers clenched in an affectionate squeeze. But the way she stared out the window in a distracted silence meant she had something on her mind. I didn't want to press her, so I waited to see if she'd open up.

She never did.

Conversation between us revolved around things we saw at the park that struck us as funny. The subject of Mikey's dad came up briefly when Sabrina mentioned how much he had missed of her son's childhood because of his deployments.

About an hour later, we were back on her street in the city. Throughout, Mikey never stirred. I found a parking space one block over. "If I carry him in will he wake up?"

"He may, but that's fine. If he goes to sleep now, I'm facing a six a.m. wake-up call," she said on a laugh.

As I removed him from his booster seat, he lifted his head, mumbled, "Don't forget my hermit crab."

"What?" I whispered once he had settled on my shoulder.

She shook her head with a grin spread over her face. "No clue."

The way his arms tightened around my neck as I carried him toward their apartment had my heart squeezing in my chest. This kid managed to get to me in a way no one ever had. Not having nieces or nephews of my own, I never really connected to a child before. Yet with Mikey, I already knew I was hooked.

Of course, being insanely attracted to his mother hooked me even more.

Once we were in their apartment, Sabrina removed his shoes, jacket, and hat and I laid him down on his bed. Again, he mumbled, turned over, and fell back to sleep.

She shut the door to his room with a small smile. "Would you like coffee?"

"No, I'm good." I walked closer to her and caressed her face. Wanting her to open up and talk to me on her own took a backseat to wanting to be sure she was okay. "You're quiet."

"I'm overwhelmed."

I tucked her hair behind her ear. "Because of me?"

"Yes." She turned away for a moment, and when her eyes drifted back up to mine, they shimmered with emotion. "I've never met a man as considerate, giving, kind-hearted, and..." A huff of air escaped while she searched for the right word. "Perfect as you," she ended her thoughts in a whisper. "It overwhelms me."

Her admission caused a surge of confusion. Part of me wanted to strip her down and replace the emotions that consumed her by taking her body and infiltrating her thoughts. But the bigger part of me knew she needed time to process this. Fuck, I *needed* time to process this.

Whatever *this* was.

I knew I battled my own mass of confusion over how quickly Sabrina and Mikey captured my heart. How the hell that happened had been all I'd been thinking about since meeting them. So, I got it, her confusion I could relate to. Add in losing her husband, finding out what he had done before he died, and having a son to care for, combined must have wreaked havoc on her thoughts.

Cupping her face, I tilted her head back to stare into her eyes. "It overwhelms me, too. I think, if we take things slow, maybe we can both figure this out together." My eyes cut to the way her lips parted. Before she could speak, I lowered my head and kissed her softly. I broke away, leaning my forehead against hers. "I'll talk to you tomorrow?"

She nodded and smiled. "Definitely."

Chapter 13

Sabrina

"CAN WE GO PLAY NOW?" Jared asked Becky. She pointed at their half eaten bagels and then looked at me for confirmation. My slight nod had her saying, "Fine." The two of them scrambled off their chairs and took off for Jared's room. "No wrestling!" she called out in warning.

Becky took a sip of her coffee before saying, "I want details." When I started circling the rim of my mug with my index finger she asked, "How's Luca?"

I couldn't control the natural smile that played on my lips thinking about our wonderful day yesterday. "He's good. We went to an indoor soccer field to teach Mikey a few things, the man is a great soccer player. The things he can do with a ball are astounding." Becky's chin was propped up on her hand, and her eyes were in a dreamlike state. Ignoring her, I continued. "Then we went to an indoor waterpark."

She let out a sigh. "I bet his body is spectacular in a swimsuit. He could probably be a swimwear model."

When I thought about his rippled torso, strong arms

and broad chest, I nodded. "He's definitely a good-looking man."

"*Good-looking*?" Becky quipped. "That is not what you call good-looking. That's what you call sex on legs. The man has it going on, and even you can't be that blind. Face it my friend, you landed a hottie."

"I haven't landed anyone. We're just getting to know each other. Plus, I need to think of Mikey. I'm not ready to jump into a relationship quite yet."

Becky's eyebrows drew in leaving a tiny vertical crease above her nose. "Nope, I'm not buying it. I know you, and you're overthinking this. From what I can tell, he's great with Mikey. So, what is going on in that head of yours?"

"I'm not overthinking anything. It's just…" I shrugged my right shoulder. "I don't want Mikey to be disappointed. You're right, Luca is great with him. He even rented an SUV because his car is only a two-seater." Becky sighed. "Yes, I know… he's perfect."

We heard a crash from the other room followed by a, "We're okay! Nothing's broken!"

Becky and I both let out a long breath. "Boys." She laughed. "What's next on the agenda with you two? If you need me to watch Mikey while you and Luca… you know." She winked. "I'm available. Hell, it's easier with two of them. At least they occupy each other. We heard a loud thud and I arched a brow. Becky smiled. "I'll go check on them."

She left me at her table with a very vivid, very real visual of Luca in that damn bathing suit. When Mikey and I left the locker room, and found Luca waiting for us, I almost swallowed my own tongue. Needing to retreat quickly to catch my breath, I went off to get us towels as a pathetic attempt to pull myself together. I was a mother, for God's sake.

As if my thoughts channeled him, my phone lit up with an incoming text.

> **Luca:** Good morning. I hope you guys are well today and Mikey wasn't up at the crack of dawn.
>
> **Me:** Hi. lol. No, he was so tired, he never woke once until 8 this morning. Thanks again, he can't stop chattering, and his friend Jared is sick of hearing about it.
>
> **Luca:** Maybe next time Jared would like to come as well.
>
> **Me:** Oh please do NOT mention that to Mikey yet. He WILL drive you crazy.
>
> **Luca:** No worries. What are you up to today?
>
> **Me:** Not much. Having breakfast with my friend Becky now. You?
>
> **Luca:** My dumbass friend Kyle is forcing us to help him move his girlfriend into his apartment.
>
> **Me:** Vanessa? That's great they're moving in together.
>
> **Luca:** We'll see. He's a compulsive neat freak and she's a slob.

I chuckled at his text, imagining it perfectly. Vanessa didn't strike me as the type to be OCD about anything.

"What's so funny?" Becky asked as she walked back into the kitchen. "They're fine, by the way. My genius son tried to get something down from the top shelf in his closet and quickly discovered shoeboxes don't make a sturdy ladder."

"Oh, those boys. I swear every day I sprout another gray hair."

She topped my coffee cup without asking. "So, what had you grinning?" Noticing the phone still in my hand she then asked, "Is that Mr. *Sex On Legs*?" Her singsong voice and the waggle of her eyebrows forced my eyes upward in exasperation. "What?"

"Yes, that was *Luca*."

"He's so smitten."

"You don't even know what the text said."

"Doesn't matter. I can tell by the dreamy look on your face that he either said something romantic or he wants to…" She leaned closer and lowered her voice. "Fuck you hard. Unless you've already done that and in that case he wants to fuck you hard, again."

"Oh my God." Another text chimed and we both eyeballed my phone at the same time.

> **Luca:** Um… based on Mikey's comment about your car being messy, I apologize if you are also a slob.
>
> **Me:** Yeah, it's me who's sloppy. (I'm rolling my eyes).
>
> **Luca:** LOL. Well enjoy your day. I have no idea when I'll be done. I'll touch base with you later?

Out of nowhere, Becky snatched my phone right out of my hand. Her fingers started moving over the screen and panic set in. "Give me that!"

"Relax. You clearly need help in seducing him." She handed me my phone, and I instantly flushed.

> **Me:** You can touch me anytime… anywhere…

anyplace.

The response was immediate.

Luca: Good to know ;)

"Becky!" I tucked my phone into my back pocket mortified at what he must be thinking right now. Then again, his cheeky response instigated salacious thoughts to take hold in my mind.

While distracted over the things he had done to me on my couch last week, Becky cackled at my discomfort. "I'm guessing from your red cheeks you are imagining him doing just that. So, you're welcome."

Luca

I THOUGHT OF SABRINA'S SILKY SKIN beneath my fingertips the entire way to Vanessa's apartment. Her text felt a bit out of character, but I appreciated it just the same. The only problem was, I was stuck moving and unpacking because Kyle was ridiculous.

When I pulled up to Vanessa's apartment, I spotted the small moving truck, Jude's BMW, and Cassie standing behind it in an empty spot with her arms crossed. I couldn't suppress a smile when I flipped on my turn signal.

Cassie scowled when I got out of my car. "Good morning, sunshine. Pleased to see me?" I clicked the fob to lock the doors.

"You're late. So far, I've been yelled at, called a few choice names, had to flirt with a traffic cop, and got flipped off by someone on a motorcycle, all because I had to save this spot for you. Where have you been?"

I kissed her on the cheek. "Who told you to stand in the street to save a spot? That's crazy."

She glared at me. "No shit it's crazy. Your insane friend Kyle asked me to, that's who."

"Lesson learned, never listen to Kyle."

"Whatever." Her eyes studied my car. "What is that? You bought a new car?"

"No, it's a rental, Miss Crabby-pants. I took Sabrina and Mikey out yesterday, and my car wasn't big enough."

Like magic, Cassie's scowl turned into a genuine smile. "I knew you two would hit it off."

My phone chimed with an incoming text.

Kyle: Did you get lost?

I showed Cassie my phone. She let out a sigh. "That man has lost his mind. Vanessa better know what she's getting into. By the way, he's dusting before wrapping her stuff. He's already unpacked and repacked some of her boxes. Maybe I should be thankful I was parking spot monitor."

We both laughed, and I slung my arm around her shoulder. "Come on, we better get up there before Jude throws him out the window."

Right when the elevator door slid open to Vanessa's floor, we could hear the yelling from beyond the closed door. I opened it to find Jude yelling at Kyle, Brae's hands on her husband's chest, because she'd be able to stop him, and Kyle with his hands flailing in the air. Vanessa walked out of her bedroom carrying a small box.

"Maybe moving wasn't a good idea," she stated as she dropped the box on the floor with a thud. "I'll call my landlord and see if I can stay."

Jude's head dropped forward, Brae's hands fell limply, and Kyle acted like his world just stopped spinning.

"Hi, everyone!" I tossed my hand in the air. Four sets of eyes stared at me. "It seems like I got here just in time." Examining the room, I saw a few boxes by the door next to a small hand cart.

"Hi, Luca." Brae walked up to hug me. While in my arms she whispered, "Please separate them. Jude threatened to put Kyle in a moving box and ship him back to Canada."

I did my best trying not to laugh at the image. Vanessa's glistening eyes roamed around the room. "I'm really sorry I mixed up the date for the movers." She sighed. "The only thing I have left to box up are the items in my bathroom. Aside from that, all boxes are packed and labeled."

After taking a deep breath, Kyle walked up to Vanessa and took her into his arms. "Nessa, it's okay. No one minds, really." He kissed her, garnering the first smile I'd seen on anyone's faces since I walked in. "I'll start loading the truck with Jude and Luca. Why don't you ladies finish packing what you need to and then we can head on over to my place."

Once we had everything loaded up, we all got in our respective vehicles, Cassie went with me, and we headed over to Kyle's apartment. It didn't take as long to unload as it did to put everything in the truck.

Vanessa plopped herself down on the sofa followed by Brae and Cassie. "Thank you for helping me today. How about we leave the rest of the unpacking until another day, and we all head out for dinner and drinks… on Kyle."

My pal's apartment morphed from a designer's dream

to a hoarder's nightmare, and I swear it caused him to twitch. But, in true *I'm pussy whipped* fashion, Kyle agreed with Vanessa's suggestion.

I hadn't heard from Sabrina since that text that still played over and over again in my brain. "Do you mind if I ask Sabrina to join us?"

Brae's face lit up. "That sounds like a great idea. By the way, when did you get a bigger car?"

"Oh, I rented it for the weekend because I took Sabrina and her son out yesterday. He's an awesome kid."

"Aww, that's so sweet, Luca." Brae put her hand to her chest. "Isn't it, honey?"

Jude glared at me. "Adorable. Can we go now? I'm starving."

Brae swatted Jude on the shoulder. "Ignore my husband. He's cranky when he's hungry."

"Don't I know it." I smirked at Jude. "Let's go, I'll call her from the car. Cass, want to come with me?"

Without any further discussion, we filed out of the apartment and headed out.

I started the car, pulled out of my spot and called Sabrina on my Bluetooth. "Hi. How's moving going?" Her sweet voice filtered through the speaker.

"Hi, there. We're done and heading out for dinner. How about I come and pick you and Mikey up and you can join us?"

"It's late, Luca."

I glanced at the clock on my dashboard. "It's only six fifteen." Out of the corner of my eye, I saw Cassie cringe, but I had no idea why. "Isn't Mikey off tomorrow?" I pulled up to a red light and now Cassie had her head in her hands. "By the way, say hi to Cassie. She's in the car with me."

Cassie mumbled. "Hi, Sabrina."

"Hi, Cassie." An audible sigh rang through the speaker. "Luca, Mikey is five years old. We've already had dinner, he needs to take a bath and be in bed by eight." The sweet voice that started off this conversation was replaced with a deflated one.

"Okay, I'm sorry. I just thought…"

"No, I'm sorry I don't mean to be rude." The light changed and I pulled ahead remaining silent. "I really wish I could, but I can't. It's been a long day and the morning comes quick. Spring Break to a kid means nothing. He'll still be up with the sun."

"Okay. I'll let you go. Good night, Sabrina."

"Good night. Have fun with your friends. Bye, Cassie."

Cassie gave me a tight grin before replying, "Bye, Sabrina."

When the phone clicked off, I let out a breath. The steering wheel felt like steel as I gripped it tighter. "Shit."

"Luca, don't be upset, it's hard with a five-year-old."

"Yes, I know. I didn't mean to insinuate it wasn't. I just called to invite her to dinner, and now I feel bad."

We pulled up to the restaurant, and even though I lost my appetite, we headed inside.

Chapter 14

Sabrina

I t DIDN'T TAKE LONG AFTER I hung up the phone with Luca for regret to set in. There were times I'd wonder who I was. So often I'd try to be the "put together single mom" and most times it worked. Except for today when I failed miserably and snipped on the only decent man who had paid attention to me since Dillon's death.

When Dillon died, my first instinct was to feel sorry for him. Every time I'd look at our son, and the world of possibilities just waiting to be discovered, I'd cry thinking his father was going to miss it all. Then I felt sorry for Mikey for not having that man in his life. Lastly, I felt sorry for myself.

There were days I'd pull up to the kiss and drop line at school trying to keep it all under control. Unlike some of the other moms who would show up with their hair done, makeup on, and in clothes that matched. I'd picture them at the breakfast table with their husbands and children, having quality family time after a good night's rest.

My mornings weren't like that. Most of the time I'd

hit my snooze button at least twice before rolling out of bed to pull on a ball cap and drive Mikey to school in my pajama bottoms and a hoodie. The thing was, as hectic, scary, and sad as it was to raise him on my own, I was happy—just tired.

As soon as Mikey was tucked in and fast asleep, I changed into my pajamas and climbed into bed. My conversation with Luca haunted me. He didn't deserve the attitude I gave him. Knowing full well I wouldn't be able to fall asleep, I called him.

It didn't take more than two rings for him to answer. "Hi."

"Hi, are you still at dinner?"

"No, I'm home." His voice sounded more solemn that the other times I had spoken to him.

"Luca, I'm really sorry I couldn't join you tonight, God knows I would have loved to. It's been a long day and unfortunately, your call came right after I finished cleaning paint off my floor."

"Did your little Picasso have *another* debacle with paint?" His tone lightened a bit.

I smiled remembering the day Mikey ran into Luca leaving colorful handprints on his pants and my embarrassing attempt at cleaning them. "Nothing like what he did to you. This time, it was my fault. It all started after I stepped on a Lego, which by the way is equivalent to stepping on a shard of glass. That was right after Mikey decided to see if putting a candy in a two-liter bottle of soda would make a volcano. Which, in case you're wondering, it does."

"Oh, no."

"Oh, yes." I rattled off the long chain of events that ended my night. "So, I had dark syrupy soda all over the floor. I sent Mikey to his room for fear something else was going to happen. After I soaked up all of the liquid, and washed the stickiness off my floor, cabinets, table, chairs, and any other surface within a six foot radius, was when I decided to clean up his toys because I was spent. I wanted to call it a day. *That's* when I stepped on the Lego, grabbed my foot in pain, lost my balance, hit the table, spilled the paint, then cleaned the paint, and answered your call."

Jesus, Sabrina... ramble much? But, damn, that felt good getting it all out.

"Ah, it all makes sense now," he said with a small chuckle. "I'm sorry you had a bad day. You know, you could've called me. I would've come over to help occupy him. I love spending time with Mikey."

"Thank you, but all of that happened within an hour at the end of the day. Plus, you were with your friends."

"You're also my friends." I smiled at his declaration. "If I was there right now do you know what I'd do?" The soft foam of my pillow cushioned my cheek as I sank deeper into it.

"What?" So many sexy scenarios flew into my brain. My heart rate increased waiting to hear what he was going to say.

"Are you in bed?"

"Yes," squeaked out sounding like I had laryngitis.

"I'd hold you." Not exactly what I imagined him saying, but truth be told, it sounded absolutely wonderful.

Part of me wanted to tell him to come over, but that wouldn't be possible. "I'd love that."

"Me, too. Are you working Wednesday?"

"Yes., Becky and I are alternating days this week."

"How about I take you and Mikey out to dinner. You can pick the place and time. This way you don't need to cook after work."

"That sounds great, thank you."

"Wednesday it is." I let out a silent yawn, but it must not have been as silent as I thought. Luca chuckled, and the deep timbre of his voice stirred me awake. "I'm going to let you go to sleep now. Sweet dreams, Sabrina. I'll talk to you soon."

"Sweet dreams, and again, I'm sorry for earlier."

"It's forgotten. Good night."

"Good night, Luca." When the line went silent, I closed my eyes, imagining the strong, kind, Italian man who found a way into my heart was with me. A comforting warmth ran through my body. Despite his comment, remorse lingered over losing my patience with him. The man was almost too good to be true. I needed to relax and enjoy his company.

Remembering how he made me feel so wanted and desired helped lessen the guilt a bit. With thoughts of Luca, I drifted off to sleep in a peaceful, content way.

A small hand shook my arm and an impatient voice repeated. "Mom...Mom..."

I opened one eye to see my son hovering a few inches above my face. "What is the first number on the cable box?"

My one eye slid shut until he said, "Nine."

Like a bat out of hell I flew up and out of bed, wide awake in an instant. *Nine*! Crap, my first client was in an hour. "You just woke up?" I asked, grabbing a pair of jeans and a T-shirt to change into.

"Yeah. What are we doing today?" The kid's appetite for activity was insatiable. We'd been going non-stop since our day at the water park on Saturday. Monday was spent with Becky and Jared at the Museum of Natural History. Yesterday I had both boys with me in Central Park where we tackled the zoo in the morning and the playground in the afternoon. Even knowing my day was jammed with clients, I looked forward to interacting with adults.

Showering before work wouldn't be happening, so I bolted into the bathroom to tame my bedhead. "You're staying with Aunt Becky. I have to work," I said while yanking a brush through the tangles in my hair.

"Aww, man. I wanted to play with Scottie today. Jared is a butthead."

"Please don't use that word."

"But he is." He sat on the toilet seat, rambling off all the reasons why his best friend was a butthead. As I brushed my teeth, I felt bad for Becky. She'd have to deal with their nonsense today while I got to be an adult.

Breakfast, dressing, and rushing around took up the next forty-five minutes of our morning. It was a miracle I only walked into the salon ten minutes late after dropping Mikey off at Becky's.

With back-to-back appointments all day long, I barely had time to breathe. Luca had texted me earlier suggesting he pick me up after my last client. We'd then get Mikey before heading out to dinner.

As it turned out, my last client was Cassie. I completely forgot she had made the appointment until Tami, our receptionist, handed me the schedule at the beginning of my day.

Her trim took no time at all, since Cassie liked to keep her hair long and straight. The natural highlights were the type some of my clients paid hundreds of dollars for. Standing behind her elevated chair, I examined her hairline once it was cut to be sure it was straight.

"So, Luca?" she asked when I was satisfied with my precision. Our eyes met in the mirror, and a wide smile spread over her pink tinted lips.

"What?"

"I like you two together." Together? *Were we together?* I guess we were dating, although it was really never discussed. "Why the look?" she asked, watching my face.

"No look. He's so great, but I'm sure you already know that. I just…"

"Worry," she finished my thought. "That's understandable."

I held her gaze and nodded. "It is, right? I keep battling with myself in my head. The way I snapped at him when he called the other night bothers me. I want to apologize to you, as well, it was a difficult day."

"No need to apologize, it's all forgotten. You and Mikey have been through a lot, but I will say, Luca is a great guy… and genuine."

"I can see that about him," I said, reaching for the blow dryer.

"Before you turn that thing on, let me say something else." She waited for me to meet her gaze in the mirror. "Sabrina, you've done an amazing job with Mikey. I told you this on several occasions. He is well adjusted, bright, funny, and a normal happy-go-lucky kid. You deserve to be happy as well. Just trust your heart, and let things happen as they should."

I nodded with a small smile. "Thank you for telling

me all of that."

"It's true." She waved her hand and added, "Okay, proceed." As I dried her hair, I wondered what Luca shared with Cassie regarding our relationship. I would never ask her, nor do I think she would tell me what he had. But I was pretty sure they must have discussed it.

After a few minutes, I switched off the dryer and finished brushing Cassie's silky locks. The salon was winding down making ringing phones and chatter less prominent than it had been an hour prior.

Twisting her head from right to left, she admired the cut and smiled. "Just the way I like it… exactly the same. Thank you for keeping it that way."

"Well, you have great hair, so it doesn't take much effort on my part." I removed the black nylon cape around Cassie's neck. "You're all done, my friend."

Based on the amount of hair I cut whenever Cassie came in, and the fact she became a great friend to me, I hadn't charged her the last couple of times. It always resulted in an argument, right before she thrusted an insanely large tip at me.

"You know this defeats the purpose," I quipped, holding up the fifty dollar bill.

"Where can I get a haircut in the city for fifty bucks? Especially one that won't have me crying because some over-ambitious stylist thinks it's her beautifying duty to rock my world with the newest trendy cut that cost me a fortune to boot." She referred to the last person who left her with choppy layers and no trust in beauticians. That incident was what had Cassie begging me to take her on as a client. With her bag in her hand, she patted my cheek affectionately. "Have fun with Luca tonight. He told me you had plans."

"Oh, he did, did he?" I teased. "What else did Mr. Benedetto tell you?"

"Not much. He barely answers my direct questions."

"He should be here any minute if you want to hang around."

"I think I will." She plopped back into the chair as I cleaned up my station. While gathering my custom scissors and cash tips, she then said, "Speak of the devil."

Luca

HI, LADIES." I STOPPED BESIDE Sabrina and bent to place a soft kiss on her lips. "Hi."

"Hi," she repeated with a smile.

Focusing my attention to Cassie, who sat beaming in the chair, I narrowed my eyes. "I thought you were getting your hair cut?"

She flipped her long locks over her shoulder. "I did."

"It hasn't changed."

"I know."

"Um… okay." Cassie and Sabrina both smiled. "Well then, it looks great."

"Thank you." She stood and gave me a kiss on the cheek. "I should get going. You're not the only one with a hot date. Have fun tonight, you two."

"What?" I snatched the crook of her elbow stopping Cassie in her tracks.

Sabrina beamed and clapped her hands. "You were sitting in my chair for an hour and this is the first I'm hearing about a date? You do know you're supposed to tell your hairstylist all the gossip, right? Is it anyone I know?"

For the first time since I've known her, I saw Cassie's cheeks turn pink. "As a matter of fact, you might. It's Mr. Carson."

"No way!" Sabrina squealed and I was suddenly the odd man out. "Oh my, God! Now I'm really mad you didn't tell me. When did this start?"

"Wait... who's Mr. Carson?" I interrupted.

Sabrina released a dreamy sigh, which wasn't something I wanted to hear after mentioning another man's name. "He's the hot first grade teacher that every mom who has a kid in Kindergarten is sucking up to in order for their kid to be in his class. Of course, all the dads prefer Mr. Carrington."

Every mom, I wondered, scanning her face as I did.

Cassie laughed. "Mr. Carrington is a great teacher and very nice in a grandfatherly way." She also sighed. *Why was everyone sighing today?* "Anyway, I need to get moving. See you two later. Have fun!"

Before I could tell her to text me when she got home, Cassie was already out the door. When I turned, Sabrina was putting her jacket on. She still had a goofy smile on her face.

"Are you ready?"

"Yes, let's go."

With my hand on the small of her back, once outside the salon I clicked the fob for the SUV and opened the door for Sabrina. "I'm right here. I got lucky."

She slid in and asked, "You still have this car?"

"Yes. A friend of mine owns the dealership. It's growing on me, so I leased it for a month to see if it's something I'd like to own. Don't get me wrong, I'm not getting rid of my Jag because I love it."

She let out a laugh right before I closed her door, jogged around the front, and hopped in. "I've heard that men have flashy sport cars to... you know... compensate."

Did she just imply what I think she did? "You're awfully feisty today. I can assure you, there is no need for me to compensate for anything. One day, I'll prove that to you." Sabrina squirmed a little and if I didn't change the subject, I was going to have a *big* problem. "So, where are we picking Mikey up?"

"You can just go to my place. I'll text Becky now to have her meet us there. She took the boys to the park this afternoon."

"Are they still at the park?"

"I haven't heard. Let me check." I watched her thumbs flying across the screen of her phone. After a chime sounded, she said, "Yes, they're still there. The same one where they play soccer."

"Okay, tell her we'll come get him there." Again her thumbs moved, and then she tucked her phone into her bag.

"Done." Before I shifted the car and pulled out into the road, I twisted to face her. Her eyes met mine and held. She tilted her head with a smile. "What?"

"You're beautiful." A pink hue tinged her perfect complexion.

"Thank you, but I feel gross. I slept late this morning and had to rush to work. I barely combed my hair. Which doesn't bode well for a hairstylist. It's a good thing I fixed it before my first client."

This woman had no clue how her natural beauty was

such a rare thing. Rather than tell her she had lost her mind, I buried my fingers into her hair pulling her head closer. Just before connecting our lips, I rubbed my nose along hers and repeated, "Beautiful."

When I closed the distance, she had parted her lips on a small sigh. Our open-mouthed kiss went from slow to smoldering within seconds. I missed those lips, and spent a few minutes devouring them while enjoying every noise that escaped her mouth.

Her eyes were still closed as I pulled away. "I've been wanting to do that since I stepped foot into the salon."

A sexy smirk spread before she said, "I've been *wanting* you to do that since you stepped into the salon."

"There's one problem with having done that now." She watched as I adjusted myself, and fuck if that tiny shift of those hazel eyes didn't make me hard as stone. "Well, yeah there's that... but also I want more of you." I skimmed my thumb along her bottom lip and then her top. "Tasting these lips reminds me of what the rest of you tasted like."

"That's not fair." Before I could respond that I agreed, she surprised me by adding, "Because I've been dying to know what you taste like."

"Fuck, Sabrina," I grumbled, shifting the gear into *Drive* while trying to imagine my parents doing it to deflate my cock.

Chapter 15

Sabrina

LUCA HAD MENTIONED TO ME at dinner that he had a gift for Mikey. I'd be lying if I said my heart didn't swell in my chest. Even more so when he told me what it was. Having had the sense to ask me first, spoke volumes.

"Go brush your teeth and put your PJ's on."

"Aww, Mom. We just got home, can't I stay up later tonight? Puh-leeeze?" He smashed his hands together, fingers pointing toward the ceiling in his typical way.

"You know the rules. Now, please go get ready for bed." His shoulders slumped in defeat. "Thank you. When you're done we'll finish the book we started last night." Without another word, he pivoted on his sock-covered feet and stomped away. When I turned, Luca had a bright smile gracing his handsome face. "What are you smiling at?"

"You're a wonderful mother. You remind me of my own, although her voice would've been a tad louder." I let out a laugh and shrugged. Mikey came sliding into the room, *Risky Business* style. "My teeth are brushed." He

151 ⚽🌼

grinned wide.

I cupped his chin with my fingers. "Good job. Hey, guess what? Luca has a surprise for you." His beautiful brown eyes sparkled.

Luca walked to the door, grabbed it from his pocket and wrapped his arm around his back shielding the surprise. "This is for you, but it comes with rules, okay?" Mikey nodded enthusiastically. "You can use this when your mom says so. If she tells you to put it away, you listen to her. Don't bring it to school unless it's show and tell and you have permission." Another nod.

He pulled out a hacky sack ball from behind his back. Mikey's small eyebrows lowered as he studied the small blue beanbag held in front of him. "What is it?"

A deep laugh came from Luca. "It's a hacky sack. It will teach you eye/foot coordination, plus balance." Mikey didn't appear as enthusiastic as I hoped he would. Luca continued, "Soccer players use it. Watch me."

Luca took a step back, dropped the ball and started bouncing it with his feet without it ever touching the ground. It was almost like a dance, from one foot to the other, behind him, in front of him, and even off of his knee once or twice. Mikey and I stared at him in awe. He gave the ball one more flick with this foot and it landed in his hand.

"That is so cool!" Rather than take the hacky sack that Luca held out for him, he launched himself into his arms. "This is the best thing ever." That balloon that had inflated in my chest earlier just doubled in size.

Mikey tried to mimic what Luca had done, but of course, couldn't. "I'll show you how to use it the next time I see you. But, if you just keep practicing starting with one foot, not letting it drop, you'll get it, I know you will."

"Okay, sweetie, it's bedtime." Without argument, he hugged and thanked Luca for the gift. "Say goodnight, and I'll be right in."

"Mommy?" His little fists rubbed his eyes. "Can Luca read to me tonight?"

My eyes went from my son's to Luca's. "Sure, if he wants to."

"Do you? I mean, will you? Please? It's not a dumb fairy tale or anything. It's a book about a dinosaur."

"I'd love to. How about your mom joins us and reads the girl parts?"

"Okay, there is one girl dinosaur, she can read that one. Even though it's old and ready to die."

"Hey," I objected.

"You're not as old as the dinosaur." Mikey grabbed Luca's hand tugging him toward his room. We smiled and allowed him to run the show.

"Would you like some coffee?"

Luca took my hand in his. "No, thank you." He guided me toward my sofa and pulled me down on his lap. "I'd prefer you."

He released my hand, and cupped my cheek. The warmth of his palm on my skin could be felt down to my toes. With a gentle pull, he brought my face to his and firm lips met mine. At first, the kisses were soft, patient.

His eyes danced over my face. "So, pretty." He traced my face with his index finger, from my temple to my chin, until his hand rested on the back of my neck. "I want to get to know you, Sabrina. Not just what has happened the past few years of your life, but all of you. What were you like as a little girl?"

I stared into his chocolate eyes. "I loved frilly things. I suppose you could say I was infatuated with pink and playing dress up. For my tenth birthday, my mom gave me a boutique princess birthday party."

He tilted his head and admitted, "I have no idea what that is."

"It was every little girl's fantasy. A limo came to pick me and nine of my friends up. We went to a salon where we had our hair, nails and makeup done by a professional stylist. Then there was a little runway, and we modeled pretty dresses. I remember studying the way the woman did my hair. It was almost down to my waist, straight, and boring, but she styled it in a way that made me feel like a princess."

"That sounds like fun." He kept his voice steady, but I was sure it sounded awful to him.

"It was the best. That was the day I knew I wanted to be a hair stylist."

"When is your birthday?"

"January ninth. When's yours?"

"September twelfth. What about Mikey?"

"July twentieth. God only knows what type of party he'll want this year. Last year was the first birthday since his father passed away. It was very strange and difficult."

"That had to be tough." Luca's thumb caressed my neck. "Tell me about him."

"What do you want to know?"

"How did you meet... get together?"

I couldn't help but smile at the memory because it was a happy time. "We met at a mutual friend's. His buddy,

Hank, was having a party for some reason or another. My college roommate, Anita, liked Hank and begged me to go with her." I closed my eyes recalling that evening. "When I saw Dillon, something clicked. He was very handsome, and suave. The man had a line for everything. According to Anita, he was very popular amongst the ladies. I suppose in hindsight that should have been a warning. Instead, I considered myself the luckiest woman since he chose me.

"It wasn't love at first sight or anything, but we started dating and when he got his first assignment after graduation, we decided to get married so we could live on base together. Shortly after, he was deployed overseas. Being married to a man in the Armed Forces wasn't easy. Every day I'd say a prayer that he was safe. About a year after we were married, on one of his leaves, I got pregnant."

"How old were you?"

I narrowed my eyes, "Is that your way of finding out my age?" We both laughed and Luca shook his head. "I'm just kidding. I was twenty-one when we married. I'll be twenty-eight in January. Anyway, we moved upstate, and you basically know the rest."

His thumb still traced circles on my skin. "I do. Thank you for telling me all of that. I'm sorry it ended the way it did."

"Me, too. I thought he was a good man. My heart shattered when the police came to my home and told me he passed away. For days, I mourned and tried explaining why daddy wasn't coming home. Then his mistress carrying his child showed up and my tears no longer fell."

"You're a very strong woman. I know I've told you that before, but it's true. Not to sound condescending, but I'm proud of you. So many women wouldn't have handled all you've been through with the grace you have."

"Thank you, that means a lot." Maybe it was a way for me to change the topic, but without thought, I raked my hand through his dark wavy hair. The soft silky strands flowed through my fingers. That's when I noticed how lush his eyelashes were. "You're beautiful," flew from my lips.

A small smile played at the corners of his mouth. "I need to kiss you some more, Sabrina." When he shifted his body, my shoulders no longer rested on his arm but that of my couch.

I stretched my neck, to give him closer access to me. Our lips met once again, savoring each other's tastes like starved lovers. We swallowed each other's moans as if we needed them for fuel. He brought his hand from the back of my neck, around my collarbone, and down the center of my chest. His thumb ever so gently brushing the side of my breast.

My back arched into his touch, wanting and needing more of it. Memories of how he touched and tasted me made my insides coil like a jack-in-the-box. His strokes were as if he were turning that handle, just a few more and the little door would fly open. If it wasn't for my labored breath, I could probably hear the circus music if I concentrated enough.

It wasn't just the way his body felt against mine or how soft and gentle his lips were, it was the way my entire body felt alive when we were together. The range of emotions he provoked, that I thought I might never feel again, brewed inside of me. One of the best things I felt with him was safe. There was something about being wrapped in his arms that was reminiscent of a child's security blanket.

Plus, he made me feel like a woman again... a desirable woman, which I hadn't felt like in a very long time. It wasn't that I didn't get approached by a man on the rare occasion I went out with friends, but this was different. He wasn't shallow or superficial. Luca cared about getting to know me below the surface, and for a widow with a child, that was a rare find. Hell, that was a rare find if I was your average single woman. Couple that with our physical chemistry, and we were both ready to combust.

"I want you so badly," Luca said as he licked and nipped the soft spot behind my earlobe. My hands trailed up his torso landing on his strong muscles. The pulse of his heart played a melody on my palms. His growing erection could be felt on my hip. This wasn't fair to him. Every ounce of me wanted to pull him into my bedroom, but I couldn't. Not with my son in the next room. We were like two teenagers, horny and lusting for each other. When I flexed my hips, he ground down on me. God, he felt good.

After a few more minutes of grinding, touching, kissing, and nipping, I knew we needed to stop. "We need to slow down." He rested his forehead on mine. "I'm so sorry, I feel like a tease."

"You're not a tease, but you're right." He didn't move right away, and I was thankful for that. When he sat up the heat that radiated between us didn't stop simply because our bodies were no longer touching. If anything, it felt hotter. "What are your plans for the rest of the week?"

"My parents are picking Mikey up before I go to work on Friday. I have a full day of appointments on Friday and Saturday."

"Do you have plans either night?"

My heart flipped at his question. "No. Why, did you have something in mind?" *God, please have something in mind.*

"As a matter of fact, I do, but you'll have to wait and see."

"You're being very mysterious, Mr. Benedetto."

"Mystery is good." He pulled me closer to him, circling his arms around my waist.

I narrowed my eyes studying him a bit before nodding. "Hmm... okay. I suppose I'll have to trust you. Thanks again for dinner, Mikey's gift, and reading a story to him. I think you made his night."

"Well, then we're even because he made mine. I'll call you tomorrow." He slid on his jacket. Damn, even that was sexy. "Good night, Sabrina."

"Bye, Luca."

Once the door closed behind him, I rested my back against it. My fingers went to my lips never wanting to forget what his felt like on mine.

Chapter 16

Luca

I'D BEEN STUCK BEHIND MY desk since the moment I arrived a little after nine a.m. Not to sound, cliché, but I was very thankful today was Friday. My week had been jammed, and once I got out of there I couldn't wait to unwind with a certain blonde. She didn't know it yet, but I planned to spend some quality time with her over the next two evenings… and I couldn't wait.

Unfortunately, there were still a few long hours to my day. Jude had back-to-back meetings lined up all afternoon, and we needed to discuss the expansion he was planning.

Needing a distraction, I grabbed my phone and sent Sabrina a text.

Me: I hope you're having a great day.

I didn't expect an immediate reply, but three little dots began to dance.

Sabrina: Just getting ready to greet my next client. Three more and I'm done. My feet are killing me. How are you?

Me: Good. Busy. Did your parents pick up Mikey this morning?

Sabrina: Yep. He was super excited to hear they were taking him to see the new Ninja Turtle movie.

Me: Well, who could blame him? Those dudes rock. Call me when you're done.

Sabrina: Okay. I need to go. Mrs. Brennan is here. Pray for me. She wants rainbow hair...she's sixty and likes unicorns. LOL

I let out a laugh. What the hell was rainbow hair?

Me: Consider it done.

Sabrina: Thanks. :)

Just as I dialed Cassie to check in on her date the other night, Jude called my office line and asked if we could meet earlier than scheduled.

"Hello?"

"I need to call you back," I said as my greeting.

She laughed on her end. "Okay. I'm on my way to get a pedicure."

"Have fun."

Grabbing my laptop, I knocked on Jude's door once before opening it. He focused on his computer monitor. "Hey, boss. Is what you're staring at have to do with our meeting?"

He clicked a few buttons on his keyboard before addressing me. "Yeah, we need to go over some ideas."

Rather than stay at his desk, we walked over to the round table with binders stacked on it. This didn't bode well for me. "What's all of this?" I asked, opening my laptop to the memo he sent me earlier.

"These, my friend, are financial reports from a couple of vulnerable companies. A few of our clients would like to invest, which means…"

"Our portfolio grows."

"Correct, and so does our bottom line." He sported the same grin he would in college when an investment paid off. "I decided instead of taking on the responsibility of running other businesses, we will continue to advise, invest, and grow our client base. In other words, we're expanding."

"Does that mean more staff?" I stared at him and he back at me knowing I already had my answer… *no*.

"Not right away, between the two of us and a couple other key staff members, we will be able to have this running like a well-oiled machine. However, there will be some travel needed to our west coast and Midwest offices. But first, we need to devise a comprehensive study, and plan before we move forward." He leaned back in his chair. "I want you point person on this. Being my second in command, you're the one I trust not to fuck this up."

"Thank you."

"Take some time and go over these files. Electronic versions have been sent to our secured drive. Let's circle back next Friday and see where we stand. Build a team, tell me what you need and it will get done." I nodded, but Jude picked up on my disappointment. "Is there something on your mind, Benedetto?"

"No, I'm good. I'm just wondering if I should cancel my plans for tonight."

Jude tilted his head to the side like a puppy trying to understand its owner. "Why would you do that? Luca, this is work. Yes, it's important and I threw a lot at you, but you need a personal life." When my eyebrows flew up and almost off of my forehead, he smiled. "Yes, I know what I just said. Before Brae, I wouldn't have felt that way, but now, knowing how much more fulfilled my life is…" He trailed off and didn't continue.

"I have plans with Sabrina this weekend. But, I don't want to let you down or this business."

"It's not in your nature. You're the most dedicated employee I have." He leaned back, and Jude the businessman morphed into Jude the sap in love. "Tell me about Sabrina."

Images of her blonde hair, sweet smile, and cute cluster of freckles popped in my head. "She's sweet, kind, caring, a hard worker, and a good person. I love spending time with her and her son… they make me happy. It's nothing like I ever thought it could be, and I enjoy being with them. You know all of this." After the day I channeled Rocky Balboa and then confided in Kyle, I called Jude to tell him how I felt about Sabrina. I also shared how I knocked our pal on his ass, and it was a shame he missed it.

"Yes, I do." Jude nodded. "I just wanted you to remind yourself why all of this can wait until Monday. Brae and I are spending Easter upstate this weekend, so I'm taking off early." It wasn't long ago, Jude was incognizant of love. It amazed me how much falling in love with someone could change your life. If I had to place bets, my money would have been on Jude being the ultimate bachelor. It was a good thing I didn't make that wager. "Go do what you have to do, buddy. All this can wait until Monday."

"Thank you, and have a good weekend. Drive safe, and stay away from the roosters." I collected the files and stood to leave.

"Yeah, I'm convinced those damn things take pride in waking me up at the crack of dawn." He laughed before shaking my hand.

"It's good to see you this way. I'm glad you're happy, man."

He nodded with a smile. "Yeah, it took an amazing woman to make me happy."

His words touched on something within me. I guessed that was true. Work, play—none of it really mattered if there wasn't someone special to share it all with. And based on the fact I was itching to see Sabrina, I had to wonder if what I saw my friend experience was indeed something I too could have one day.

Tapping my fingers on the steering wheel while I sat at the red light accentuated my impatience. You would think living in New York as long as I had, I would be used to ridiculous traffic… tonight I just wanted to get to Sabrina.

When I pulled up to her salon, there wasn't a spot in front. I saw her through the window and pulled around the block finding a place to park not too far away. As I made my way down the street, I saw the woman she had been talking to sporting multi-colored hair. Who knew rainbow hair literally meant an array of different colors.

Rather than go inside, I leaned up against the lamppost on the sidewalk caddy corner to the salon's entrance. People rushed by me to get from point A to point B. No one gave rainbow lady, whatever her name was, a second thought. That was what I loved most about this city—you could be yourself. Either in black slacks, leather jacket and Italian loafers, or a woman with hair that resembled the front of the Lucky Charms box, it didn't matter.

Then I saw Sabrina. The spring early evening breeze picked up the ends of her hair revealing her slender neck. Just as I was about to move toward her, she pulled out her phone, tucked a few strands of her hair behind her right ear, smiled, and brought her phone to that same ear. Seconds later mine rang.

"Is this the beautiful Sabrina Callahan?" I took two steps forward.

Her smile widened. "Hi, Luca."

"I love when you wear blue." She gazed down at herself and raised her head to find me standing in front of her. Still talking into the phone I said, "But then again, you're gorgeous in anything... or nothing."

We both lowered our phones and tucked them into our coat pockets. "Hi. This is a surprise. I didn't expect you to be here."

Leaning forward, I softly kissed her lips. "A pleasant surprise I hope."

"Very." Her hazel eyes sparkled. "What are you doing here?"

"I thought we could grab dinner."

"That sounds great, but I'm exhausted." My expression must have mirrored my disappointment. "What would you think of grabbing takeout and heading to my place?"

"I like that idea. I'm parked around the corner."

Once we were both settled inside my car, I asked, "What are you in the mood for?"

Mischievousness flickered in her eyes. "Can I be

honest?"

"Yes, of course." I pushed the ignition button and listened to my car come to life.

A pause made me pivot my head toward her before shifting into gear. Her eyes connected and held mine when she said, "You."

One tiny word caused desire to snake through me like a fallen powerline full of electricity with no hope of settling.

"I just decided we're grabbing pizza from the place on your street, because my navigation is set on your address… do not pass go… do not collect two hundred dollars." I pulled out into the road, speeding a bit too fast for a one-way street in the East Village.

"Well, it's a good thing their pizza is decent," she quipped, playing along.

Throwing her a sideways glower that could be misconstrued as anger, I said, "Sweetheart, I don't give a shit if it tastes like the box it comes in."

How did one manage to get to their destination only minutes later, in spite of the typical traffic that clogged the streets on a Friday evening? Have the woman he was into say that she wanted him.

A small smile played on her lips the entire time I drove, and after we parked, I dragged her by the hand into the pizza parlor. Without bothering to ask her, I said to the man behind the counter, "One pie please. And I'll take anything you have to go now."

"The mushroom just come out. You take that?" he asked in broken English. I wasn't a mushroom fan, but fuck I'd pick those suckers off one by one to get out of there quickly.

"Yep, that's good."

165

Less than five minutes later, we were in her apartment with a mushroom pie. I placed the box on her counter, and when I turned Sabrina was standing right behind me. "Can you hold off on eating right now?"

"I can."

"Good." She skimmed her hands up the smooth leather of my jacket until they reached the back of my neck. "I've been thinking about you all day, Luca. Specifically, kissing you."

"What a coincidence," I admitted. Placing my hands on the curve of her ass, I pulled her against my body and took control of the situation. Her soft lips parted the moment mine touched them. The stress of my week disappeared with each stroke of my tongue along hers. But when she pulled away, I failed to hide my disappointment.

Without explanation, she removed her jacket, and then held a hand out for mine. I followed her lead, watching as she turned to hang them both up in the small closet by the door. The way her jeans molded over her ass, down her slim legs, stirred me up.

Still silent, although I could read her mind based on the vibe she gave me, she took my hand and led me to her couch. Standing before it, she repositioned her hands on the back of my neck and said, "Now, where were we?"

This time I grabbed her ass, forcing all the space between us to disappear. "Right here," I said, before molding my mouth over hers. The second kiss unleashed a fury of groping and dragging off our shirts that quickly became a nuisance to our touches.

She helped me, I helped her, and by the time I stood shirtless and shoeless before her, my cock screamed to be let out. This level of lust wasn't a new thing for me.

I'd been there before where all I wanted was to get to the end result. With Sabrina, for the first time in my adult life I wanted the journey more than the act.

I skimmed the back of my hand down her neck and over the curve of her breast. The smooth white satin of her bra felt cool beneath my touch. Her skin pebbled with goose bumps, and when I reached where her nipple hid behind the fabric, I ran my thumb over it to feel it harden before pinching it.

Flecks of gold and green blazed in her eyes. I felt her fingers work the button and zipper of my jeans. Judging from the pause, I worried if she was nervous about what would soon happen.

"Sabrina, you don't have to—"

"Yes, I do. I have to, Luca. I *want* to. Since the night you made me feel so wanted and desired, right here on this couch, I've been wanting to do the same for you." With a deliberate determination, she tucked her fingers into the waistband of my jeans and boxer briefs. As she slid them down my legs, she lowered her body before me.

I didn't know what was hotter, having Sabrina on her knees with my cock a whisper away from her gorgeous lips, or knowing what she was about to do with them. She helped me step out of my jeans and underwear before pushing on my thighs until I fell backward onto the couch. Now naked and ready for the taking, every part of me thrummed with unbridled anticipation.

I truly didn't know what I wanted to happen first— her hands on my scorching skin or her lips tasting me, because either scenario was too much for me to imagine. And you'd think I'd be prepared. But when she wrapped her hand around my cock while sucking on the tip, I swear I almost came right then, right there.

Instinctively, my fingers threaded in her hair, cupping her cheeks with my palms. A groan vibrated around my dick causing me to push forward. Sabrina hollowed her cheeks sucking hard, and it was my turn to groan.

"Fuck, that's so good." I held her head possessively relishing in the warmth of her mouth. Perfect suction, her tongue… the way it stroked me, circled me, was all too much. When she brought it up and dipped it into the slit at the tip teasing me, I bucked like a man possessed.

It wasn't until she took me to the back of her throat when that threat became a bona fide concern. The combination of her hand now cupping my balls, her hot mouth devouring my steel rod, and the longing I saw on her beautiful face, made it almost impossible to hold back.

Somehow, someway, I did. I managed to find a way to hold off the inevitable as Sabrina continued to gift me with one of the best blow jobs I'd ever received. I wanted it to go on and on. I wanted it to end. I wanted…

She stopped with most of my length in her mouth, and swallowed. I forgot what I wanted and released a dirty grumble. "Sabrina… you need to stop, or I'm going to come in your mouth."

She ignored me.

She sucked harder.

I swore and then came.

Chapter 17

Sabrina

THAT WAS BY FAR THE hottest thing I'd ever witnessed in my life.

Luca's head fell backward on the couch. The length of his lashes rested on the skin beneath his eyes while they remained closed.

All the while, I watched in awe. He was stunning. His sculpted chest rose and fell with each breath as he attempted to calm his erratic breathing. A sexy trail led to just the right amount of hair that framed his long, thick shaft. Trimmed neat, it caused another wave of desire to course through me.

When I lifted my gaze from his manhood to his face, he was watching me with hooded lids.

"Come here." His hand gently gripped my arm pulling me toward him until I was straddling his bare legs. Our eyes connected in a way they never had before. It was an unspoken language that we had just learned. No more words were necessary.

My pulse beat wildly until it thundered in my ears. Everything about what just happened felt so right... so good… so natural. Being the woman to bring Luca to such euphoria gave me my own high.

There was no doubt in my mind, that in a short period of time, this man carved out a place for himself in my heart. Not wanting to wait another second, I brought my lips to his. His manhood, rubbed against my denim covered body, coming to life once more.

Large, soft hands cupped my cheeks. Our kiss was tender, not rushed or too demanding. It was thoughtful, deliberate, and full of mutual adoration—it was *us*.

"Sabrina." The seductive way my name rolled off his tongue caused my desire to escalate. He paused, letting out a breath. His eyes felt tethered to mine, neither one of us wanting to break our connection. "You're incredible. Not only because of what just happened, but everything about you."

My God, this man always had the right words. Like an idiot, I had nothing. I searched my brain for some sort of a response, but the ability to speak eluded me. I could have admitted that was just a teaser for me, and I desperately wondered what he would feel like inside me. I also could have admitted I never felt such deep-rooted desire as I did in that moment. The scary part was I couldn't remember ever feeling that way with Dillon. But how could I admit to having such a profound response without sounding insane?

Luca must have sensed how emotion prevented me from speaking. Taking the burden from me, he pulled my mouth closer for another long, hard kiss. The longer it went on, the more I wanted it to. I gripped his hair, digging my fingers into his silky strands. I shamelessly rubbed myself over his hardened length. I pathetically moaned into his mouth, sounding more like an alien than a human.

He was first to pull away, and my cheeks flamed red from embarrassment. "I'm sorry. I don't know what has gotten into me."

Lie.

Big fat lie.

He was getting into me, but not in the way I wanted. I needed to get a grip, I was a mother for God's sake.

"Sabrina, I believe I'm at a disadvantage." His two large hands gripped my hips and pushed them down just enough for me to feel his so called *disadvantage*. "I'm naked, you're not, and I want you to be."

My brilliant response was an audible swallow... a puff of air... and a squeak.

He chuckled before burying his face in my neck. "You're so adorable."

"I feel like an idiot. Luca, I haven't... it's been... I don't know..."

When he pulled back, the humor had fallen off his face. "Hey. It's okay. Let's have that poor excuse they call a pizza, maybe watch a movie, take it slow."

His eyes widened when I shook my head. Finally finding my words, I blurted out, "No. I want you, not pizza." The surprised expression morphed into a sly grin. "It's rare that I have a night to myself and a hot naked guy on my couch for the taking."

"Is that so?" he asked, tracing the smooth edge of my satin bra with the pads of his thumbs. I felt them skim over my breasts until his fingers met at the clasp on my back. He paused and brought his nose to mine. "Having you on my lap wearing that sexy bra is driving me nuts, Sabrina."

The way his chocolate brown eyes drilled right into mine, with heat radiating from them that was hard to ignore, had me feeling more wanted than I'd ever felt in my life. The taut fabric slackened as he pulled the straps forward until my bra released my breasts.

Anticipation, or maybe it was anxiety, furled in the pit of my stomach over what was about to happen between us. What we were about to do would change everything.

With the lightest touch, he first traced one nipple and then the next. His eyes were filled with pure heady need, as if nothing would be as important to him as I was. Whether that was true or not became secondary. In that moment, everything in my being felt Luca needed me. That revelation made me brave.

Enough so, I leaned forward and initiated a very seductive kiss. The insecurities I felt just a few minutes earlier were gone, simply because of the way he made me feel.

After a few tongue-tangled kisses, I stood and held my hand out to him. "Are you sure, Sabrina?"

"I am." The conviction in my voice was unmistakable. He laced our fingers, stood proud and tall, and allowed me to lead him toward my bedroom. On the way, we passed Mikey's room, and with a tilt of his head, he smiled.

I flipped on a light, and then thought, *now what?*

My room wasn't large by any means, and it lacked the warmth found in a woman's bedroom. The bedding was plain and nondescript. Unlike my living room that was warm and inviting, my bedroom was blah. The only personal touches could be found in the framed pictures of Mikey on my dresser. All of that was a purposeful decision. Anyone could have lived in this room that held no evidence of a marriage that was a farce.

If Luca noticed the lack of personality, he didn't let

on. Instead, he pulled me into his arms and placed a tender kiss on my lips. "Let's catch you up," he said, working the button and zipper on my jeans. The man's confidence was an aphrodisiac as he stood naked before me.

His warm large hands elicited goose bumps to break out all over my skin as he skimmed them down my thighs to remove my jeans. Leaving me in my pale blue bikini panties, he stood back a step to admire me.

"You're so beautiful." I never saw myself that way. Cute, yes, but not beautiful… especially the last year of my life. Yet, hearing him say that to me, and it wasn't the first time he had, I believed him. Standing before this god of a man, I felt adequate to be with him.

With Dillon, I never felt popular enough, confident enough, or pretty enough beside him. I always felt, if given the opportunity, someone else would catch his attention. How so very right I was, and thinking back it now seemed so obvious.

I just hoped I was enough for Luca.

Luca

GODDAMN, THIS WOMAN CALLED TO me like no woman ever had. What was it about Sabrina that pulled me toward her?

My eyes feasted on her smooth pale skin, the way her perky breasts sat high on her chest, the way her slight belly and hips screamed all woman. She bit on her bottom lip as my eyes continued to devour her.

"Talk to me," I demanded in a gruff voice.

"I haven't been with a man this way since Dillon." I watched her raise her chin with a defiant determination. My heart sunk at the notion that she wasn't ready, but when I went to speak she lifted her hand to stop me. "I'm so glad it's you, Luca."

A surge of concern took over. This woman just offered me her vulnerable heart. By letting me into her life, her son's life, the responsibility should have sent me running.

Inexplicably, it did the reverse.

I stepped closer and lifted her into my arms. An unspoken agreement passed between us as I stared into her eyes. A slight nod encouraged me, her hand on my chest spurred me on, but it was her simple statement a few seconds ago that sealed my purpose. This woman needed to be doted on, worshiped, and I was just the man to do that.

The smooth comforter felt cool beneath my overheated flesh as I laid her down beside me in the center of her bed. She moved her hand from my chest to my jaw, leaned in, and kissed my lips.

With that simple kiss, my self-restraint cracked and released all my pent-up desire. The kissing and touching that had happened between us up until that moment paled in comparison to where I wanted to go. Never breaking the connection between our lips, I caressed her skin from shoulder to breast. Palming its weight in my hand, I could feel her nipple harden each time I squeezed.

Like a bee to honey, my tongue savored her sweetness. Circling the sensitive area, before pulling a pebbled nipple in between my lips, caused her to push it further into my mouth. From left to right and back again, I gave both sides of her equal pleasure.

A light gentle scrape of her nails on my scalp created a carnal reaction. My nips became forceful sucks, my grip tightened, squeezing her firm flesh while I continued to pleasure her. I skated my hand along her torso until I felt smooth satin.

Pulling back, I looped my fingers into the waistband of her underwear. "Lift." When her hips rose, I slid them down her toned legs until I flicked them to the floor. "Stunning."

As much as I wanted inside this woman, I needed to take my time. Rushing our first time would be wrong on so many levels. Her thighs parted exposing her perfect pink flesh. I licked my lips at the memory of what she tasted like, but this time when she came, I wanted it to be around my cock.

A slight tremble of her thighs brought a smile to my lips. Sabrina wanted this as much as I did. Her impatience, desire, and need were evident in each subtle movement. Not wanting to wait a second longer, I slid one finger up and down her slick wet heat. Glancing up, her pretty eyes were closed, her lips slightly parted to release every audible breath.

"Fuck. My condom is in my wallet in the other room."

"Closet." She lifted her arm and blindly pointed toward the wall. "There's a Jimmy Choo shoe box in there." Dumbfounded, I stared at her until she opened her eyes. "Becky gave me a *get over a cheater* gift. It'll have what you need… and then some." Her face flushed. "On second thought, maybe you should go get yours."

"No way, you've intrigued me." Even though I was wasting time, I couldn't wait to see exactly what she was talking about. Sliding the door open, I found the box on the top shelf. There was a surprising weight to it. Flipping the lid off, I studied the contents that were more like something Vanessa would have, not innocent Sabrina. Taking inventory, I said, "A blindfold, handcuffs, a dildo, lube, batteries…" Sabrina's face was now shielded by her hands. "And finally, a sealed box of gold medal standard, lambskin condoms of champions… ribbed for her pleasure… and yours."

A muffled, "Oh my God!" echoed behind her hands. She peeked through her fingers as though she was watching a horror movie. "Becky gave that to me months ago."

"Remind me to thank her."

Sabrina propped herself up on her elbows. Rather than embarrassment flashing in her eyes, I saw desire. She smiled. "I don't need any of those artificial stimulators… I have you." Little did she know what those words just did to me. "I think I'll be regifting them back to Becky for her birthday."

"Sounds like a plan." Not waiting a second longer, I opened the box, ripped the foil packet, and sheathed myself before kneeling between her legs. Her knees dropped to either side as an open invitation. Positioning the head of my dick at her entrance, I leaned forward, laced our fingers together above her head, and pushed into her.

Tight warmth encased me as I rocked back and forth. I had a feeling making love to her would come more naturally than just fucking because nothing we had experienced thus far could be considered anything less.

Our bodies moved in unison; my lips dusted kisses on different parts of her face down to her slender neck with each thrust. There wasn't one part of me I didn't want connected to her. Sabrina's fingers clutched my hands tighter the closer she came to her climax.

The need to memorize her expression compelled me to study her. Holding our visual connection, while our hips moved faster searching for that euphoric moment, I watched her lashes flutter before her lids slid shut.

"Open your eyes, Sabrina... watch me."

I wasn't sure if it was my command that caused her to come, but feeling her tighten around me, unleashed my own release. We kept our eyes trained on each other, riding out our peak together.

When our muscles relaxed, I cupped her face and brought my lips toward hers. Just as I expected, this was more than sex. It was as if our souls and heart merged as easily as our bodies had. Every part of this experience with her wasn't anything I had felt before, and I could easily become addicted.

She continued to stare into my eyes. "What are you thinking?"

"I'm thinking you've become my addiction."

Chapter 18

Sabrina

SUN PEEKED INTO MY ROOM alerting me it was
morning before my alarm clock did. Heat radiated
off the naked body next to me. I quietly rolled to my side
to face him. His soft brown hair was wavy and messy
creating the sexiest bed head. I envied the way the ends
of his long dark eyelashes curled up. Light scruff lined his
jaw and peppered his face. Part of me wanted to reach
down and touch it, but I also didn't want to wake him.
Not when I could take my time and study him. His cross
shifted while he slept and now rested on his collarbone.

My eyes raked down his smooth taut skin that covered
his muscular chest and torso to that delicious V that
women lost their minds over. I'd never been with a man
who had such a defined physique, and seeing one in
person, I now understood.

The white bedsheet laid just low enough for me to
enjoy his pleasure trail, and just high enough to cover the
part of him that brought me to such heights last night.
Becky would tell me how white spots would dance under
her eyelids, and how she could be transported while

having an orgasm. I used to think she was exaggerating, but after last night, I now understood.

Not wanting to take a chance of getting caught, I made sure he was still sleeping. Eyes closed, steady breaths, peaceful expression—perfect. I bit the corner of my bottom lip, very gently took the white sheet between my fingers, and lifted to play a bit of peek-a-boo.

My brain scolded me to look away while my eyes chanted *don't you dare*. Needless to say, my eyes won. I swallowed the sigh that was on the tip of my tongue and just stared in grand appreciation.

"Good morning." His deep voice caught me off guard. Despite that, I didn't lower the sheet. Why bother? I was busted anyway. "See something you like?"

My brain quipped, *told you so*. Regaining my composure, I summoned the confidence I had last night. "As a matter of fact, yes."

"I'm glad to hear it." He sat up and tugged me to nestle against him while resting his hand on my bare ass. With his other hand, he pushed the hair off my forehead before kissing it gently. "For the record, I see something I like as well."

"You do?" A funny expression crossed over his face.

"Why do you doubt me, Sabrina? You're a beautiful woman."

I wanted to say, *no one has ever called me that before*. And, it wasn't that I needed constant reassurance and compliments. Actually, I was used to not getting them. On occasion, Dillon would appreciate a dress I wore or if my hair was styled the way he liked it. The way Luca doled out the flattery supported the type of man he was. Sure, Luca was stunning, and his confidence made him even more attractive. But now, having gotten to know him a bit, I felt his romantic side was what made him even sexier.

"Sabrina," he prompted.

"I don't feel beautiful sometimes. Dark circles and stretch marks will do that to a woman."

He pushed me onto my back, hovering above me. A mixture of anger and disbelief altered his handsome face. I expected words to discredit my insecurities, but instead I got actions. Luca kissed my neck, moved down to my breast kissing each in turn, and then to my stretch marks to place kiss after sweet kiss over them. The kisses weren't sexual or erotic, but they still caused an immediate response in my body. If he took those kisses any further, it would be impossible to stop him.

His devious grin revealed just what ran through his mind. "Luca, can you hold that thought? I'd love to stay and play all day, but I need to shower and get ready for work."

He dropped his head onto my belly and groaned. "I can join you and wash your back."

God, I hated that I had to adult today. "I'll never make it to the salon on time if you do. Raincheck?"

"Fine." Moving back up to come face to face with me, he placed a chaste kiss on my lips before resuming his position on his back. "I'll make coffee, you get dressed, and I'll drive you to work."

"That would be great, thank you."

I eased away from him and out of bed. My gut instinct was to tug the sheet off the bed to expose him while covering myself up. For some reason, feeling his penetrating gaze, and remembering his words a minute ago, emboldened me to walk around my room collecting clothes all while he stared without apology. "You're making this very hard for me, Sabrina," he said with a smirk.

"Sorry." I had to control my expression at seeing just how hard it was for him. But if I went anywhere near that bed, I'd never get to work. So instead, I smiled coyly before darting down the hall toward the bathroom.

Twenty minutes later, I stood in my kitchen watching Luca cooking at my stove while shirtless, barefoot, and in his dark jeans. Damn, he was perfect. His hair still stuck up in places from sleep. The way the denim hung low on his hips revealing nothing but skin meant he was commando.

He turned his head when he spotted me. "I hope you like eggs, because I'm making you a breakfast sandwich. I wasn't sure how much time you had, so if you need to take it with you, you can."

"You made me breakfast?" He let out a laugh and probably thought, *duh*! But, in all fairness, I couldn't remember the last time someone made me breakfast. Aside from Mikey pouring me a bowl of cereal, that was it. "I have enough time to eat here, thank you."

The egg flipped in the air with a flick of his wrist. "Cheese?"

"Yes, please."

In no time at all, I had a breakfast sandwich sitting on the plate in front of me worthy of being photographed for a restaurant's menu. "I would've poured your coffee, but I didn't know how you took it."

"Black."

"Great, that will be easy to remember for next time." He winked and sat down next to me.

"Aren't you going to eat?"

"I will later. After I drop you off, I'm going to the

gym." He patted his bare stomach, giving my eyes an excuse to ogle a bit. "I need to keep in shape since my girl likes what she sees."

His girl.

Damn, I could get used to this.

The sandwich tasted even better than it looked. I covered my mouth with my free hand and said, "Thith ith tho good." He chuckled as I swallowed and tried again. "Sorry. It's delicious." It truly was, and I appreciated the second bite more than the first.

"I'm glad you like it. I have a couple of other culinary tricks up my sleeve."

This time I swallowed my mouthful before I spoke. "I remember you telling me you learned from your mom. What's your specialty?"

"You'll have to wait and see," he said matter-of-factly. "Speaking of, what time will you be done today?"

"My last client is at three."

He leaned over and ran his thumb over the corner of my mouth in such a casual way while having no clue my heart pounded over the gesture. "Can you meet me at Greenmarket?"

"On First Avenue?"

"Yes. It's a short walk for you. We can shop for our dinner ingredients together. It's supposed to be a nice day."

My brain quickly ran through a scenario that could happen tonight—a romantic dinner after which Luca made love to me all night in his bed. There was one huge problem with that wonderful chain of events, I had to drive to Queens in the morning to celebrate Easter with my family.

"What?" he asked, picking up on my dilemma.

"Nothing. I just need to be at my parents' house fairly early tomorrow."

"Okay, so I'll drive you back to your apartment."

Shit, I couldn't believe I assumed he'd ask me to spend the night. While internally chastising myself, he took my hand in his and flipped it over to kiss my palm. "Sabrina, what is running through that head of yours?"

"Nothing," I repeated. "Thank you again for a great morning… and night."

A slow, sexy smile lifted the corners of his lips. "You can thank me properly later."

I finished my breakfast and stood to place my dish and mug in the sink. "I'll do this, go get ready." As Luca began washing, he added, "Pack a bag." His words halted me in my tracks. Sensing my confusion, he turned off the water, wiped his hands on a dishtowel, and walked over to where I stood in the doorway. Chocolate brown eyes searched my facial expression, "Did you think I was driving you home in the middle of the night?"

"No…" I shrugged at the way he quirked a brow in challenge. "Fine, yes. I wasn't sure."

"Well, now you are." After placing a chaste kiss on my lips and a firm slap on my ass, he pushed me toward my room and said, "Chop… chop."

Luca had me at work fifteen minutes early. He double parked in front of the salon and twisted in his seat. "Meet me at the entrance of the market."

"I will." My eyes cut toward my overnight bag that sat on the back seat. "I can't wait for tonight."

He placed a hand on the back of my head and pulled me toward him. "Me, too." I felt his fingers tighten over my hair just as his firm lips met mine. It wasn't a quick peck by any means. Luca was about to send me off with desire coursing through every part of my body.

He dipped his tongue inside and coaxed mine into his own mouth. I followed his lead to continue the erotic dance he initiated. His other hand held my face as he deepened the kiss between us and sucked on my tongue.

An immediate shot of electricity traveled from my mouth and ended between my legs.

Luca pulled away with a groan. "Go, before I drive us right to my place." Based on the condition he had just worked me up to, I couldn't guarantee I'd argue if he did. "Have a good day, dear," he said as I let myself out of the car. Giving him a brilliant smile, I blew him a kiss and dashed into the salon.

Three steps in, and I came face to face with a grinning Becky. "Holy hell." Ignoring her, I walked around where she stood with hands on her hips toward my station. "Hey, missy. Spill it."

"There's nothing to spill." I figured I had about three minutes before she'd beat the information out of me. With her eyes trained on my back, I removed my tools from my work bag to place them on my counter. None of the other stylists were due to arrive until ten. Becky opened the salon an hour earlier for me on the Saturdays that I worked. "Coffee is up?" I asked, walking myself to the break room to grab a cup.

She was right on my heels, zipped around my body, and planted herself at the entrance of the small kitchen at the back of the salon. "You walked out of here last night after doing Mrs. Brennan's clown do. And today you sit in front of my place of business sucking face with that hot Italian. So, you have two choices. You either tell me what went down between Mrs. Brennan and now, or I'll go full stalker mode and ask him myself."

I knew she'd make due on her threat. The woman was relentless when she wanted info. "Fine," I conceded. "Let me get my coffee, call Mikey to say good morning, and then I'll tell you what happened."

She tapped her wristwatch and released an exaggerated sigh. "Fine. But not the abridged version."

"Yes, the abridged version." I pushed her aside to get to the caffeine I desperately needed from a second cup. "I haven't been with a man since Dillon. There is no way I'm telling you every detail." I carried my cup to my chair and sat with a huff.

"Don't be so selfish, Sabrina." She had the nerve to stand beside me with a pointed authoritative finger in my face. "I have no prospects in sight and the least you can do is give me something to work with."

"You were just with someone last week."

My statement caused her mouth to hang open in an unflattering way. "That doesn't count. It was meh at best. I need new material to fantasize over. It's the little things in my sad life."

"There will be no fantasizing over Luca."

She released a shot of air through her nose. "Oh, that ship has sailed, my friend."

Chapter 19

Luca

I SPENT MOST OF MY MORNING at the gym. The way Sabrina appreciated my physique was enough incentive to add a few pounds to the bar and run an extra mile or two. With Jude at his in-laws' farm, Kyle was my gym-partner in crime.

Of course, conversation centered around Vanessa and Sabrina. Unlike Kyle, who had no problem sharing details of their very hot, very active sex life, I chose to keep what transpired during my night with Sabrina to myself. Kyle knew we were dating, and that I was happy… and that's all he needed to know.

After two full hours of a grueling workout, I set the weights back onto the rack and wiped my neck with a towel. "I'm outta here. Say hi to Vanessa. What are you two up to tomorrow?"

He followed suit, wiping his brow with a towel and sitting heavily on a bench. "Vanessa is anti-holiday, so we are heading to Atlantic City."

"Well, good luck. We all know how much you suck at cards."

"I'm a lover not a gambler, Benedetto."

"So you say. See ya, Cleary." I headed to the lockers to grab my bag. Not bothering to shower at the gym, thirty minutes later I was in the luxury of my own bathroom.

I loved my apartment. Although sleek and modern in architecture, my interior decorator managed to bring warmth with the furniture and fabrics in each room. From my living room, you could exit onto a glass-encased balcony with an amazing view of upper Manhattan. That was where I spent many hours enjoying the tranquility away from the crazy busy life I lived.

While in my shower, my thoughts went to Sabrina. Having her see my space, getting to know me in my own environment, and spending quality time together excited me. Hell, just thinking of making love under the rain showerhead I currently enjoyed, in my bed, and maybe even while she was pressed up against the glass door to my balcony, forced me to turn the dial to cold. It was her I wanted, not my own hand.

Besides getting myself and my apartment ready for my time with Sabrina, I managed to scour through some of the portfolio's Jude had asked me to review until it was time to head out.

A few hours later I was engulfed in floral and spicy scents while I waited outside of the market for Sabrina to arrive. My fingers toyed with my keys in my pocket. The digital clock on my phone read just after four p.m., and Sabrina should be getting out of work soon.

I knew I was going to beat her there, but better than the other way around. I sat on a bench outside of the market watching people come and go. A guy walked out holding a flowers in one hand as a little girl skipped alongside him. Couples, families, and singles, milled about.

If you would have asked me a few weeks ago which category I fell in, there would be no doubt what it would be. Now, after meeting Mikey and Sabrina, I wasn't quite sure. I knew I wanted to be a couple with Sabrina, and would make that happen, but would she want me to be part of her family? That was the question. Of course, it was too early to delve into that portion of our relationship. Hopefully, one day I'd have that answer.

Growing up, I was surrounded by large families. My mother had four siblings, and my father had six. I had countless cousins and there was never a point when I felt alone. We were a tight knit group. So when I left Italy, it was a major shock to not only my system, but theirs.

There were some days that I thought about moving back. As time passed, that option didn't make sense… my life was here. I had my friends, work, and now I had a woman who got under my skin.

My knee bounced in anticipation of wanting to see Sabrina even though it had just been hours since I dropped her off. I found myself wondering how her day went, if she had any other customers who wanted unique hair, if she had told Becky about us. It wouldn't bother me if she had, it would almost make it more real, not just to me, but to her.

It wasn't much longer when I spotted her silky blonde hair coming toward me. Her jeans accentuating her legs, the strap of her purse crossed her body between her breasts while the bag bounced on her hip with each step she took. Her hazel eyes scanned the area. I stood and raised my hand to capture her attention. When she spotted me, my heart began pounding in my chest. The smile that grew across her face, coupled with the sparkle in her eyes, made me feel alive.

"Hi," she said as she stopped in front of me. "I hope you haven't been waiting long."

"Hey, there." I wrapped my arms around her and pulled her against me. "No, not long at all. How was your day?" Releasing her, I linked our fingers together and we started toward the entrance.

"It was good, busy, but good. How was yours?"

"Dull, which is how I prefer my Saturdays." Taking a basket, I said, "Well, your day is about to get exciting."

"Yeah, what's the plan?"

"First, I thought we'd get our ingredients, then go to my place and cook dinner. The rest of my plans I'd rather show you rather than tell you."

She bit her bottom lip. "Is that so?"

"It is," I replied with a wink.

We made our way over to the vegetables. I had no idea of what I'd make, since I didn't know her likes and dislikes. Most of my culinary skills were based on what my mother or grandmother made, and everything seemed to go back to what I grew up with.

"This is going to be fun. Finally, cooking for someone with a palette that expands past chicken nuggets and macaroni and cheese." She let out a laugh, then added, "And cereal."

"I don't know, that son of yours didn't seem too finicky when I've eaten with him."

"Yes, because you were there. Mikey seems to have taken a very strong liking to you."

"That kid is the best." I walked toward the tomatoes, picked one up, felt it for ripeness. She nodded and a couple more followed into our basket.

We shopped like this for an hour. What I realized was

we generally liked the same things, except she had an aversion to artichokes, which I happened to love.

"How could you not like these?" I asked holding the glorious vegetable in my hand. "This is their prime season." Her nose crinkled, and she shook her head. "You have no idea what you're missing." I chose four that I liked and put them in the basket.

She quipped, "You must really like them."

"Sweetheart, by the time we're done with dinner, you will like them." Not letting her rebuke my comment, I told her to pick something, but I liked almost everything, so whatever was fine with me.

Sabrina stopped in front of the Brussels sprouts. Shocked that she liked them, I nodded with a smile. Truth be told, I didn't care for them, but I didn't let on. I played the same card with my mother when she wanted me to try new things. "You like Brussels sprouts?" Three lines formed on the bridge of her nose and I instantly knew she didn't like them.

"Sure, don't you? We should get some." I pulled a plastic bag off the roller and started to open it.

"No, I don't like them."

I let out a laugh and kissed the top of her head. "I don't either, it seems Mikey's eating habits didn't fall far from the tree."

She smacked my chest with her open hand. "That's not true. Just because I don't like artichokes and Brussels sprouts doesn't mean I'm picky."

"Spinach?"

"Love it."

I continued, this was a fun way to get to know her. "Broccoli?" She nodded. "Cauliflower."

"Yes. I actually make a great cauliflower rice. Mikey has no idea what he's eating." Her laugh sounded like a melody with a little bit of sinister laced in it. She put a head of the white vegetable in our basket.

"Do you eat anchovies?"

"Paste yes, the entire fish, no."

"That makes zero sense to me."

"Not really. The entire fish is boney and ugly. In paste form it's easier to handle." She shrugged when I stared and blinked at her.

"So, does that mean you don't eat any seafood? I was thinking scallops for dinner."

"Oh, I love scallops. I don't consider them fish," she offered with a shrug.

My chuckle was instant, and pulling her into my arms was automatic. "You're so adorable," I said before once again kissing the top of her head.

When we had a basket full of things she agreed on and some I insisted on, we left the market. On the way out, I bought a bouquet of flowers similar to the one I gave her once before, and handed them to her. "For you."

Just like she did the first time, she lowered her nose to the blossoms with a smile. "Thank you, I love them."

$Sabrina$

"LUCA, THIS IS MAGNIFICENT." I stared out at the Manhattan skyline in awe. "I'd be out here all the time."

"I am." His tone caused me to twist my gaze to his

face. The dim evening light did little to hide the retrospect I detected in his voice. He was so devastatingly handsome in his white button down shirt and casual denim, but in that moment I could see his vulnerability. I suspected there were layers of Luca Benedetto I had yet to discover.

He leaned his elbows on the banister and sighed. "My mom goes to church to think and contemplate things...I come out to my balcony. Even in the dead of winter, at the end of my workday I enjoy taking a few solitary minutes to stare at the view and detox." A warm smile spread over his lips as he turned his attention to me. "If it doesn't get too chilly, after dinner we can sit out here with our wine."

"I'd like that." He took my hand and led me back into his apartment. It was the perfect mix of masculine and class. In spite of the modern architecture, his furniture and accessories were warm and inviting. A glass wall separated his living room from that stunning balcony. The modern black kitchen cabinetry was topped with immaculate white granite. Even the gray slate tile floor contrasted yet complimented the soft pile cream area rug that covered a good portion of the living room.

His bedroom was as sexy as he was. Rather than the blacks, grays, and creams that carried through the rest of his place, warm wood furniture mixed with silky bedding in shades of blue made me want to snuggle up with him for days on end.

"Okay, now that you've been given the grand tour, ready to make dinner?" he asked, still holding my hand as we walked toward his incredible kitchen.

"I almost don't want to mess it up." The confused expression on his face forced me to elaborate. "Your kitchen looks too pretty to cook in."

"Don't be silly, I cook in it all the time." Patting one of the barstools at the island, he commanded, "Sit."

"I want to help," I argued.

Smugly, he folded one cuff up at a time to reveal his masculine forearms... strong forearms were my thing. "You will. But, right now I want you to relax."

How could I not be relaxed? This was heaven for me. I was having an adult night with one of the sweetest men I'd ever met. I loved my son dearly, but one could only take so much of Cartoon Network.

Soft music drifted through the apartment with a woman's melodic voice singing lyrics in Italian. I smiled as Luca moved around his kitchen pulling ingredients from the market bags and from his fridge.

"White or red?"

"Whatever you're having." After pulling out a bottle of chardonnay from his wine fridge along with two wine glasses, I watched as he opened it and poured us each a glassful.

He raised his glass and said, "To getting hit in the head with a soccer ball." I laughed at the memory before tapping my glass to his.

"To finger paint on the pants," I added.

It was his turn to laugh. "I guess we owe that little dude for bringing us together."

We both took a sip of the wine. Its smooth full-body flavor assaulted my taste buds. Luca's eyes fixed on mine over the rim of his glass. In them I could see a mixture of desire and admiration, and once more I felt wanted.

"Okay, time to wow you, Ms. Ricci," he said with a wink. The fact he used my maiden name thrilled me in an inexplicable way. When he pulled out the artichokes from the bag with a devious smile, I wasn't sure he was aware he had. "I'll convert you yet. This recipe is my nonna's. How is it you're part Italian and never had a stuffed artichoke?"

"They look like they'd hurt when going down."

He gifted me with a devious grin. "It's impossible to hurt when going down." And just like that, the need to tear that white shirt off his body and have my way with him consumed me.

Ignoring his comment for the sake of dinner, I changed the subject. "I picture you as a little boy helping your grandmother." What was odd, the image I had in my head of Luca as a young boy was of Mikey. The color of their eyes and hair were so similar, my son could pass as Luca's.

"I really never did. I was too interested in soccer and playing outside. Weird that I picked things up, though."

Luca jumped into expert chef mode, chopping and slicing as we fell into a comfortable chat about our lives. His claim that I'd help turned out to be a lie. I think he passed me a pepper, cutting board, and knife just to shut me up.

I never had a man cook me dinner before, and debated on telling him so. Part of me wanted him to know how much I truly appreciated all the little things he'd done for me. Some would consider them silly, superficial. I treasured the art of romance, craved it. Sure, Luca had so many qualities that made him a catch, but damn his romantic side could no doubt have me falling in love with him.

And that scared me to death.

Chapter 20

Luca

S HE PUSHED MY HAND AWAY with a firm nod of her head. "Please, no more."

"Say it." Her hazel eyes cut to mine and held. "Say, it Sabrina and I'll stop."

"Fine. I love stuffed artichokes. Happy now?"

"Very." I tossed the leaf I held on my plate and tugged her onto my lap. My lips molded over hers tasting the wine mixed with a hint of the seasonings I used for dinner.

Yes, the scallops, rice and wilted spinach were delicious. But fuck, watching those gorgeous lips slide over each artichoke leaf that I hand fed her was the best part of the meal. "I hope you're happy. I can't move," she added before gulping down the last of her wine.

When she placed her glass on the table, I leaned in to nuzzle her neck. "You just sit here then."

"You're treating me like a queen. Thank you."

"For?"

Her gaze moved toward the empty plates and then the

flowers I bought her before coming to land on my face. "Everything." The sincerity in her voice touched me. Especially since I hadn't done anything special. Other women I dated expected fancy meals at high-priced restaurants as part of the dating process. Then there was Sabrina who truly appreciated a simple meal made from ingredients found at a farmer's market.

"I liked cooking for you. I'd like to do it again." I placed another soft kiss on her lips before adding, "Maybe if I can get you to love artichokes, I can also convert Mikey."

"I may have to place a wager on that one." She glanced at the clock on my microwave. "Speaking of, I better call him before it gets too late."

"Go ahead, I'll clean up. What time do you need to leave in the morning?"

"Around ten. My parents like to go to the eleven o'clock mass. They have an Easter egg hunt for the kids afterwards."

"Sounds fun. Then what happens?"

"Just lunch with my parents." She suddenly scooted off my lap and walked toward my living room to grab her handbag. "It makes me nervous when I don't hear from them," she admitted with her eyes pinned to the screen of her phone.

"Usually no news is good news."

"In my son's case, no news means he's negotiating something he's not allowed to do or have…" After a pause she added, "or for a lesser punishment." I chuckled at her statement, imagining a wide-eyed Mikey trying to talk his way out of trouble.

Just as I stood from my barstool, she came over with her phone. "Hi, Ma. How is he?" After a few loud words came, Sabrina pulled the phone a few inches from her ear. She hit mute, and said, "My mother thinks you need to shout into cell phones. Hopefully, she won't say anything too embarrassing."

With an exaggerated eye-roll, she unmuted the call and listened as her mother recounted details of Mikey's day. I heard every word she said as if she were on speaker phone. Sabrina remained silent, every so often she'd release a sigh.

Clear as day, her mother then said, "The little booger invited all the kids to sleep here tonight. That's when I put my foot down. Now that we'll have a full house tomorrow, the last thing I need are six kids running amok all night. Of course, your father just laughed and said we'd manage."

"Wait, *how many* are coming tomorrow?" Sabrina asked.

"Including us, twenty." At Sabrina's audible groan, her mother quickly added, "It's no big deal, you know I make enough to feed the whole town. Although I switched the menu up a bit from lasagna to baked ziti. It's easier."

"Mom, do you need me to come help tonight?" I stopped stacking our dirty dishes and waited.

"No dear. You had a busy week. Take the night to relax. We have it covered." Not bothering to hide my relief at her mother's response, Sabrina's lips twisted into a smirk as she noticed my smile. Relaxing was one way to put what we'd be doing tonight.

"Okay, can I talk to him?" Her mother passed Mikey the phone. The moment his little voice began speaking, it didn't stop for a full five minutes. "Mikey, you'll have plenty of fun tomorrow. Now, get ready for bed, and stop giving Grandma a hard time, or you will not be participating in tomorrow's egg hunt."

Silence filtered over the phone. The poor kid was probably debating his options. Sabrina asked if he understood her threat. When she said, "Thank you. Sweet dreams. I'll see you tomorrow," I had to assume he conceded.

"Good Lord. This kid," she said with a firm shake of her head. "Never ending. Where does he get the energy?"

"He's five."

"It's not enough to have a full day tomorrow packed with activity, he needs to have a sleepover to boot?" Remembering her mother sharing that their quiet Easter was now a full production, I wondered if Sabrina would ask me to join them. I also wondered why she hadn't asked what I was doing tomorrow.

Assuming she had her reasons, I decided to commence with the relaxing part of our evening. I placed our dishes in the sink before walking around the island to stand beside her. "Cleaning up can wait. I'd rather do something else right now."

"Yeah?" she asked with a smile. "What would you like to do, Mr. Benedetto?"

"You."

The smile instantly fell off her face when she twisted her stool to face me. I stepped in between her legs while at the same time grabbing her ass and yanking her closer to eliminate the space between us.

Although she didn't respond to my edict, the way her hazel eyes stared into my soul said just what I needed them to—*yes*. The way she skimmed her hands up my shirt before linking them behind my neck said—*I want the same*. And when she pulled my face down toward hers to initiate a kiss that rocked my soul, that said—*I'm yours, Luca.*

Our kiss was full of need, full of longing. The longer it went on, the more she blurred my world. Every hour I spent with her made me want two more. This thing between us was new, yet it felt so familiar at the same time.

I lifted her easily and carried her to my bedroom. It was still early, and we had all night, but I needed her then and there. Anything else I wanted to experience with her, specifically getting to know her better, could wait. The one and only thing I craved, the only thing I needed more than my next breath was an intimate connection.

Placing her down at the foot of my bed, I never broke eye contact as I began unbuttoning my shirt until it hung at my sides. Her line of sight traveled over my body caused me to internally shatter... and not in a bad way. In a *way* I never had felt before, a pleasurable one. She reached for the button of my jeans and unfastened it.

I expected her to continue with the zipper, but instead she stepped back to admire me once again. With my jeans and shirt unbuttoned and gaping open, I may as well have been naked in the way she appreciated me. Her gaze had the same effect on my cock as if it were her hands, and not her eyes, that traveled over me.

She moved closer, her hands roamed over my shoulders to push my shirt off. It fell to the floor. The feeling of her cool hands on my scorching skin caused my resolve to snap. Propelling me into removing every article of clothing she wore until she was standing bare and beautiful before me.

Not a word was spoken between us. There was no need. I removed my own clothes before leading her to lie on my bed. Once we were side by side, our naked bodies aligned from head to toe, I held her face in my palm. "Sabrina, I want nothing between us. Do you trust me?"

Her nod was immediate. "I'm on the pill, Luca. Do you trust me?"

"Completely." I did. I had no doubt I could trust everything about her. The fact she did as well caused a surge of possessiveness to overwhelm me. I wanted to own her in every way. This was just the beginning.

With our gazes tethered, I rolled her backward and positioned my cock at her entrance. Her wet warmth stole my breath. I couldn't be sure if it was the lack of latex separating us that made it feel so fucking good, or if it was because of Sabrina. But one slow thrust, and I already knew I had never experienced such pleasure as I was about to.

We moved together effortlessly. Hands, lips, eyes, connecting throughout our love making enhanced every move we made. Moans and sighs came as we got closer and closer. "Sabrina, I need you to come with me."

Her response was an audible swallow and a short nod. Watching her face as her orgasm began, and feeling it build and crest around me, had every molecule of my body sparking almost painfully. It was her turn to watch me as I fell apart from the inside out.

I wanted to say filthy things to her, admit to all the dirty thoughts that ravaged my mind. But something else took over the carnal need to own her, and for the life of me I had no idea what that was. Confusion and desire, mixed with lust, made the combination both dangerous and terrifying. The only thing I could manage to say as my release ripped through me was, "Sabrina."

I couldn't get enough of her, and as a slow tear leaked from her eye and traveled down her face I worried she'd always hold back a piece of her heart.

After dropping her off at her apartment, it took less than a minute for me to miss her company. Last night had been one of the best of my life. Enjoying the entire evening together, making love, talking, sleeping with her wrapped in my arms was nothing short of perfection.

That was the mark of a perfect connection. When outside influences weren't needed to enjoy being with someone, that had to mean something. The human race seemed to be addicted to stimulation that came from shallow and meaningless social standards. Not once had I checked my phone while with Sabrina. The entire time we were together I had no other thoughts but her.

As I drove myself back to my apartment on Easter morning, the significance of that religious day didn't go unnoticed in comparison to the levity I felt for the first time in my life. I felt alive, optimistic, and anxious to see her again.

My dash lit up with an incoming call from Cassie. "Hey."

"Hi, my friend. Are we still on for dinner later?"

Since all our friends ditched us, and with Cassie's family in Florida for the holiday and mine in Italy, we decided on dinner and a movie. "Yeah. I'm on my way back to my place. I'll pick you up at six?"

"Sounds good. How was your date with Sabrina?"

"Fantastic."

A small gasp preceded her, "Really? I'm so happy for you guys." At my silence she then added, "What's wrong?"

"Nothing. We had a great night. I really like her, Cass. The problem, I don't know if she feels the same. Her actions say she does, but at times she still holds me at arm's length."

"Like when?"

I slowed my car at the light and paused to choose my words carefully. "Like today, at first she said it would be a quiet Easter with her parents. But then when her mother said it became a big affair, with a bunch of guests, she never asked me to join them or even what I was doing today." Once the words were out, I realized how ridiculous they sounded. "What is wrong with me? Of course she shouldn't have invited me."

Not more than a second of silence passed before Cassie countered with, "There's nothing wrong with you, Luca. In fact, you're perfect in every sense of the word. She's been through a lot in the past year. I'm sure she's apprehensive."

I knew this, I did, but I wasn't like her husband. I had never cheated on a woman nor did I plan to. "I understand." This wasn't a conversation I wanted to have in the car. I really wanted to talk to Cassie. She had a different perspective on things. "What are you doing now? Let's spend the day together. We can still have dinner, but why wait?"

"Laundry, that's what I'm doing. But, you're right, this can wait. I'm waiting for a load to finish drying, so I can be ready in about thirty minutes. Are you still close to my apartment? I'll make coffee if you want to come by now."

"I'll stop and grab bagels."

"Oooh, yum. A cinnamon raisin for me please."

"Be there in a bit."

Exactly thirty-five minutes later, I knocked on Cassie's

door. Her eyes went wide when she saw the white bakery bag in my hand. "I swear I could smell that bagel before you knocked."

I gave her a kiss on the cheek as she stepped aside to let me in.

She snatched the bag from my hand, opened it, stuck her face in and inhaled before sighing. "Heaven." When she pulled her face back, she smiled. "It's still warm. I love them when they're like this."

"Me too."

Cassie retrieved two plates from the kitchen and poured us each a cup of coffee. We sat at the table and rather than eat, I stared at the circular bread in front of me. "Luca, what are you thinking?"

"Do you think Sabrina is ready?"

Her eyebrows scrunched together. "Ready for what? A relationship?"

"Yes. I need to talk to someone about this, but since you're also friends with her, I don't want you to feel uncomfortable." I almost added, *I really need to talk to you.* Talking to the guys about this felt foreign, yet with Cassie it felt normal.

Her dainty fingers plucked a raisin out of the bagel before taking it into her mouth. "To tell you the truth, I wondered if she was. But, she's seems so happy when she's with you. There's a lightness that you bring out in her. Not to mention the way Mikey took to you."

Mikey.

That was another issue in itself. It would be hard enough if Sabrina didn't want a relationship with me, but that meant I'd never see him either. The thought of that entire scenario forced me to place my bagel down and push the plate aside.

Her eyes softened. "Maybe she didn't think you wanted to go?" The tone of her voice raised an octave at the end of her question.

"Of course, I would have wanted to. I figured if she *wanted* me there, she would've asked."

"You've only been seeing each other a short period of time. If it were me, I don't know that I'd be ready to invite a man I was seeing to meet my parents so quickly. What would you have done? If your family were here and not in Italy, would you have invited her?"

"Without a doubt." That was the truth, too. "She could've just said we're friends even though we were more or even that I was helping Mikey with soccer. I understand the entire *meet my family* scenario and the weight that carries. But, it could've been informal, just like the gathering."

"I'm sorry, Luca." She covered my hand with hers. When our eyes met, she asked, "What are you thinking? I see your wheels turning."

"I feel like I'm being compared to a ghost." There. I said what had been on my mind. While I had held a sleeping Sabrina in my arms, I wondered why she hadn't asked me to go with her. I could understand if it was a small family gathering, but it wasn't. She said she trusted me. Hell, we had unprotected sex… that in itself spoke volumes. Deep down though, I didn't think she trusted me not to break her heart.

Chapter 21

Sabrina

I T SOUNDED MORE LIKE CHRISTMAS than Easter. Kids scurried through the grassy courtyard in search of plastic goodie-filled eggs. You'd think these kids had never had a piece of chocolate before the way they squealed when they found one. Naturally, the boys made it into a competition.

When no more were to be found, Mikey ran toward me. He slid on his knees, coming to a halt and no doubt leaving a patch of green on each knee of his new Easter khakis. Colorful plastic ovals knocked around in his basket. "Look, Mommy. I must have twenty eggs."

Another little boy, did the same next to him. "I bet I have more."

Mikey shook his head. "Nuh uh, Simon, I do." They both started counting and when Simon counted four more than Mikey, the taunting began. Just as I was about to interject and put a stop to this nonsense, my son said, "Who cares? I bet you can't do this."

He stood up and pulled out his hacky sack that had become his new obsession. Mikey played with that every day. In a short amount of time, he had become better and better at keeping it off the ground.

"That's so cool," Simon said, and before I knew it, other kids had gathered around watching Mikey. The tip of his little pink tongue peeked out of the corner of his mouth as he concentrated. "Where did you learn how to do that?"

His words were staccato breaths. "My best friend gave it to me." The small beanbag toy fell to the ground. "It's called a hacky sack, and it's going to turn me into a great soccer player. I might even go pro one day. Luca is the best soccer player in..." His brows scrunched together. "Mommy, where is he from?"

I stood staring at my son. My heart started beating a bit faster when I saw he gained my mother's attention. "Italy, honey."

"Yeah, that's right, Italy," Mikey said without hesitation. "They're like the best at this sport, so I don't care if you got the most eggs because I got Luca."

The sound of my own swallow filled my ears. "Mikey, don't speak to him that way."

Of course, he ignored me and continued. "We're always together. He's my private coach, and I'm going to be as good as he is one day... maybe even better. He said so himself."

Simon narrowed his eyes at my son. "Then where is he?" he asked with a five-year-old's attitude.

Mikey squinted. "Mom?"

What did I say? I didn't invite him? "Oh, honey, I think he had plans."

"Let's call him. I know he'd want to be here." Then Mikey reached into my purse, with the agility of a Ninja, and grabbed my phone.

"What are you doing? Give that back to me."

Mikey's little fingers tapped my screen, and he held the phone face up in his palm.

Before I knew it, Luca's deep Italian voice came over the speaker. "Hi, beautiful."

"Um... it's Mikey."

"Hey, little buddy, is everything okay? Where's your mom?"

My mouth opened, yet Mikey answered for me. "She's right here. We just had an egg hunt."

Luca laughed. "I bet that was fun. Did you get a lot of eggs?"

"Yes, but not the most."

"That's okay. What's up?"

"Can you tell my friend, Simon, that you are the best soccer player in the world and my coach?"

Luca didn't reply as quickly as Mikey would have appreciated. "Am I on speaker phone?"

"Yeah, Simon's here. When I told him all about my best friend, he didn't believe me because you're not here." My heart sunk with a weight of regret.

"Hi, Simon. Mikey is telling you the truth, I'm a very good soccer player, but decided not to go pro. Because of that, I can't claim the title of best in the world."

"But you are," Mikey chimed in. "You're better than my coaches."

I covered my mouth with my hand to stifle a laugh knowing full well Luca fully agreed with that assessment. "That's true."

"See!" Mikey said to Simon. "Thank you, Luca."

"Can I talk to your mom now?"

"Yup." He practically tossed the phone at me and ran off with Simon and the other kids.

After clicking off the speaker function, I brought the phone to my ear. "Hi."

"Good morning. Happy Easter."

"Happy Easter. I hope he didn't interrupt anything."

"Just having breakfast with Cassie."

A wave of unnecessary and irrational jealousy washed through me. "Oh, tell her I said, 'hi.'" Taking a breath, I added, "Would you like to come to my parents' for lunch? It might get a little insane due to the number of people who are going to be there. But, I'd love it if you were one of them… bring Cassie."

"What time?"

"One."

"Text me the address, and I'll ask Cass, too."

"Okay, see you soon."

I watched my son having a fun time. Children's laughter played like a song in the background. Mikey giggled while tapping kids' heads in a game of duck duck goose. Minutes later my mom stood next to me. "Should I set another place at the table?"

"You heard that?"

"Some of it, yes."

"I hope it's okay that I invited him and Mikey's teacher?"

"Of course it's okay. Sweetheart, I know this is hard on you. I saw Michael's face when he was talking about Luca. This man isn't Dillon… rest his soul." The sarcasm dripping from her words was unmistakable.

Yeah, his cheating soul. It broke my heart that mourning for my late husband ended so abruptly thanks to his mistress. "I know that. But, having my son's heart broken again isn't an option. I'll do whatever I need to insure that doesn't happen."

Her kind eyes that could always see right through me softened. "Are you sure it's just Michael's heart you're protecting?"

"No, I'm protecting my own too, I know that. It's probably why I didn't ask him over today. It scares me to already feel so much for this man."

She smiled. "Sweetheart, you need to live life. Not just for your son, but for you, too. If this man makes you happy, then allow yourself to enjoy it. Our hearts are meant to love, and you have so much love to give. Don't be afraid to open it again." I nodded. "Now, I need to get home and start preparing the table."

I knew she was right. I sent Luca my mom's address and as soon as I pressed the green send button, my heart felt lighter. This was right. Having him with us today should have never been a question in my mind.

Luca

CASSIE WAS ALL SMILES WHEN we walked up to the front door of Sabrina's parents' home. "Nice touch." Cassie smiled at the flowers I held in my hand for Mrs. Ricci. With a slight tremble I pressed the circular button on the door frame. "Are you nervous?"

I studied my petite friend with amusement. "Yes, a little bit." Cassie laughed at me. "Some friend you are, I should have left you home."

She smacked my arm. "I'm just trying to ease your

worries. Relax, Luca, they'll love you." Even with the top button open on my button down light blue shirt, it still felt as though it was closing around my neck. With a curved finger, I hooked the fabric and pulled to allow me some give. "Wow, you are nervous," she quipped.

"Thanks, Captain Obvious."

When the door swung open, Sabrina took my nerves and my breath away. Her dress fit as though it were made for her. Pink flowers that dotted the white material matched the color of her lips. Lips that I had kissed and who had kissed me back not less than six hours ago, yet all I wanted to do was devour her all over again. "Hi, come in."

I moved aside to let Cassie pass first. "Thank you for including me today," she said pulling Sabrina into a hug.

Taking that minute to gather my thoughts, and force my body to not ravish hers, I waited for her eyes to land on me. I chastely kissed her cheek and felt it rise in a smile beneath my lips. With my lips close to her ear, I whispered, "I'll kiss you properly when we're alone. There are about twenty pairs of eyes watching."

When she turned around, a very attractive woman walked toward us. The resemblance to Sabrina was uncanny. "You must be Cassie, I'm Isabelle, Sabrina's mother. Mikey and Sabrina speak so highly of you." They shook hands. "I give you all the credit in the world for doing what you do."

A blush colored Cassie's cheeks. "Thank you. And thank you for having me in your home."

Her mother turned her attention to me. "Mom, this is Luca. Luca, this is my mother."

"Well, aren't you a handsome man." My lips curled up at the corners. "Sabrina, you didn't tell me how handsome he was."

I laughed when Sabrina shielded her face with her hands. "These are for you." I handed her the flowers. "You and Sabrina could be sisters." Tossing in a wink for good measure, I added, "Are you sure you're her mother?"

"Smart, charming and easy on the eyes. And your accent... you sound like my husband's Great- Uncle Antonio." Her mother looked at Sabrina, whose cheeks deepened in hue. "I'm going to go put these in water."

Sabrina ushered us into the living room where several people were chatting and laughing amongst themselves. A man stood and the way his eyes appraised me, there could only be one answer as to who he was.

"Luca, this is my father."

He extended his hand to me. "Sebastian Ricci."

"It's a pleasure to meet you, Mr. Ricci. I'm Luca Benedetto." His grip was firm, but his smile was kind, just like his daughter's.

"Please, it's Sebastian."

"Luca!" Mikey's voice boomed through the room. "You're here!"

Just as he did other times he saw me, he launched his body toward mine, forcing me to catch him mid-air. "Hey, buddy."

"I knew you'd come. Can you come out back with me? I have my hacky sack, can you show everyone how good you are? I learned some tricks too that I want to show you." When he stopped to take a breath, he finally acknowledged Cassie. "Oh, hi Miss Brooks." His attention span was short lived. "Come on..." He tugged my hand.

"If you'll excuse me, sir?" Sebastian regarded us with

amusement, as did Sabrina. "Want to come with us?" I asked her. It was clear my pleading eyes were for naught since she just smiled and didn't budge.

Outside kids were laughing and playing. Mikey tapped a boy on his shoulder. "Luca, this is Simon the one that didn't believe me."

Simon zoned in on me with eyes as wide as the sun. "Hi, Simon. So, do you play soccer too?"

He shook his head. "I'm more into basketball." Appraising me he said, "Can you dunk a basket?"

Mikey chimed in, "I bet he can." His eyes zipped toward me. "Can you, Luca?"

"Only if I'm standing on a ladder." The two boys broke into a fit of laughter.

Mikey handed me his hacky sack. Without hesitation, I did what Mikey had asked me to do—showed off.

Laughter and stories flowed throughout the dinner conversation. Every so often, I'd catch Sabrina's eyes making me wish we were alone. Her family and friends were very welcoming. Her father and I even shared a few stories about Italy. It had been a while since he had been there, but talking to him made me miss my family more than I already did.

When the party was over, Mikey, who should have been hopped up on sugar, appeared to be exhausted. The kid refused to admit it and fought Sabrina tooth and nail to stay longer. On our way out, Cassie and I walked Sabrina to her car passing mine on the way.

"Wow!" Mikey exclaimed. "It's the Batmobile!" Unknowingly, he pointed to my car. "Mommy, look how cool that car is."

Sabrina smirked at my prideful face. "That's Luca's car."

His eyes widened. "Can I ride in it?"

I pushed the door lock prompting the handle to pop out. "I don't have a car seat, buddy, but you can sit in it for a minute. One day, if it's okay with your mom, I'll take you for a ride."

"Cool!" I opened the door for him to slide inside. "How fast does it go? I bet it goes really fast."

The kid reminded me of myself when my dad got his first Alfa Romeo. All I wanted to do was ride around with him at top speed—which thanks to my mother didn't happen. Sabrina's face mirrored the one my mom used to give my dad.

"Pretty fast, but we don't live on a racetrack, so we won't be speeding."

"Aww, man."

"Come on, Mikey, we need to get you home." Sabrina's mom voice prompted him to get out. "Tomorrow's a school day."

With a pout he asked, "Can you come over and read to me again?"

I kneeled down to his level. "I need to take Miss Brooks home, she also has school tomorrow. But, I'm going to follow you guys to make sure you get home okay."

Cassie smiled and said goodbye to the both of them before sliding in the seat Mikey just vacated.

"You don't need to do that," Sabrina said quietly for my ears only.

Ignoring her, I asked, "Buddy, which car is yours?"

His tiny hand lifted and pointed to a red Honda CRV that was parked a few spaces away. Sabrina put her hand on her son's shoulder and shook her head as we all started walking toward her car. After she clicked open the door, she said, "Hop in, Mikey, and buckle up."

"Drive carefully. I'll be right behind you."

"Luca…"

"I'm following you, Sabrina." Not giving her room to argue, I said, "Bye, Mikey," before turning to leave.

Chapter 22

Sabrina

THE PAST FEW WEEKS HAD been nothing short of astonishing. That would be the only word I could use to describe my life since meeting Luca. From the first day we locked eyes, I knew he was something special. Fear of the unknown encapsulated me on so many levels, but I finally began to trust that not every man could break a woman's heart.

To some people, I appeared to be a widow who had quickly moved on from the death of her husband. But they didn't know the real reason my grief was short-lived, and I wouldn't taint Dillon's name for my benefit. Just like everything else in life, it would flush out on its own when his mistress's child came around.

My parents suffered along with me once Dillon's dirty secret was revealed. After meeting Luca on Easter, they were thrilled for me... and for Mikey. They watched his relationship with Luca and even my father approved. I had to laugh when he told me so since it took months for my late husband to gain his approval. But, that was what made Luca different.

Tonight, was date night. Becky and I had a very busy day at the salon, and my mom picked Mikey up from school for me. What I didn't bargain for was the fact that his soccer coach surprised us with a scrimmage the next day. My parents, who would normally take him if I couldn't, had a church event to go to and planned to take Mikey. Of course, now that he knew his friends were playing soccer, that was all he wanted to do.

When my phone rang with a FaceTime request from my son, I knew what was coming.

My finger tapped the green circle. "Hi, baby. Are you having fun?" I propped my phone on the vanity and slid an earring in continuing to get ready.

"Mom, please?" His hands pressed together in front of his face.

"Honey, I wish I could take you but I can't. I tried to get out of work." I slid my other earring in and picked up my phone to finish getting ready. Guilt flooded me, but there was nothing I could do. I had asked Becky what Jared was doing, but he was going to see his paternal grandmother since Mother's Day was tomorrow.

When the buzzer rang, I carried the phone with me to the door. Luca stood there with a smile on his face. "Hi, beautiful."

"Is that Luca?" Mikey's voice rang through my phone's speaker.

Luca stood next to me and angled the phone so he could be in the camera's spot. "Hey, buddy. Are you having fun?"

"Can you take me to my soccer game tomorrow? Mommy has to work and Grandma and Grandpa can't take me. I don't want to miss it. Puh-leeeze?"

Luca let out a laugh and turned to me. "If it's okay

with your mom, I'd love to bring you."

"Sweetie, your grandparents have the day planned with you."

"Mom, they're going to a church thing to serve food. They won't care." He turned away from the phone and yelled. "Grandma, do you care if Luca takes me to soccer?"

My mother appeared on the screen. Her eyes went wide as did the smile on her face when she saw Luca. "Hi, you two. Sabrina, it's fine with us. We feel horrible as it is. You can come back on Sunday for brunch as planned... both of you."

"See! Luca, can we go in your car?"

"One thing at a time, buddy. I'll get the information from your mom and I'll pick you up in the morning. We will let you know the time, okay?"

"Yes!" He fist-pumped in the air. "You're the best."

"Hey..." I said with a pout.

"I mean you're the second best. No one is better than my mom. Okay, I gotta go eat dinner. Bye. Love you."

The moment the screen went dark I set my phone aside and asked, "Are you sure about this?"

Luca wrapped his arms around my waist bringing me flush against his body. "Positive."

Without hesitation, I linked my fingers together on the back of his neck. "You're a special man, do you know that?"

He lowered his head resting his forehead against mine. "You have no idea how happy you've made me." Soft lips caressed my cheek, jaw, and finally my lips. It wasn't a hasty or aggressive kiss, it was tender, loving, and all Luca. Like a free fall off of a cliff, I could feel my heart doing the same. It hadn't been very long since I met this wonderful man, but I knew deep down, in the middle and on the surface, I wanted more with him.

From my experience, the feelings I had weren't infatuation, they weren't lust, and should have probably scared me. The fact that they didn't spoke volumes. There was one person that I was concerned with and that was my son. He had already fallen for Luca, and I wasn't far behind.

"Let's go to dinner before I decide to have you instead." Luca's deep voice caused my insides to quiver.

Desire accentuated the beautiful brown eyes I'd come to adore. With every breath I took, I wanted him more and more. "I am hungry." I smirked and may have batted my eyelids a few times.

A low growl rose up his chest. Strong hands cupped my face. "When we get home, you're all mine… do you understand?"

"I'm yours now." Using his wrists for balance, I gripped them. "Kiss me again, Luca."

Not a millisecond passed before he devoured my mouth with his. Luca's tongue danced with mine. He tasted of mint and his own uniqueness—a blend that I started to crave. Our hips pressed together, and I felt his obvious arousal. It was as if my entire body wanted to climb him and tangle around him like a vine to a post.

His hand grabbed my right ass cheek forcing us closer together. When our kiss broke, our breaths were audible. I no longer wanted to go to dinner, but he laced our fingers together and pulled me out of my apartment.

I turned to lock the door, and he pinned me up against it. Nose to nose, he skimmed the knuckles on his right hand down my cheek. "Later. I'm going to give you so much pleasure, you're going to wish you didn't have any neighbors."

Luca's last comment about giving me pleasure didn't bode well when we were going to dinner and had no chance of acting on it. Since leaving my apartment, said pleasure was all I could think about, and feigning innocent thoughts was hard as hell. Somehow, I managed to eat, smile, and laugh at the appropriate times, even with thoughts of what was to come later that evening bouncing around my brain like a ball in a pinball machine.

Throughout dinner, his hand placement, his whispered promises, and his casual lip licking turned the blood in my veins into molten lava.

So, as we got into his hot car, and he asked if I was up to hanging out with his friends at Dispatch for a few drinks, it took every fiber of my being not to hiss, "*Are you freakin' kidding me?*"

He immediately picked up on my scowl. "What?"

"Nothing."

He gave me a smirk I wanted to wipe off his face with my lips, grabbed my hand, and kissed my knuckles. "Sure looks like something is on your mind, Ms. Ricci." The deep throated chuckle he then released meant he was so on to me. "We can skip drinks, if you're cranky."

"I'm not cranky," I lied. I was *very cranky*.

"Just say the word, and we can head home and meet my friends for drinks another time."

I narrowed my eyes and bit out, "No, I could use a good stiff one."

"Then a stiff one is what you'll get... later," he said

with a wink.

I both hated and loved how much he enjoyed torturing me. This man brought out a side of myself that I didn't know existed.

Luca continued to tease me with his sexual magnetism until the moment we walked up to the table where his friends were sitting. Four pairs of eyes landed on us. "Well, if it isn't Mr. Romeo," Vanessa said with a huge grin. "And his Juliet?"

"Funny," he said, but never denied her observation. "You all remember Sabrina?"

They waved at the same time I did. Luca and I took the two empty chairs, and his arm immediately circled my shoulders. "Happy Mother's Day," Brae said with a smile. "Are you doing anything special?"

"Thank you. Just brunch with my parents. Even though I'm a mother, I feel it's more about celebrating my mom."

"I agree," Brae added with a nod.

"No way. I expect to be celebrated on Father's Day once we have a baby," Jude interjected.

Vanessa scoffed. "Soren, every day is like Father's Day for you. Get real."

As they bickered, Luca's hand traveled down my back and came to rest low on my hip. The feel of it sparked all the desire I had stomped down since leaving my apartment. I twisted my head, and he caught my eye.

"I know that look," Vanessa said, wagging a finger between us. "Honey, there's a small closet in the back by the ladies' room. No one will see you. Trust me."

Brae gasped, "V."

"What? Kyle and I used it just last week. No one

knew. Just wait for the music to start so no one hears you screaming. Unless you're not a screamer, then go any time."

Kyle lifted a finger in an *aha* moment. "Nessa, we need to revisit that closet." Not five seconds later, the music began, the two leered at each other, and bolted.

"Seriously?" Jude asked Luca.

"That surprises you?"

"Fuck no. I'm jealous." He turned to his wife and her head shook from side to side before he could say another word.

"No way. You'll have to wait until we get home."

Jude seemed appeased with what Brae said, because he didn't argue but instead nibbled on her ear while whispering things that caused her to blush.

The way the friends spoke so openly about their sex lives made me feel a bit better that I hadn't turned into a complete nymph these past few months. That's what I felt like, a woman who couldn't get enough and wanted more each time she got it.

"Want to dance?" Luca's question brought me back to the moment.

"Sure." I was about to excuse ourselves, but Jude and Brae wouldn't have noticed as long as their lips were latched in a heated kiss. *Had everyone been abducted by horny aliens?* Maybe there was a full moon?

Luca took my hand and led me to the crowded space. Bodies pressed together as Ed Sheeran's *Thinking Out Loud* played. The moment we found a corner for ourselves, Luca pulled me into his chest and began swaying us to the music.

"Do you remember hearing this song in my car?"

"I do. I said I loved it."

"I remember. And so many times since then I wanted to think out loud whenever I was with you." He rubbed his nose along mine before pressing our mouths together. The people around us disappeared as Luca probed my lips with his tongue. As I listened, every lyric Ed Sheeran sang suddenly had a whole new meaning.

"You know, if you did... think out loud that is... it would make dating so much easier." My fingertips fiddled with his hair that laid on his neck.

"Sweetheart, trust me if you knew everything I was thinking, you might not like it."

Tilting my head to the side, I studied his eyes. "Try me."

His lips twisted into the sexiest grin I'd ever seen. "Right now, for instance, I'm thinking how much I wish your body was lying beneath mine. Our skin would be touching like we are now, except we would be naked. Then, my hands would explore every inch of your bare skin, all while my mouth made love to yours."

I forced a swallow and nodded urging him to continue. "Then..." He brought his lips to my ear. Warm breath sheathed my skin causing my body temperature to rise. "I'd tell you to spread your legs before I lowered my head to lick you until you came in my mouth." At those words my body reacted and my panties dampened more than they were. "And that's just the beginning. The rest I'd like to leave as a surprise."

"Yes. In my opinion, your words are better than Ed's." Lust blurred my vision. I wanted Luca so bad. Based on the heat in his eyes, and the hardness between his legs, he felt the exact same way. Twisting my head, I nodded toward the hall containing the closet Vanessa informed us of and wondered if she and Kyle were done using it.

Just before I could voice my own thoughts out loud, he leaned closer and said, "We need to leave... now."

Chapter 23

Luca

MY ENTIRE BODY FELT STIFF, but with her nakedness pressed up against me all night I wouldn't dare move a muscle.

Between the time we left Dispatch and arrived at her apartment, we had worked ourselves up into quite a sexual frenzy. Sabrina wasn't happy with my teasing, and that caused her to reciprocate in evil ways making the drive home very difficult for me.

By the time we clamored through her door, the only thing either of us were capable of at that point was a quick punishing fuck against her wall.

Not bothering to fully remove any of our other clothes, within seconds her jeans were in a puddle on the floor, mine were hanging around my ass, and her legs straddled me as I pushed hard and fast inside her.

Lacking was our normal romance, regardless, it was still one of the best encounters we ever had. Through the grunts and thrusts, the crushing kisses and painful gripping, we came together, and the result was perfection.

It had been the first time we allowed ourselves to be so carnal and crude. Afterward we calmed down a bit, the next time was the complete opposite—slow and deliberate. We ended our night in her bed, taking turns bringing the other to a new height of pleasure. Tit for tat, every one of the affections I lavished on her body she had reciprocated on mine until our final act. With Sabrina straddling my lap while I remained buried within her silky heat, neither of us were capable of speaking. As for myself, I couldn't conjure up even one word that could summarize the significance of what passed between us.

What seemed like mere moments later, the sound of her alarm cut through the peaceful silence. She moaned, reached behind her to quiet it, then buried her face into my side. "I don't want to go to school," she murmured in a whiney voice.

I kissed the top of her head with a chuckle. "I know. And I'd love nothing more than to convince you to play hooky and stay here with me all day. But I'm sure you have more rainbow hair on your agenda today, and I have an eager soccer player on mine."

"Five more minutes." When she wrapped an arm around my body, bringing her bare boobs even closer to my side, and hooked her toned leg over mine, who was I to argue? In the process, the top of her thigh rested against my hard-on causing her eyes to fly open. "Well, hello there."

"It's your fault," I said with a shrug. "He's not used to having a sexy naked woman waking up beside him."

Shyness mixed with flattery in her hazel eyes. "He's not?"

"No, he's not." I pushed her hair off her warm face. "This isn't a normal thing for me, Sabrina."

Her tentative smile grew into a brilliant one. "I like knowing that."

"It's the truth. What else do you want to know?"

"Have you ever been in a serious relationship, Luca?" Based on how quickly her next question came, my guess was she'd been thinking about it.

"As serious as one could get at the age of seventeen." She smiled. "We were just two kids who were infatuated with each other." I almost felt by not being in love before, it had prepared me all along for what I'd be experiencing with Sabrina. Every part of our journey so far had been new and confusing to me, yet because of that, I appreciated it all the more. I bent and placed a soft kiss on her forehead.

"What happened?"

"We grew apart, she stayed in Italy, I moved here. But, even if I didn't move, we never would've lasted. Aside from her, no other steady girlfriends." She cocked a brow. "You seem surprised."

"I am. I mean look at you. It baffles me that some wonderful woman hadn't snatched you up and held on for dear life."

I gestured at the way her body was wrapped around mine, and grinned. "You mean like now?"

She pulled her lip in between her teeth to stop from grinning as well. "Have I snatched you?"

"In every way, Sabrina. Consider me officially snatched. I'm not an angel by any means, but I never had the opportunity to crave more with a woman. And I'm not just talking about the sex, although with you it's been… "

"Amazing," she finished my sentence.

"More than. With you, it's more than just an act to get to a climax. Do you know what I mean?"

"I do."

I palmed her cheek, skimming my thumb along her bottom lip. "I enjoy being with you." Just before I reached her lips with mine, she pulled away and bolted out of bed. "Where are you going?"

"You brushed your teeth, cheater."

"I got up earlier, peed, and used your mouthwash. I hope that's okay?"

"That's fine, but I also have to pee really bad, so don't move," she said while moving toward the door.

"Wait, you can't stand there all naked and gorgeous. Worse yet, you can't leave me like this," I groaned, pointing to my now very obvious arousal. She had the nerve to giggle at my quandary.

"I'll just be a minute." The sight of her naked ass walking out of the room left me hanging in so many ways. But when one minute turned into three, I couldn't stand it any longer and took matters into my own hands. Time was of the essence, and there was none to waste.

I found her washing her face. Through the mirror, she watched me move past her to the shower. Without a word, I turned the water on, held my hand beneath the steady stream, before lifting and carrying her in with me.

"What are you doing?" she asked, amused.

"I going to repeat last night. First, the beast in me will fuck you hard and fast until you scream my name in this shower. Then, the romantic in me will repeat the process only softer and slower until you scream my name in your bed. I don't care if you're late, if the building catches fire, or if your neighbors call the cops."

With the warm water pelting our bodies, I turned her around, placed her hands on the tile wall, and started to do just as I promised.

Sabrina

THE SMILE ON MY FACE was constant, as was the galloping in my heart. Whenever my mind drifted to Luca, I bounced between feeling like a giddy schoolgirl and an insatiable woman in need. Remembering how he brought me pleasure with his lips, his tongue, his fingers, and ultimately his tireless erections caused my libido to once again soar.

I managed without a sex life for way too long, and never really missed it. Yet, there I was after only a few hours without him, squirming while attempting to go about my day. For the record, I deserved a medal. No one was onto me, except Becky. From the moment I walked into the salon this morning, she narrowed her eyes and accused, "You're hiding something."

How she knew that I'd never know, but the woman was a human lie detector. The more I ignored her questions, the more she asked.

The salon was now empty, and as she locked up after the last beautician left for the night, she turned on me with a pointed finger. "I've waited long enough, missy."

"You've lost your mind."

"No, I haven't. You have. You are head over heels for that man, why can't you admit it?"

I nestled my custom scissors in their padded leather container and zipped it up with a sigh. "Okay, I am."

She came closer and placed her hands on my shoulders while staring me into the eyes. "Then why do you look like your puppy just died?"

A weight settled on my chest. How could I explain this to Becky when I couldn't explain it to myself? "Deep down I'm so very happy, and at the same time I have this unsettled feeling growing in the pit of my stomach. It's like I'm a wearing a constricting pair of SPANX and just want to yank them off and be free. Does that make sense?"

Becky stared at me. "You lost me at SPANX," she said as she walked to the front desk.

I followed, and leaned against it while she counted today's till. A ponytail holder caught my attention. Holding up the circular object, I said, "See this?" She nodded. "Okay, well you know the more you wrap it around someone's hair the tighter it gets?" Another nod came. "And when you think that maybe it could take one more turn, it snaps in your hand?" Her brows then furrowed. "That's how I feel. I'm starting to want so much with him but what if it snaps?"

"So, you're scared." She slid the deposit money into a bank bag. "That's normal. We all think when it's too good to be true it is, but it isn't." I opened my mouth, and she put her hand up. "No. Don't you dare compare him to your late husband. He is nothing like Dillon." She peered out the front window and then back to me. "This is how I see it... you can spend the rest of your life waiting for that proverbial shoe to drop or you can go outside and be happy."

Using the eraser end of her pencil she pointed out the window. There stood Luca holding a bouquet of Gerbera daisies in one hand and my son's in the other. Mikey had a balloon with *Happy Mother's Day* printed on it in his other hand.

My eyes filled with tears. "Thank you, Becky." I slung my bag across my body.

"That's what I thought you'd say. Now, go on. I have a last minute client coming in." She started shooing me out the door.

"Who? You just closed everything."

She winked. "Not everything. Now, get out of here. He's going to be here any minute and I need to put something more comfortable on like... nothing."

"Oh my God!" I started laughing. "Only you, Beck." Before leaving I gave her a hug, "Thank you."

"No thanks needed. Now, get out." She swatted me on the butt as I walked out the door.

Pure joy surrounded me. "Hey, you two." I leaned down and hugged Mikey. "Hi, sweetheart. Did you have a good day?"

He handed me the balloon. "Happy Mother's Day... early."

"Thank you, honey." I took his little hand in mine and looked at Luca. "Hi, thank you for watching him."

Luca smiled and continued to hang on to the flowers since I didn't have a free hand. "We had fun, didn't we, buddy?" Mikey nodded. "But, we're not done yet." He opened the back of his SUV and helped Mikey climb in. "Buckle up." After the click of the safety belt, Luca shut his door.

He opened mine, kissed me on the cheek, and when I was settled in my seat, he handed me the flowers. "Thank you, Luca." I tucked the balloon under the dash. "For everything."

"Mom, where's the..." He turned to Luca, his forehead creased in confusion. "What is it called again?"

"Colander."

I had to bite the inside of my cheeks to keep from laughing. Since getting to our apartment, flipping between giggles and tears had occurred no less than four times. Luca and Mikey informed me I was not to move from the couch because they were cooking me dinner.

"Yeah, that."

"It's in the cabinet next to the stove. Look for a silver bowl with holes in it."

He hopped off a small step stool. A cabinet door opening and the sound of pots clanking meant he had no clue what to search for. Luca caught my eye and winked.

Donning matching *Kiss the Cook* aprons, the sight of them working side by side caused my heart to swell with unbridled emotion. Whatever Luca did, Mikey mimicked.

He kept giving Mikey simple tasks to do while he tackled the more difficult ones. Whatever it was they were making smelled delicious, and I couldn't wait to dive into what my two favorite males made special just for me.

After some more clanking, a dropped dish, and a fit of giggles over hearing Luca's story of the time his grandmother made octopus for dinner, I was summoned to the table.

"Close your eyes, Mom," Mikey said as Luca took my hand. Once I was helped into my chair, my son commanded, "Okay, open them. Ta-da!" He waved his hand over a steaming platter of pasta. A green salad, and a basket of garlic bread toasted to golden perfection completed the meal. "It's called car-boon-air-ia."

"Carbonara," Luca corrected.

"That's what I said."

"Good job." I clapped my hands while sporting one

of the biggest smiles I'd ever had. "It looks so yummy."

"Dee-liss-e-oozo."

Luca camouflaged his chuckle with a cough as I said, "Yes, I bet it is delicioso. You two did all this by yourselves?"

Mikey scooted onto the chair beside me as Luca took the one across the table. "We did. Luca taught me some Italian, and I helped chop up the bacon stuff."

"You used a knife?" I asked my son, but lifted a questioning brow at Luca.

"Luca bought me a special one." Mikey bolted off his seat to go grab a kelly green plastic knife off the counter. "Give me your hand," he said with the knife poised to cut. I followed his request, and he dragged the serrated edge over my palm. "See, it doesn't cut people. It tickles."

"That's very cool, baby."

My son began firing off random thoughts and his new Italian vocabulary, including bella, ciao, basta, and aspetta… which I knew meant wait and predicted would become his favorite word soon.

Luca served us both some pasta. Mikey dove in and moaned in appreciation, making a liar out of my claim he had a limited pallet. We took turns answering his questions and nodding at his observations. And the entire time Luca and I exchanged a myriad of meaningful glances between us.

Luca

SABRINA CLOSED MIKEY'S DOOR BEFORE joining me on the couch. "It's when he puts up the biggest fight that he's the most exhausted. Already out like a light." It had only been fifteen minutes earlier when I finished reading his favorite book. She watched us from the doorway as I sat on the floor with him on my lap. The shimmer in her eyes made me wonder what ran through her mind at that moment. What stopped me from asking was the possibility that a memory from her past caused the melancholy.

"He had an exhausting day," she said before releasing a yawn. It was the first time Sabrina and I had some privacy since we picked her up at the salon. As she snuggled against me, I played with the silky strands of her hair while filling her in on my day with her son. Giving her a play-by-play, I took her from the soccer field to the market to Mikey's convincing argument that his mother loved the movie *Cars*.

"Him and that damn movie," she said.

"Honestly, I kind of liked it," I admitted with a smirk. During the movie, Mikey sat between us on the couch announcing what was about to happen before it did.

"Of course you did. Men."

I chuckled easily. "What is your favorite movie?"

"Kiddie or adult?"

"Kiddie, for future reference."

"I love *Finding Nemo*. Mikey and I used to snuggle together and watch it on Sundays." I remembered Sabrina telling me that she and Mikey had movie days. A vision of them huddled together on the very couch we sat on caused me to smile. "Mikey outgrew that a few months ago. One day he decided it was dumb. That was when he moved on to anything super hero, Ninja Turtle, or automotive."

"As did you."

"Exactly," she said with a firm nod. "I can't remember the last time it was about me. Which leads me to today." She twisted in my arms and blinked back tears. "Luca, today was just so lovely. Thank you."

I skimmed my fingers over her cheek. "You don't have to thank me. You're a wonderful mother, Sabrina. You deserve to be appreciated."

"Well, I appreciate what you did. Dinner was delicious... or I should say dee-liss-e-oozo. My dad is going to be thrilled hearing Mikey speak Italian. Lord knows, he's tried and failed." Her gaze landed on the colorful Gerbera daisies that sat in a pretty vase on her table. "The flowers, the balloon, and everything you did with Mikey was very thoughtful."

She lifted her face, and I met her halfway. Our kiss started slow and sweet before taking on a life of its own. There was so much that felt right with the way we made out like teenagers on her couch... but only one thing that felt wrong. It couldn't go any further because Mikey slept in the next room.

As if reading my thoughts, she broke the kiss with a gasp. "Oh my God. That was a bad idea."

"My sentiments exactly," I grumbled while adjusting myself in my jeans. "Sweetheart, I hate to say this, but I think I should go."

Chapter 24

Luca

A SOLID KNOCK ON THE doorframe caught my attention. "Were you just whistling, man?"

Why bother denying it? "Yep," I said with attitude.

The all-knowing smile on Jude's face spoke volumes. Yet, he still felt the need to say, "What's up with that, Andy Griffith?"

"Who the fuck is Andy Griffith?"

"No clue. But Brae's dad references him all the fucking time when he whistles."

I couldn't help but laugh. "That's *your* father-in-law."

Jude made himself comfortable in the chair in front of my desk. "He was a package deal, and I'd take ten of him if it meant I had Brae."

A sap in love. That's what he was.

Normally, I'd have a witty or sarcastic retort, but for some reason, Mr. Ricci popped in my head so I kept it to myself. "So, what brings you in here?"

"What do you know about the Callo Corporation?"

It didn't take much time for me to reply. "It's only one of the largest growing manufacturing businesses in Europe. According to the trades, since they've expanded into the US, they are quickly rising into the top 100 on business insider's lists. Why?"

"I called Anthony Callo, the son of the founder and CEO of the corporation, congratulating him on their success." A sly grin appeared on his face.

"And of course, you offered our services since he would need someone to manage his finances, especially here."

He nodded thoughtfully. "Exactly. Their net was 1.2 billion last year." I let out a whistle. "Anthony will be traveling here next month. I'm not sure when and neither is he. But, he said when he gets here he will give us a call."

"Fantastic. What can I do in the meantime? I'll assume you have a game plan already formulating in that head of yours."

"I want you to take point on this. Naturally, I'll be there as well, but when I spoke to him, he sounded exactly like you did when you got to Yale. His English was extremely broken. You, being from his homeland will serve a great purpose. More than you already do."

Ideas swirled in my head. "I'll create a proposal. Did he send you any financials or are we going off public record for now?"

"I'll email what he sent. We need this one, Luca. This could put us on the map."

"Don't you mean control the map?"

Jude let out a hearty chuckle. "I want Soren Enterprises to *be* the map." He stood. "I'm excited about this one, Benedetto." His eyes danced, his jaw was stern, and I knew what that meant... *I will be in Forbes top 100 before I turn 31.* It used to be 30, but that ship had sailed.

"I'm on it, boss."

"Let's go grab a bite to eat."

Ten minutes later we walked into the small café-style restaurant around the corner. We ordered our meals. Jude and I started discussing our game plan for Callo. According to Anthony, he was visiting a few companies in the city. This information sparked both of our competitive nature. Of course, this was what normally happened when a top-rated company searched for the right person to handle their outside investments. It was as if vultures could smell the blood. The difference with Soren was we planned on swooping in before any bloodshed occurred.

Over our club sandwiches and fries, we plotted out our plan of attack, so to speak. We were out of the office for over two hours. Jude brought up his calendar. "Fuck."

"That doesn't sound good, did you miss a meeting?"

"No, but I'm going out of town for Brae's birthday next month. I want this wrapped up by then."

"If you're not here, I'll take care of it. Trust me, I can handle it."

"I have no doubt, but…"

"Don't. Your wife will be disappointed. Like you've said, love first, work second. Right?"

He smirked at my comment. "Eighteen months ago I wouldn't have agreed with you, but yes. Love always comes first. By the way, we're thinking of buying a home in the Hamptons. We found one we like and are renting it for the summer. Plan on coming out the weekend of the Fourth of July. I'm going to tell Cleary, and Brae is inviting the girls. Feel free to bring a date. Speaking of, what's new on the Sabrina front?"

The sound of her name brought a wicked smile to my face. I'd be lying if I said I hadn't been thinking of her. In all of my adult life I had never thought of a woman as much as I did Sabrina. Everything about her made me happy. From the way the sun caught the natural highlights in her hair, to the way she walked. If I let myself think of anything sexual, there would be no way to hide my thoughts.

"Everything is great, thanks. I spent Saturday with her son, and then Mikey and I cooked her dinner as an early Mother's Day gift," I said matter-of-factly.

Jude stared at me. "Wow, you got it bad. When's the last time you cooked for a woman?"

I had to think about it and the answer would probably be my own mother but that most likely didn't count since my grandmother did most of the work. I just chopped tomatoes and grated cheese. Rather than answer, I just shrugged.

He snickered, "That's what I thought." That's when my best friend gave me a genuine smile. "I'm happy for you. She's definitely a keeper and her boy seems to like you."

"I love that kid."

Jude's eyebrows shot to his hairline. "What about her?"

Either my heart was swelling or my ribs were shrinking, but my chest started to tighten. "She's special." That was all I could offer. Even if I was feeling love or extreme *like* toward her, I wanted her to be the first to know.

He gave me his trademark nod alerting me I wasn't fooling anyone. "We should get back to the office."

Mere minutes later that was exactly where we were. Me in my office and Jude in his, both plotting out ways to land Callo and in the back of my head, I thought of Sabrina.

Sabrina

YOU WOULD HAVE THOUGHT THIS was my first time applying mascara. Why in the world I was so nervous going out with Brae and Vanessa sans Cassie, baffled me. No, that was a lie. I wasn't baffled. These women were part of Luca's circle. If Becky wasn't watching Mikey for me tonight, I would have brought her with me like Linus would his blanket.

When Brae called to ask me to go out for a girls' night, I was excited. Then once I had Mikey situated, the nerves kicked in. I stared at my reflection and wondered if I was trying too hard. As it was, I had changed outfits three times and wound up wearing the first one I tried on. I reached into my pink V-neck sweater and adjusted my boobs—even they felt crooked to me. *Calm down, Sabrina.* I chanted in my head. I sprayed on a bit of perfume, gave my hair one more smooth over with my palms, before heading out to meet my Uber at the curb.

A neon sombrero flashed as the sedan pulled up in front of José Ponchos. When I walked in I scanned the bar for the ladies. Brae spotted me and thrust her hand in the air signaling me to their table.

"We're so glad you're here." She gave me a hug and then Vanessa did the same.

"Thank you for inviting me. I've never been here before."

Vanessa flagged down a waiter. "The margaritas are to die for, you'll love them."

Tequila had never been a friend of mine, but why not? It wasn't as if we were doing shots, and a cocktail or two wouldn't be bad. When I was younger, I dubbed tequila, "talk-ee-la" since my lips moved faster than my brain. Many a night did I say something I didn't intend to.

When the young waiter appeared, Vanessa ordered a refill for herself since Brae was still working on the one she had, and one for me. Once again, my nerves spiked. After meeting these girls a couple of times, I could see that their group of friends were more like a family.

Brae shimmied in her seat and then looked at me. "How was your week? I think I'm going to start coming to you to get my hair done. My stylist moved away and my new one, Enrico, isn't going to work out."

I hated hearing horror stories about hairdressers, but, she had perfect hair. "Why?" My head tilted to the left and to the right to check out her shiny tresses. "You have beautiful hair."

Vanessa laughed. "Oh, it has nothing to do with the man's talent."

Confusion set in. "I don't understand? Did he say something rude?"

Brae shook her head. "No, nothing like that. Let's just say Enrico could double as a movie star, and he's straight... a combination that didn't sit well with Jude."

Vanessa shook her head in mock disgust. "You should've told Jude he batted for the other team. It's hard to find a good stylist and that man had talent. Plus, your man is just as hot if not hotter."

Without pause, Brae added, "Hotter. But, I suppose if his stylist could double as a lingerie model, I wouldn't care for that. Thankfully, she could double for my grandmother."

The waiter delivered our drinks. After the tart liquid caressed my taste buds, I added. "I wouldn't care for that either." They both waited as I took another sip. "Wow, this is really good."

Brae and Vanessa eyes remained focused on me. "Why would that bother you?" Brae asked.

"When I was in cosmetology school, a lot of the girls would say how they loved giving attractive men haircuts because they could use their boobs to flirt."

"Shut up!" Brae exclaimed.

"I could see that," Vanessa chided. When neither of us said anything, she added, "I mean, they're eye level with the man. I suppose I should be thankful Kyle goes to a dude."

Brae flung her hand in the air. "Change of subject." That was when she pinned me with her eyes. "How's Luca?"

Vanessa leaned forward, elbows on the table, her laced fingers supporting her chin. "Yes, dish. We want to hear all about him."

It was then I knew my face turned the same shade as my sweater. "He's good." No, that wasn't the right wording. "This past Saturday he took care of my son, since I had to work, and then the two of them made me dinner. It was—"

Before I could complete my sentence, Vanessa finished if for me. "Fucking romantic, that's what that is. Hell, did I get the only one who doesn't cook?" She sipped her chartreuse colored drink. "Jude-alicious cooks for that one, Luca cooks for you, and Kyle orders in dinner."

"Jude-a-what?"

Brae waved her off. "Ignore her. It sounds like a great night. So, you two are getting close? Jude said Luca went to your parents' for Easter."

I did a recap of my relationship with Luca, adding a sigh here and there followed up with a smile. All this talk of him made my insides coil. Shit. As if on cue, my phone vibrated in the back pocket of my jeans.

"Excuse me. This could be about Mikey." When I saw Luca's name, I slid the bar to the right opening the text.

> **Luca:** My ears are burning. Are you talking about me?

I gasped.

"What is it? Is everything okay?" Brae's concern prompted me to show her the screen. Vanessa feeling left out, snatched it from my hand.

"Oh, this is too good. May I?" Switching the straw from her water glass to her margarita, to suck it down, and before I could object, her thumbs went to work.

Vanessa squirmed a bit and let out a giggle. My heart felt like it was going at rapid speed.

After every chime she pulled the phone closer to her chest and farther away from me. Suddenly using a straw didn't seem like a bad idea.

After the last chime, Vanessa jutted out her bottom lip in a pout. Then my phone rang. Without hesitation, she answered. "Well, hello there. How did you know it was me?" I dropped my head in my hands causing it to spin a little, while Brae patted my shoulder in support. "Fine, hold on." Vanessa graciously offered me my phone back, adding, "The jig is up."

Not knowing what the text said, I cringed a little

before I said, "Hi."

"Hey, how's it going?"

"Can I call you right back? It's loud in here and I can't really hear you." I clicked the call off after he said okay, and scanned through the text.

> **Me:** They should be on fire. I'm telling the girls about how you make my toes curl.
>
> **Luca:** Is that so?
>
> **Me:** It is. I can't wait to see you again.
>
> **Luca:** I can't wait to see you too.
>
> **Me:** The way you kiss me makes me so wet, Mr. Romeo. The next time we're together, I'm going to climb you like a tree.
>
> **Luca:** Vanessa... give Sabrina her phone back.

"Oh my God, Vanessa?"

Brae read the messages and tsk'd. "V, really?"

"What? Was I wrong, Sabrina? Doesn't he make your toes curl? You can't tell me he isn't an amazing lover. Couple that with how he treats you, and your toes should curl like a poodle's coat after it just got out of a bath."

"Excuse me a second. I need to call him back." I hurried out of my chair and headed toward the front door. As soon as I breathed in some New York air, and tried to slow the merry-go-round in my head, I tapped on his name.

"Hi."

Everything Vanessa said was right. Even the way he sexily said that two-letter word made me want to leave and go to him. "Hi, I'm really sorry about that."

"You weren't talking about me?"

"No, we were." I let out a small giggle. "But not as detailed as Vanessa would want you to think. I don't kiss and tell."

"Good to know." He paused. "So, I *don't* make your toes curl?"

"No comment." The cool brick of the building chilled my back when I leaned against it. "I wish you were here."

"I wish I was, too. Cleary and Soren have been kicking my ass at pool. Is Mikey out all night?"

"Yes, he's sleeping over at Becky's. Why?" My fingers started fiddling with the edge of my sweater.

"Let's ditch our friends. My place or yours?"

A groan crawled up my throat and into the receiver. "Yours."

"I'll come and pick you up in thirty. Will that be enough time?"

I felt like saying too much, and even though I wanted to be with him sooner rather than later, I didn't want to ditch Brae and Vanessa. "Can we make it an hour? I don't want to make a bad impression. You know, ho's before bro's." *Ho's before bro's?* Yes, talk-ee-la stuck again. "You know what I mean."

He laughed. "One hour. I'll pick you up. Jude told me where you all were."

"See you soon." I paused. "And Luca… just so you know, you do make my toes curl and much more." I pressed the red dot ending the call and walked back inside.

Chapter 25

Luca

THE ELEVATOR PINGED AND OPENED on my floor while she still worried her bottom lip. I stopped us in the hall and tugged it from between the confines of her teeth. "Stop. After your phone call, no sooner had I said that I was ditching our pool outing when Jude and Kyle dropped their cues on the green felt before stalking toward the door."

"I just feel bad. They went through the trouble of inviting me."

"If you ladies want anyone to blame for ending your girl's night out early, then blame my two horny friends."

She threw me a sideways grin. "Nice try. From what I hear, the three of you are all pretty similar in that department."

"It's our women," I retorted just as I opened my apartment door. "You ladies bring out the beast in us." At her silence, my eyes searched her face for a reaction to my claim. "What's running through that pretty head of yours, Sabrina?" A slow smile spread, lighting up her eyes. "That look has me even more curious."

"I like your inner beast."

"You do, huh?" I asked, as I removed my jacket and tossed it not caring where it landed.

She nodded shyly. "He makes me feel wanted."

With my eyes pinned to hers, my response held no levity. "Oh, you're wanted, Sabrina." It was almost comical when her bag fell to the ground with a thump, yet neither of us laughed. I stepped closer and began unbuttoning her jacket next. "But a beast won't be appearing tonight." I didn't stop with her jacket and continued to stare right into her soul while my fingers gripped the hem of her soft pink sweater.

"He won't?" My only response was a slow, methodical slide of my head from right to left. "Why?"

"I have other plans in mind for tonight. Maybe in the morning I'll ravage you like an animal in my shower, or with you spread across my kitchen island. But tonight, you're getting the real Luca." The motion of her swallow caught my attention just before I lifted her top over her head and dropped it to the floor. A lace bra of the palest shade of pink melded with her skin tone, creating an open canvas for my lips. But we were still vertical in my foyer, and I needed her horizontal on my bed to do what I had in mind.

Without any further explanation, I lifted her and carried her right to my bedroom. Once I placed her in the center of the mattress, I appreciated the beauty before me. "Sei bellissima."

"Hearing you speak in Italian while staring at me with those sinful brown eyes of yours is the best kind of foreplay."

"Here comes more foreplay, Sabrina." Her admission forced me to give her a play-by-play on all I planned to do to her, in Italian. I wouldn't translate with words, only with actions. With each detailed account of where my lips would travel from hers down and over every inch of her body, the reaction I received proved her comment was true.

But first and foremost, I needed her naked. One by one, I removed her heels and when she wiggled her pink painted toes I took a moment to knead them with the pads of my thumbs eliciting a sexy groan to escape her lips.

The next article to come off were her jeans. As I unbuttoned and unzipped them, I admired how they seductively molded over her body before rolling the tight denim down until her legs were freed.

"Gesù Cristo," I muttered the Lord's name from seeing her in a whimsical pair of white panties with pink polka dots all over them. My heated gaze caused her to bring her thighs together. "No," I said with a firm shake of my head. She hesitated a pause, and then widened her knees just enough for me to see what she tried to hide a few seconds ago… her wetness revealed in the way the polka dots over her crotch appeared a tad darker than the rest.

I wasn't even aware that my hand moved down to adjust the uncomfortable confines of my jeans until her eyes tracked me doing so. As she continued to stare, I took the opportunity to remove the clothes I wore. They were nothing less than a nuisance to what I needed at that moment. I stopped when I had nothing left to remove but my boxer briefs. The reason I had, Sabrina's gaze stopped raking over me and settled on the very obvious arousal that I couldn't hide. She licked her lips and lifted her gaze to my face.

It seemed an eternity by the time I shed that one last piece of fabric I wore as well as removing her bra and panties. I settled over her while forcing myself to keep the pace that I had started with. Because that beast she claimed she loved lay right beneath the surface, ready to claw his way out.

The reasons I wanted all of her, and to give her all of me, may have been a cowardly way to convey how I felt about her. But, somewhere along the line I realized that I fell in love with Sabrina in every way. What was about to happen needed to be a preview of what would come for us with each day that passed. Words could be scary, and I hoped I could transfer my emotions by making love to her. Just she and I, with our hearts and bodies connecting in the most intimate of ways.

I held her face with one hand, and pressed my lips to hers in a sweet, soft kiss. During that intentional connection, the tear that hit my thumb solidified she felt the same way that I did.

"Luca," she said as a plea. Through the tone of her voice I knew she needed more, she wanted everything from me. By saying only my name and nothing else, Sabrina revealed she also struggled with the right words to say.

Kissing along the track where her tear fell, I moved over her and slid inside her warmth just as I said, "I know."

Sabrina

SINCE WALKING THROUGH HIS DOOR, Luca hadn't broken eye contact once. I meant it when I said the way he looked at me, and the way he spoke in Italian, was the best kind of foreplay. His tenderness forced my heart to swell with more emotion than I'd felt in a long time. It over spilled, and affected every part of my body, resulting in a deep-rooted need to bottle this moment and remember it forever.

Truth be told, that scared me. Nothing was forever, I learned that the hard way. And if I allowed my head to play a logical part in this wonderful experience, I'd run away just to protect my heart.

Luca moved in and out of me with slow measured strokes. Each time our eyes would connect, I felt more exposed. As the saying went, *eyes were the windows to your soul*, and maybe that was why my lids slid shut. Because how could I tell a man who I had only known for a few months that he owned my heart? He claimed he knew... and I prayed he did.

Skin on skin our bodies were one. Pulling my legs up, I wrapped them around him and linked my ankles together, holding him to me as close as I could.

"Guardami, Sabrina," he whispered, his voice throaty. At my hesitation, he added, "Eyes on me." I obeyed, and saw his weren't lustful or dark, but instead filled with raw desire. The reality and weight of our stares created a wave of feelings to course through me. Stray tears seeped from the corners of my eyes landing on my ear. "Please don't cry, sweetheart." But his soothing voice caused a few more to spill.

Every inch of us was connected, and that euphoric feeling began to coil inside of me. Butterflies took flight as my impending climax approached. My heart expanded with each breath I took. I wanted to remember this moment—this feeling.

Luca took my right hand that was on his waist, and raised it above my head, linking my fingers with his. He then did the same to my left. His movements grew faster, my heart raced, our lips met, and I was lost... lost in a man who I just gave my heart to.

He gripped my fingers tighter with his, while his hips continued pistoning against mine. "I'm so close, Sabrina. The way you feel around me... I never want this to end."

Those words caused my climax to rumble through me. It was an ache of the best kind. "Neither do I." My admittance came through challenged breaths.

He smiled and slowed down until he stilled. Then with the utmost tenderness, he lowered his lips to mine and gave me a kiss that I knew I would never forget. Each unspoken word was heard through that kiss. Every emotion I held, with fear and love dominating, traveled from our lips straight to my heart.

Without a doubt, it was the most intimate moment of my life.

When I opened my eyes, it took a few seconds to remember where I was. The naked body spooning behind me, combined with his measured breaths, reminded me of the magnificent man I had just spent the night with.

One strong arm draped over my hip possessively while his hand splayed below my belly button. The warm skin of his broad chest pressed up against my back felt like a comforting blanket. Waking up in Luca's arms probably ranked among my top three favorite things since meeting him... things one and two were a bit more obvious.

But as much as I wanted to stay there all day, I needed to adult and pick up my son. I reached for my phone on the nightstand, but a strong arm held me firm after having moved just an inch. "Good morning, sweetheart," his deep voice rumbled behind me.

"Good morning. I was trying to see what time it is," I said, gripping his forearm with my hands to give me some wiggle room. That second time he allowed me to move, raising his arm as I leaned forward to grab my phone. "It's seven," I said out loud. Relief that it was still early had me relaxing back into his hold.

"Mmm, so I can enjoy you a bit longer?" he asked, eliminating the space my moving had added between us. Every inch of his body aligned with mine from head to toe. I felt his lips on my shoulder before he began leaving soft kisses over my skin.

"Yes, we have time. Becky said to come by around ten or so. She promised the boys pancakes."

"Well, yay for pancakes," he said directly into my ear. When goosebumps spread over my skin, I felt Luca smile against my neck. Firm lips pulled on my earlobe while his hand found one of my breasts. "What are you guys up to later today?"

"It's supposed to be sunny and warm. I thought I'd surprise Mikey with a trip to the beach to watch the fishing boats. Would you like to come?"

His hand stilled for a moment. "Are you sure?"

I twisted in his arms and propped my head on a bent arm. Confused as to why he would ask me that, I replied, "Yes, I'm sure. Why?"

"Sabrina, I'd love to spend every moment with you two. I just want you to be sure you want me there. I know spending Sundays with Mikey is important to you."

"There are two reasons I'd like you to come. Mikey enjoys your company… and you're important to me… to us."

A smile spread over his gorgeous lips, and with it my heartbeat sped up. "I know." There were those two words again, and I loved how much meaning they held. "You and Mikey are to me as well. You do know that, right?"

"I do," I said without a doubt. He'd proven as such these past few months.

"Good." He mimicked my posture, holding his head up on a bent arm. "Speaking of a beach, Jude and Brae are thinking of buying a place in the Hamptons. They're renting it this summer and invited us to come out for July 4th weekend. But if it doesn't work out for you, I'm sure we can pick another time."

"Mikey is away that week. He'll be upstate with my in-laws," I said with a frown.

"You're worried about that?"

"I am," I admitted with a sigh. "I trust them, but that town is so small I worry Mikey will hear or see something by accident. I can't stop them from seeing their grandson, though."

Luca tucked my hair behind my ear. "I understand your concern. But you can't worry about something that may not happen."

"You're right, but I worry about everything... especially when it comes to Mikey."

His hand found my breast again, and his eyes focused on the way he ran his thumb over my erect nipple. "I'll do my best to distract you that week." He dipped his head to suck on my other nipple, causing an electric zing to travel right from my breast to my core. "Shall I demonstrate how?" He stopped long enough to ask. When I moaned and arched my body as a response, he added, "I'll take that as a yes."

Chapter 26

Luca

I T WAS A SPECTACULAR JUNE day, and the park bustled with activity. The noise of kids playing and parents cheering drowned out the sounds of nature around us. It still drove me nuts watching these so called coaches waste the talents of the soccer prospects running around like chickens without their heads.

Most of the time I stood with my arms folded in a defensive stance on the sidelines. My pacing caused Sabrina to shoot me a sideways look. Then there were the times I went to open my mouth and her hand would clamp over it before any offensive words came out.

"Next year, I want to coach that team," I said into her ear. Her expression was part amusement, part something else I couldn't read. "What?"

"Okay, Ronaldo. Let's take one season at a time."

"Whatever."

Sabrina's parents stood next to us. Her father nodded at me in agreement. However, her mom's expression mirrored Sabrina's. Maybe it was a guy thing, but knowing I wasn't alone in my opinion made me feel a bit better.

So, there I was *trying* to behave myself, and I didn't remember anything in my life ever taking as much effort. With minutes left to the game, suddenly Sabrina gripped my arm in a death hold and gasped. We watched together as Mikey sailed down the field, controlling the ball like a tiny professional while leaving the rest of his team and his opponents in the dust.

"Oh my God," Sabrina said quietly, contradicting my very loud, "Go, buddy!"

Just as Mikey reached the net, he faked left and kicked right, sending the ball over the goalie's right shoulder and into the center of the goal.

"Holy shit!" I screamed, earning a few glares in the process. Surprisingly, Sabrina ignored my outburst. Her arms flew up over her head as she and her parents cheered for her son. On the field, Mikey's teammates surrounded him. The sight of his grinning face practically brought tears to my eyes. He wasn't mine, but he may as well have been. Pride swelled at the sight of *my boy* taking the skills I had taught him and excelling at a sport we loved.

In a matter of seconds, Sabrina was in my arms and giggling as I spun her around. "He is going to be so excited over this," she stated the obvious. Of course he was, based on the way his electric smile lit up his adorable face. We spent the last short minute reciprocating with our own grins.

The moment the ref blew his whistle, Mikey came charging right for us. "I did it! I won us the game!" he yelled before jumping into my arms. I lifted him easily, using my other arm to bring his mother into our circle. Even though an official score wasn't kept, the kids knew the final score. Sabrina cupped his sweaty head and kissed him on the forehead. "Eww, Mom." I set him down to do the exact same thing. "Eww," he repeated after my smooch.

"That goal deserves a kiss from all of us," Sabrina's mother said, planting a kiss on one reddened cheek while her dad planted his own on the other.

"I agree all goals should be celebrated with a kiss," a female voice said as she approached. Sabrina laughed at her friend Becky, who began to bend toward Mikey's head all while her scarlet lips were puckered and ready to strike.

He thrusted his hand up, stopping her in her tracks. "No way, Aunt Becky!"

"Fine. High five then," she said, lifting her hand so Mikey could slap it with his. Her son did the same to Sabrina, and me, just as we heard a commotion from the other side of the field.

Mikey's coach began yelling for his team, who were currently scattered all over the field celebrating in their own ways. "Rebels and parents, please come over to the bench."

Sabrina took my hand and led me to where the team began sitting in a circle on the grass with their respective parents behind them. Being included left me speechless. The coach began speaking, complementing the team on great season. He then acknowledged the parents and thanked them for their support.

My girl squeezed my hand, awarding me with a smile. That simple gesture meant as much to me as being included in this celebration. One by one, the boys were called by name and given a small trophy. I wondered if there was an MVP statue for Mikey in that box, but knew better than to mention that to Sabrina.

The entire process was over in minutes, making me

laugh that snack break actually took longer than the trophy ceremony. While the team munched on their treats, Sabrina introduced me to a few of the other parents. The men shook my hand cordially, and the woman offered a variety of flirtatious greetings. I couldn't guarantee I'd remember one name out of the lot, because hearing Sabrina saying, "This is my boyfriend, Luca," kept playing over and over in my head.

Mikey ran toward us with Oreo residue all over his lips. "What are we doing now? Can we celebrate?"

"Of course. Wherever you want to go," I said as his mother attempted to wipe the crumbs with a tissue.

"Oh, can we go to Great Adventure?"

"Um… no," Sabrina interjected. "It's too far, and it's too late, and I don't think Grandma and Grandpa want to go to an amusement park."

"Luca said wherever I wanted to go," he pouted.

"I have an idea." Mother and son waited expectantly. "Let's get cleaned up first, and then I'll tell you," I said, which was code for—*after I run it by your mom.* Sabrina quirked a brow in question and with a tilt of her head summoned her mother to come over.

Catching the hint, Mrs. Ricci took her grandson's hand. "Mikey. Grandpa and I are going to head home." She then added, "Sabrina, we'll go clean our little champion up before we go."

"Thanks, Mom." Sabrina handed her mother Mikey's duffle bag and watched her parents walk off with him chattering about something animatedly.

"What exactly are you planning, Mr. Benedetto?"

I pulled her into my arms to sweeten the deal. "I'm thinking we make the kid happy, but instead of Great Adventure we head to Point Pleasant."

"New Jersey?"

"Yeah. It's such a nice day, and it's barely noon. He can hit the rides, we can have an early dinner, walk on the beach, maybe get some ice cream. What do you think?"

"I think you're too good to be true."

"Well, I agree. You can pay me later," I said, placing a chaste kiss on her lips.

We waited for her parents to bring back a cleaner Mikey. Once they appeared, Sabrina hugged them goodbye. "We'll see you on Wednesday, then?"

Sabrina nodded with a smile. "One, sharp."

The Ricci's said their goodbyes to me and Mikey, leaving the three of us to get on with the celebration.

"What's Wednesday?" I asked, hoping all was okay.

"It's my graduation! Can you come too, Luca?"

Sabrina placed a hand on Mikey's shoulder. "Sweetie, I explained that Luca works during the week. We'll celebrate with him afterwards."

"I'll take the time off," I blurted out.

"Really?" The wonderment on his face melted my heart.

"Yes, I promise."

Mikey raised a fist in triumph. "See Mom, he *can* come!"

My eyes cut to Sabrina's, worried I overstepped. Part of me felt slighted over not being asked. I understood she didn't want to put me in a position to have to say no, but if it meant a lot to him, then it meant even more for me to be there.

While Mikey skipped ahead, she touched my arm and with a small smile mouthed, "Thank you."

Sabrina

THE ELEMENTARY SCHOOL'S AUDITORIUM BEGAN to fill by noon. My parents walked in taking the two seats to my left, while my sweater rested on the seat to my right saving it for Luca. Mikey couldn't contain his excitement during breakfast this morning. After each spoonful of Rice Krispies, he would tell me another part of the ceremony his class practiced.

Every few minutes I'd tap my phone to check the time. It was almost about to begin, and Luca's chair was still vacant. I thought of texting him but didn't want to in case he was driving. Disappointment was obvious each time I saw the door open to see it wasn't him entering.

My mom caught my expression. "Maybe he's stuck in traffic." I forced down a swallow and nodded. All I could think of was something happened. There would be no way he'd break his promise to Mikey. He knew how much it meant to him.

Fifteen minutes later, the principal stepped to the microphone in the center of the stage announcing the ceremony would begin in five minutes. My phone vibrated and when I saw his name appear in a text message, my heart sank.

> **Luca:** Sabrina, I can't make it. Jude is away and an important client needs to meet today instead of tomorrow because he's returning to Europe tonight. There's no way for me to reschedule it. I need to take care of this. I'm so sorry. Please tell Mikey congratulations for me.

Was he kidding? My heart fell like a skydiver without her parachute. I gripped my phone, surprised it didn't crack in my hand. This was all my fault. I should have nipped it in the bud when he promised Mikey he'd be there. As his mother, I knew better making such a promise could lead to heartbreak, and that was exactly what was going to happen to my son.

When the lights dimmed I noticed my mom, whose sad eyes mirrored mine. "Is he okay?"

"He's not coming."

She placed her hand on my shoulder. "I'm sure it couldn't be helped, Sabrina."

"I understand that, but Mikey won't."

Shutters clicked on cameras as each student took their prideful place on the stage. Mikey spotted us sitting in the first row, but his wide smile faded when he scanned the chair next to mine. Rather than confirm his suspicion that Luca was a no show, I just gave him a wave followed by a thumbs up.

Throughout the various songs, short speeches, and the handing out of their completion certificates, my adorable innocent son, kept an eye on the door. The only smile he gave was when I took a picture of him accepting his kindergarten diploma while standing next to the principal and Cassie.

When I caught Cassie's eyes she gave me with a knowing expression. I wondered if he texted her too? When her smile faltered, I guessed he had.

After the pomp and circumstance, the children descended the steps to greet their families. Each one of them were happy, except for Mikey who looked as though he was about to cry. Steeling myself, I plastered the biggest smile I could muster on my face. There was no way in hell I was going to let Luca's absence ruin this moment for my son.

"Sweetie." I knelt down. "I am so proud of you." After a good hard squeeze, I released him to allow my parents to congratulate him next.

He gave them a timid smile before asking me, "Where's Luca?"

Dread filled me because my son was once again going to be crushed. "He couldn't come, but he wanted me to congratulate you."

"Why not? He promised."

"He had a work meeting come up. He's sorry."

Cassie approached us and put her arm around Mikey. "You had such a great year. I'm going to miss having you in my class."

Mikey nodded but didn't say a word. In all the happiness that surrounded us, my son appeared to be in a spotlight of sadness. My heart ached for him and the longer his smile was a frown, the more irritated with myself I became.

My parents pulled Mikey to the side to take a picture with each of them leaving me with Cassie. When she placed her hand on my forearm, I had to fight back the tears that were forming.

"Luca texted me. He feels horrible."

Knowing how close she was with Luca, I needed to choose my words wisely. "I know he does, but look at my son's face."

She nodded. "I knew the exact moment he realized Luca wasn't coming."

There weren't any words that I could add to her statement. Cassie continued to try to placate the situation, but there was nothing she could say that could change the outcome.

"We need to get going. We don't want to miss the cupcakes."

With a knowing nod, Cassie gave me a tight smile. "Have fun." She walked away to visit with some of her other students.

Taking Mikey's hand in mine, we walked to the gymnasium where refreshments were provided. Thankfully, Jared spotted him and the two went off to enjoy the treats.

Becky walked up to me licking vanilla frosting off her thumb. "I thought Luca was coming?"

"So did I." Even Becky flinched at my snark. "He had a meeting and couldn't leave work."

"That stinks. I bet he's sad he didn't see Mikey graduate. That man loves your son."

She was right. I knew he loved him and wanted to be there, but that didn't negate my son's fragile state of mind. "I'm sure he is."

"I don't doubt that he'll come by when he can. Then Mikey can show him his certificate and you can share the pictures you took. It won't be the same, but I'm sure he'd appreciate it."

"Beck, did you see Mikey's face? The kid was devastated. I need to worry about him before I worry about Luca seeing a picture."

"Yes, I understand. I just meant..."

"I know what you meant... and I appreciate it. But, my head isn't there right now."

Her ex-husband walked up to us and placed his hand on her lower back. "I need to get going. I'll pick him up after work." He kissed her on her cheek before heading out.

"That was interesting," I said to her. "He kisses you now?"

She shrugged. "Whatever. He's still an asshole."

That was the first time I genuinely smiled all day.

Mikey and I had a nice quiet dinner—the complete opposite of what I had pictured. Each attempt to keep his spirits up had failed. By the time we finished watching, *Monsters, Inc.*, a movie that would normally have my son laughing, Mikey yawned.

"Are you tired, honey?"

He nodded. "Has Luca called you?" I shook my head and led him to his room. Tears welled in his little brown eyes until they spilled down his face. "He lied." Throwing himself on his bed, I watched his chest heave with a hitch. "Just like daddy promised he wouldn't go away anymore, Luca broke his promise, too. I'm never going to lie to someone I love. I hate him… I hate them both."

I laid beside him and pulled him into my arms. "No, you don't, honey, you're just disappointed, there's a big difference. Plus, you shouldn't hate anyone." My son's tears dampened my cotton shirt. "Shh, it's okay. I'll always be there for you. That's a promise you can count on."

"I love you, Mommy."

"I love you, more. How about a bedtime story?"

"No. I don't want one tonight."

Sadness washed over me when he refused one of his favorite rituals. My hand rubbed his small back in an attempt to soothe him but nothing was working. Knowing my son the way I did, I knew it wasn't just Luca's absence. It was the memory of pure devastation coupled with confusion that resurfaced in his mind.

After I kissed his wet cheek goodnight, I cuddled up beside him holding onto him as he cried himself to sleep. I felt this had little to do with Luca, and all to do with old wounds reopening. And as I stared at my son's face, one that resembled his father's, I wondered if his little heart would ever mend.

Chapter 27

Luca

ON A DEEP BREATH, I pressed the white button next to her last name. Several long seconds passed, and her voice still hadn't come over the intercom, forcing me to press it once more. Finally, a groggy Sabrina asked, "Who is it?"

"It's me." It took longer than it should have for the latch on the door to release. Once it did, I didn't hesitate to walk in carrying the gift I bought for Mikey's graduation, and one that meant a lot to me.

Normally, she would have been waiting for me in the threshold, but not tonight. I rapped my knuckles on the metal door. Three locks sounded before she appeared. Her eyes didn't meet mine, nor did she smile.

"Hi." I pecked her lips as she let me pass. Glancing around the room, I noticed Mikey's school supplies and folders on her coffee table. When I heard the door click closed, I turned to face her. "Did I wake you?"

"No, I was just lying down."

Her pretty face was clean of makeup, making the redness around her eyes even more predominant. "Are you okay?"

"Not really," she responded without hesitation. Sabrina wrapped her arms around her body, accentuating how the oversized T-shirt and sweatpants she wore hung on her frame.

"I'm so sorry I missed it. I really am, Sabrina." The only response I received was a halfhearted nod. "Can I talk to Mikey? I'd like to explain."

The woman I'd come to love was expressionless. With every beat of silence that went by, I knew deep down I had my work cut out for me.

"He's sleeping," she said with a resigned tone. "He's had a long day… and night. We both have."

Setting his gifts on the small table on top of some of his schoolwork, I took a few steps closer and wrapped her in my arms. Limp arms hung at her sides, yet I refused to let go. "I'm so sorry. You have no idea how badly I wanted to be there today. But this client…"

"Don't," she whispered, stepping out of my hold. Determination replaced the defeat I saw in her when I walked in. "It's done. I understand the obligations that go hand in hand with your job, but Mikey doesn't. This morning, he couldn't contain his excitement. It was as if he was hopped up on sugar." I smiled knowing exactly what that meant.

"After meeting you, I started to feel desired. It was something so foreign, yet wonderful. I went from being a military wife, to a mother, to a widow, and somewhere along the line I lost myself. I had all of titles, which I was proud of, but something was missing. Over the past few months, I've come to realize that something was you."

Taking her trembling hands in mine, I asked, "You're worthy of those feelings and so much more. Knowing I am responsible for that makes me happy. I'm failing to see how that's a bad thing?"

"Because dating wasn't on my radar, it wasn't even a blip on the screen. This all happened too fast and maybe it shouldn't have."

"Are you saying you regret our relationship?"

"I regret bringing a man into his life too soon after he lost his father."

There was no way I could hide my disbelief. I felt like she was a different person than the woman I came to know, to love. I had always felt she compared me to a ghost without intending to, but hearing her now only solidified my suspicions.

"You keep comparing me to Dillon. I can't compete with a ghost. I know even if he didn't die, you wouldn't be together because of the other woman. From what I know of your late husband, I'm nothing like him. I'd never hurt you the way he did or take our relationship for granted. I thank God every day for bringing you and Mikey into my life. Do you really think that little of me?"

"I don't think little of you, Luca. You are a wonderful man. I also thank God for bringing you into our lives, and I couldn't have asked for a more genuine, kind, caring person to have spent the past few months with."

"So then why push me away? Is this really about Mikey, Sabrina?"

"It's all about Mikey. I was swept away with my own happiness that I didn't stop to think what would happen if my son grew attached so quickly. Here's the thing, if we started dating conventionally, and not because of a soccer ball my son kicked at your head, I wouldn't have even introduced you two yet.

"Do you know how he fell asleep tonight?" I

remained silent to allow her to admit what was on her mind. "He cried to the point where his body trembled, something he hadn't done in months. In his young impressionable mind, he can't distinguish the difference between why his dad left and why you were absent.

"Do you know during the entire ceremony today, he kept looking at the door waiting for you to walk through it? That damn empty chair next to me was his sole focus. It was a constant reminder that you weren't coming. That his mother let him down."

"You didn't. I did."

"No, *I* did. The day I started a relationship with you knowing full well that we weren't just a couple, we were a threesome. I set him up for disappointment." I stared dumbfounded into her misty eyes.

"Sabrina… if I could just talk to him and explain."

"I think that would make it worse." She let out a long breath. "I'm not blaming you, Luca. This is all my fault. I brought a man into my son's life when he was still grieving the loss of his father. I should have known better than to allow you to promise him anything. You can't do that to a child. You're not a parent, so I don't expect you to understand."

I could feel my ribcage begin to close around my heart. No, I wasn't his parent, but I loved him as if he were my own. All I wanted was to protect that boy, love him, be the male influence he needed.

Before I could argue, she captured her resolve, straightened her spine, and said, "This can't go on."

"What can't?"

She pulled her hands from mine. "You're a wonderful man, Luca. If Mikey was older or my situation were different, we wouldn't be having this conversation right now. The fact is, we were dealt a shitty hand, and because of it I need to make sure my son is always my first priority." She shook her head from side to side. "I should have listened to my gut."

"What was your gut telling you?"

"It was too soon." She wiped the tears that fell with her fingertips.

I took a step toward her. The need to comfort her overwhelmed me. But when she took a step back, I knew everything between us had changed.

"I think you should go."

"Sabrina, please don't do this. Let's sit, talk this out. What happened today couldn't be helped. I can come back in the morning when he's awake and explain everything to him. He might not understand at first, but at least let me try. I love that little boy more than you'll ever know, and the last thing I'd want to do is hurt him, or you."

She took a few steps away and picked up a crinkled crayoned drawing. "See this?" I stared at the artwork of a man, woman and boy, with green scribbles beneath their sneakered feet and a soccer ball between them. At the top it said, *My Family.* "He was so excited to give this to you today. When we got home, I couldn't find it in his book bag. You know why?" I shook my head. "Because he threw it away. So, now you see why coming back tomorrow isn't a good idea. Witnessing the hurt my son felt today, reversing all the progress he made after his father's death, broke my heart."

"What are you saying, Sabrina? I need to hear the words. Don't force me to guess." I silently prayed to God that my instincts were wrong... that this wasn't the end of us.

"I'm sorry, but I don't think we should continue to see each other." Her voice quivered as she confirmed my suspicion. "I need to end it."

The skin on my face prickled. "I don't believe you. This can't end, Sabrina. We're just getting started. There's so much ahead of us... so much I want to share with you. I'm begging you to please reconsider. You deserve to be happy, and by being with me I thought you were."

"My happiness isn't what's important—Mikey's is." When my jaw went slack she added, "I know he's happy when he's with you. But, he's just too young to understand when life gets in the way and stops someone from being there. It took a lot for him to move on after his father's death, but in one day I saw the child that he was a year ago resurface... withdrawn, sulking, crying, angry, blaming himself. It's not right, Luca. He's five years old. He should be unaware of life's cruelties; but he isn't unaware, and that's his sad reality."

"I get it. I understand where you're coming from, but we fit. The three of us fit perfectly, and to ignore that would be a shame. In a year, he may not remember this. We can help him move on, create new happy memories to replace the bad ones." I took her hand and led her to the couch, forcing her to sit beside me. "Are you scared to move on? Is this what this is about?"

"Of course I'm scared," she responded defensively. A heavy sigh filled the pause before she added, "You asked me not to compare you to a ghost, and that was a fair request. But, Mikey is doing just that. He compared you to Dillon, and said just like his dad promised that he wouldn't go away anymore, you broke your promise as well." She lifted her eyes, crushing me with the sadness in them. "Luca, he said he hated you *both*." Tears spilled, the sight of them adding to my torment, and combined with her words they sliced me open.

"And I hate myself for disappointing him." Bottom line, I hurt her son. Like a mama bear protecting her cub, I could see Sabrina wouldn't back down. Remembering my own mother and the ends of the earth she'd go to just to protect her kids, how could I not understand Sabrina was doing the same?

"I feel like we're getting nowhere. You said you understood. Please stop fighting me on this, Luca, and respect my wishes."

Whatever was left of our connection snapped with her last comment. It was evident her mind was set and nothing I could do or say would change it. I could feel the pressure building within me... and there wasn't a damn thing I could do about it.

Sabrina

IT DESTROYED ME TO SEE him so broken, but a flash of Mikey's face as I held him in my arms earlier overruled Luca's pain... and mine.

"Can I say goodbye to him? I know he's sleeping, but please allow me that."

After a short pause I agreed. "Okay, but please don't wake him."

I watched Luca disappear into Mikey's room. Not being able to stop myself, I inched my way closer to the open door. Luca was squatting next to Mikey's bed with his elbows resting on his knees.

"Hey, buddy." His soft voice echoed in the quiet room. When it hitched, he brought his hand up to his cheek in a swiping motion. "I'm really sorry you were sad today. I'm so proud that I got to know you." He paused and his back heaved. My first inclination was to comfort him, but I remained still.

"Do you know how happy you've made me? How much I loved watching you play soccer and being able to help you?" He quietly cleared his throat. "I know gifts aren't important, but I brought you a couple. One is very special to me and there isn't anyone else I'd rather give it to. I hope you like it and that it reminds you of our time together."

Luca sniffed causing more tears to stream down my face. "This is really hard. I have so much I want to tell you, but it can't all be done in a few minutes. If there's one thing I need you to know, it's that I'll always be here for you, Mikey. It doesn't matter how much time passes, you'll be on my mind as you grow into a teenager, and then an adult. More importantly, you'll be in my heart."

With a gentle touch, he swiped Mikey's bangs to the side, leaned toward him and kissed his forehead. "I love you, Mikey. You've become one of the most important people in my life. Because of you, I met your beautiful mom and I'll forever be grateful. She's very special to me, as are you, and I hope when you think of me you'll smile. Take care of your mom, she loves you very much."

When Luca stood, he remained standing over Mikey, watching him sleeping peacefully for a few long moments. Not wanting him to see me, I turned and walked back into my living room.

Pained bloodshot eyes looked at me as Luca took a few lethargic steps into the room. I'd never seen such devastation on his face before. I couldn't stop more tears from falling. When he reached toward me, I allowed him to wipe my cheeks with the pads of his thumbs.

"I'm so very sorry, but I understand." He brought his lips to mine and I allowed him to give me one last kiss.

"I'll be sure he gets your presents."

His eyes followed mine to the wrapped boxes sitting next to the crinkled artwork. "Can I have that, please?"

Wordlessly, I lifted the drawing and handed it to him. Luca stared at it before I noticed a spot on the paper dampen with a tear. "I'm sorry, Luca. I know you love my son and how hard this is for you. It's not my intention to hurt you by keeping you from him."

"That's not all of it." He walked up to me and cupped my face with a gentle touch. "This isn't just about Mikey... don't you understand?"

"I know it's not. We had a great time, and I'll miss that."

"It was more than just a great time. I fell in love with you. I love you, Sabrina." Before I could process what he said, he walked toward the door.

"Daddy!" Mikey's loud squeal caused both of our heads to snap toward his room. Luca lunged forward.

His hard chest hit the palm of my hand. "You need to leave."

"Sabrina..."

"Mommy!"

"Go, Luca." Panic caused him to stop in his tracks. I had to ignore the tears that sprung in his eyes, the fear and worry clearly etched in the lines of his face. My son needed me, and nothing else mattered at that moment.

As I walked into my son's room, the sound of my door clicking closed echoed in my apartment like an atomic bomb had just detonated.

Forty-five minutes passed before Mikey settled back

down. Exhaustion settled in every bone of my body. Robotically, I walked to my front door to lock it. Noticing Mikey's drawing missing, I lost my fight to stay strong and allowed my body to slump next to the gifts that remained on the table.

Grief overcame me…more than it ever had before. This was an entirely different loss. Breathing became more and more difficult as the sobs took over from remembering the devastated look on Luca's face.

Physically, he may have been gone, but lingering was the scent of his manly cologne. It permeated the air around me, reminding me of our intimate moments. Also lingering were the emotions he left behind, leaching their way into the confines of my heart, my lungs, and the blood in my veins. Despite all the crushing pain I felt in the center of my chest, a numbness spread throughout me from head to toe.

In the few months we spent together, Luca left his indelible mark on me, a permanent tattoo. Unlike a tattoo that could be removed one day, this one was ineradicably etched on my soul. And I was left to figure out how to move on now that I'd been branded by him.

Chapter 28

Sabrina

SLEEP EVADED ME MOST OF the night. Every time I heard a sound, my eyes would fly open praying Mikey hadn't woken up. The way he called for his father, and then for me, would plague me... not to mention the sadness on Luca's face before he left.

Since the sun was up, I decided to be as well. Before hopping in the shower, I peered in Mikey's bedroom. He had kicked off his covers, but he slept peacefully—thank God.

Twenty minutes later, I sat at my kitchen table drinking my coffee wondering what this day would bring. I had never been so thankful that I decided to take the rest of the week off. The shuffle of little feet on my carpet grabbed my attention.

"Hi, Mommy." His hands balled into fists as he rubbed the sleep out of his eyes.

"Good morning, sweetie." I stood and gave him a hug. "Are you hungry? How about I make you your favorite chocolate chip pancakes this morning?"

"Okay." Sadness still coated his voice. "Do we have

Nutella?"

The fact he asked for his new favorite, rather than his usual whipped cream, caused pressure to build behind my eyes. This was going to be a rough day. "We sure do," I said with the perkiest voice I could muster. How sad the sight of that chocolate spread Luca had bought him could awaken every emotion all over again. I poured him a glass of milk and began to make his breakfast.

Mikey sat quietly watching his favorite cartoons waiting for his pancakes. Once they were done, he took a seat at the table next to me. "What are we going to do today?"

"Well, since I have the day off, I thought maybe we could go to a movie. Would you like that?"

He shrugged. "There really isn't anything good out."

"Hmm…" I replied tapping my finger on my chin. "How about the zoo? You love the animals."

"That might be fun. After that, can we go to the park and feed the ducks?"

At this point, if it made him happy, I'd let him feed just about anything if it was safe. "We sure can. Would you like to invite Jared to go?"

"Is it okay if it's just you and me?" He speared a piece of his Nutella-covered pancake with his fork and slid it into his mouth.

"Of course. There's nothing I'd like more than hanging out with my favorite guy." I sipped my coffee. "Finish your breakfast and after you're dressed we can go."

The Bronx Zoo bustled with kids who were on field

trips to adults just wandering around watching the animals. For such a crazy place, it was a calming experience. Mikey hadn't brought up Luca's name, and since I put the gifts in the hall closet, he wasn't reminded of him not being there yesterday.

We spent a few hours walking from exhibit to exhibit, eating popcorn, and of course, watching the elephants get their bath. He laughed when one swung their trunk knocking over the large bucket of water. Hearing and seeing his joy was the best part of my day.

Later when we got to the park, we sat on a bench waiting for the ducks to come closer. Mikey walked to the edge of the small pond and left a trail of bread to lead the ducks to where we were.

His little feet swung back and forth waiting for his plan to work. Off to the side sat an empty soccer field. "Can I play soccer again next year?"

"Of course, sweetie. You know at camp, they play soccer." Last summer after we moved to Manhattan, he went to a day camp while I worked. It was a great distraction for him. He loved the counselors and there was never a day I had to worry about him being safe or happy.

"That's right. Wow. This year I'm going to be even better thanks to…" His brown hair fell forward as he dropped his head.

And there it was. I had been waiting all day for him to think about Luca. Thank God, the sound of ducks diverted his attention. "Look," I whispered, pointing to a mama duck and her ducklings waddling closer to us.

"Cool!" He stuck his hand in the Ziploc bag, grabbed a small piece of bread, and held his hand out flat waiting for one of them to come and get their snack. A huge smile grew raising his sweet cheeks until the corners of his eyes crinkled. "It feels so weird. Like it should hurt, but it doesn't. Do ducks have teeth?"

And just like that, my little boy was back. Without a care in the world, just as it should be, we sat there most of the afternoon; laughing, trying to guess which duck was a boy or a girl, and searching for teeth.

It had been one week since Mikey's graduation and thankfully he hadn't had any more nightmares. Even his spirits were better, which was more than I could have said for myself. Becky and I sat on my living room couch while Mikey played with Jared in his room.

Becky had been the first one I confided in after my breakup with Luca. Although she understood my attitude toward the situation, her sadness was evident.

She swirled her straw in her glass of iced tea sending the ice cubes and lemon wedge around in a circle. "Have you spoken to Luca?"

I made sure the boys were out of earshot. "No. He sent a text last Friday asking me if Mikey was sleeping better, but that was all."

"He has been, right? Have you spoken to the camp counselors? How did he do this week?"

"Yes, they said he had a great week, and Mikey told me the same. He loves it there, so I guess he's doing much better." Laughter flowed from his room to where we were sitting, bringing a smile to both our faces.

"And you?" She sipped her drink. "How are you doing?"

"Good." I made patterns in the condensation on my

glass. When I looked at her she wordlessly nodded. "What?"

"I call bullshit. You aren't good. You're anything but good. One of the nicest, sweetest, and let's not forget most gorgeous men I've ever met, fell in love with you and that little boy in there." When I opened my mouth she shushed me. "No, I've been listening to your reasoning for the past week. Actually, since the day you met him. First came the excuses, and then once you finally let him in, and allowed yourself to enjoy life, you had a setback." She put her hand up, palm facing me. "I'm not saying you weren't justified, but your son is fine. I hate that he's had to learn hard lessons at such a young age, but what's the lesson now?" She paused. "Has he asked for Luca?"

Once I swallowed the knot in my throat I nodded. "Yes, a few times."

"Wait, a few… of course, not counting the four times he's mentioned him since we've been here?" She crossed her arms in front of her chest and glared at me. "Sabrina, he's fine." Her lips twisted from the sarcasm. "But you're not. You're a mess." I peered down at my black capris and white T-shirt. "Not what you're wearing, but you're just not *you*.

"Don't be ridiculous." I stood and walked into the kitchen to set my half-full glass on the counter."

"Have you given Mikey his presents yet?"

"What presents?" His little voice shocked both of us. Every day I opened that closet and thought about the gifts that sat on the top shelf. One day, I even went as far as taking them down, only to put them back. I didn't know how Mikey would react and what effect they would have on him and on me.

Becky mouthed an, "I'm sorry," before telling Jared it was time to go. Mikey watched them walk out the door, and then his eyes scanned the room. "Where are my presents?"

Taking slow tentative steps toward the closet, I opened the door and pulled out the gifts. His eyes lit up like stars when he saw two professionally wrapped boxes. "Wow!" He took them from my hands and sat down on the couch. "Can I open them?"

I sat next to him. "Yes." Before he ripped the paper as though it were Christmas, I told him to read the card first.

He held it out. "Can you read it to me?"

My tongue dampened my lips as I pulled the card from the envelope. The front had an illustration of a young boy thrusting his hand in the air with the words, "Way to go!" at the top. When I opened the card I saw Luca's handwriting.

MIKEY,

CONGRATS, BUDDY! I AM SO PROUD OF YOU. YOU'RE GOING TO MAKE A GREAT FIRST GRADER! I CAN'T WAIT TO WATCH YOU WALK ACROSS THE STAGE TODAY. THANK YOU FOR INVITING ME.

LOVE,

LUCA

After I read it out loud, I realized I should have read

it to myself first. Mikey, smiled. "He *did* want to be there."

I stroked his head with my hand. "Of course he did, sweetheart."

"It wasn't his fault, Mommy. Do you think he feels bad that he missed it? Did you send him pictures?"

Before I could even conjure up a reply, he started opening the smaller of the two boxes. He gasped. "Wow, it's just like Luca's car!" Mikey studied each side of the box containing a model car of a Jaguar F-Type. He was right, it was an exact replica.

As quickly as he unwrapped the first gift, he moved on to the second. Tossing the cover aside, he tore through the tissue paper and pulled out a red jersey. When he held it up, tears welled in my eyes. The number ten was stitched on in white, with the name Benedetto across the shoulders. Mikey spun it around. "There's grass stains on it."

Lying in the box was another small note.

MIKEY,

THIS WAS MY HIGH SCHOOL TEAM'S JERSEY. IT BROUGHT ME A LOT OF LUCK AND I WANTED YOU TO HAVE IT.

LOVE,

LUCA

Without hesitation, his head popped through the neckline. Stretching his arms to the side like a T he modeled the shirt. "How cool is this? Take a picture!" A small Italian emblem rested on the right side and what I assumed was Luca's school's name laid across Mikey's belly.

I did what my son asked and snapped a few photos with my cellphone. "Okay, got it. That was very nice of him."

"He's the best. Can we call him?"

The smile on my son's face negated all of my reasons not to. After a brief hesitation and more prodding from my son, I reluctantly pressed a couple buttons and wished for his voicemail. Two rings later, my wish wasn't granted.

"Hi." His voice hit me square in the chest.

"Hi, Luca. I'm calling for Mikey. Hold on."

Mikey pushed one of the sleeves to his shoulder only for it to fall down to his wrist before taking the phone from me. "Hi, Luca." His little chipper voice made a liar out of me. "Thank you so much for my presents. I love them."

He remained silent listening to whatever Luca was saying. After a nod here and a nod there, he finally spoke again. "When can you come over and help me build the car?"

I reached to the phone and hit the speaker button just as Luca replied, "I don't know when I can, buddy. I need to go out of town for a while." Mikey's smile faltered.

"That's okay, we can do it when you get home."

"Can I talk to your mom, please?" Luca's deep voice sounded pained.

Mikey handed me the phone, and I placed it back in handset mode. "Hi... hold on a minute." I pulled the phone away from my mouth. "Michael, do not open that box yet! There are small pieces, and you could lose them."

"Okay!" sounded from his room. "Don't forget to send Luca the picture."

I raised the phone back to my ear. "Sorry, about that. He's excited."

"I'm glad he liked it. He sounds good. What picture?"

"Hold on." I pushed a few buttons. "I just sent it."

When my text sounded, he laughed. "It looks good on him."

"That was a very generous gift. He's going to cherish it and most likely sleep in it until I allow him to wear it in public." The only sound I heard was Luca's breathing. "How are you?"

"Busy… you know, the usual. I'm actually at the office now trying to get last minute details ironed out before my trip."

"So, you're going out of town?"

After a few beats of silence, he asked, "What is this, Sabrina?"

"What do you mean? Mikey wanted to talk to you."

"What do I mean? I've spent the last ten days trying to figure out how to move on. Making small talk isn't helping. Don't get me wrong, it's wonderful to hear your voice and Mikey's, but you're killing me. I'm glad Mikey liked his gifts, and that both of you sound happy. That's all I ever wanted. So, if that's it, then I need to get back to work."

"I'm sorry. I'll let you go." Tears fell freely from my eyes. I didn't even bother to swipe them away—what would be the point, they would just continue to fall.

"Bye, Sabrina. Take care of yourself."

"Luca…" My words lodged in my throat. "Have a safe

trip."

"Thank you."

When his name disappeared from my screen, I dropped my phone to the floor, my head to my hands, and cried for what we once had.

Chapter 29

Luca

FOR NINE MINUTES I STARED at my phone after I hung up. The next eight were spent smiling at the picture of Mikey wearing my jersey. Add another sixteen of me ignoring the pile of paperwork on my desk while memories of a certain blonde and her son took over my brain. It was fair to say I wouldn't be getting any more work done.

I had a ton to do at the office, and even more at home. But based on my sluggishness over the past ten days, every simple task took a fuck-ton longer than it should have. With a sigh, I packed up what I needed for the trip to L.A. and headed out of the quiet office. Maybe I'd have better luck at home, although I doubted it.

I couldn't even blame my lack of focus on the fact I spoke to them for the first time in ten days. Because to be honest, even during the silence, concentration was non-existent. Except for one text asking Sabrina how Mikey was sleeping, there was no communication between us. That didn't mean the need to see her hadn't consumed me. A few times during this past week I'd walk by the salon in hopes to catch a glimpse. Through the window, a smiling Sabrina was enough to appease my curiosity. She seemed happy and appeared to be just fine.

Wasn't that what I wanted?

But in one fell swoop, by just speaking to Mikey, hearing the obvious normalcy through the phone, made me equal parts sad and angry. I missed that kid so much, and his mother even more. After she pushed me away, I sympathized with her motives. That five minute phone call I received out of the blue effectively reversed any understanding I held for the situation.

During the trek from the office to my apartment, I flip-flopped at least a dozen times between not wanting to leave New York and feeling it might be just what I needed at the moment. Some distance could do me good, because for the life of me I no longer understood why we were apart. For the first time in ten days, my anger took over my sadness.

One thing I was certain of, she wasn't ready to move on. I didn't know if it was his betrayal that seeped into her conscience and caused a lack of trust, or if she wasn't feeling the same toward me as I felt for her. Either way, to force something that wasn't meant to be would only result in more heartbreak... for me, for her, and for Mikey.

Just as I stepped through my door, my phone chimed with an incoming text.

> **Cassie:** Are you alive?
>
> **Cassie:** I'm about to call John Walsh.
>
> **Me:** No need. I'm breathing, does that count?
>
> **Cassie:** Where are you?
>
> **Me:** I just got home.

Cassie: Coming with food. Chill the wine.

Me: I'm busy.

Cassie: Doing?

Me: Washing my hair.

Cassie: Cut the shit, Luca. I know.

Me: Know what?

Cassie: The reason you've avoided people since graduation. Do you think I believed your lame excuses? I gave you space, but your time is up. Be there in twenty.

My gut wanted to tell her I needed more space, especially after today. But a pang of regret hit over the distance I put between one of my best friends and me. I really hadn't socialized with any of my friends. With Jude and Brae still in Hawaii, Kyle and Vanessa busy with work, and Cassie taking a child psychology course at NYU, it had been easy to lie low. Like Cassie said, my time was up.

True to her word, my doorman announced her arrival twenty minutes later. I propped a shoulder on the doorframe of my apartment door waiting for her to appear. The elevator doors opened, and upon seeing me she shook her head. "Going for the Paul Bunyan look?"

I ran a hand over my overgrown scruff. It had started because I couldn't be bothered to shave every day, but now I liked the way it felt like a mask. "You don't like it?" I asked, moving aside to let her pass.

"If you sported a clown wig and a red nose, you'd still be a hottie, my friend."

"Gee, thanks."

She raised the brown bag in her hand. "I was in the mood for Greek." Before I could say, that was fine with me, she pointed to the beach ball Mikey made in her class, that was on display in my living room. "He was very proud of how it turned out."

I smiled. "He should be." As I pulled out dishes, silverware, and glasses, Cassie sat quietly. I glanced over my shoulder with a smirk. "Cat got your tongue, Brooks?"

"Nope. Just waiting for your undivided attention, Benedetto."

After grabbing a bottle of wine from my fridge and serving us each a glassful, I sat with a huff and raised my hands. "So? What's new?"

"Funny. What the hell happened?" From the bag she pulled out a greek salad for herself and a gyro for me.

"Have you spoken to her?" I asked, curious if Sabrina had reached out to Cassie.

"No." The fact she hadn't hurt a lot. A sick part of me stupidly thought if Sabrina had been as distraught as I was she'd want to talk to Cassie about it. Apparently, not.

Cassie took a sip of the wine before going on. "That day, she was upset. When I tried to talk to her about it she kind of dismissed me. I was concerned, and with you being swamped at work I didn't want to add to your stress. But then Becky called me just before I texted you."

"What did she say?"

"That she was at Sabrina's earlier and was concerned that she seemed miserable."

I knew the feeling. Staring at my still-closed styrofoam container, I asked, "And Mikey?"

She waited for me to lift my eyes to hers. "That was why Becky reached out. She gave me the rundown on what Sabrina said happened after the ceremony. Yes, that day Mikey was not himself. But since then, he seems absolutely fine."

"I surmised that after I spoke to him." Cassie uncrimped the silver edge on the tin holding her salad and waited for me to elaborate. "Sabrina called me today. Mikey wanted to thank me for the graduation presents I left with her. Cass, he sounded normal, with no evidence of the way Sabrina said he acted when I didn't show. I felt awful that day, for disappointing him and her. I listened to her make excuse after excuse on why she felt us starting a relationship was a stupid idea."

"You don't believe her?" she asked, before stabbing some leafy greens with her fork.

I shook my head as she ate the forkful of salad. "I do. Before I left her apartment that night, Mikey had a nightmare." Remembering his scream haunted me. "It was at that point, I thought I understood where she was coming from. But now, just like then, I think there's more to it all, and…"

I stopped myself from revealing too much. Sabrina's story wasn't mine to tell. Amending what I was about to say, I flipped open the lid to my dinner and added, "I don't doubt that to a five-year-old, missing something as important as a graduation seemed like the end of the world. I know enough about kids to know they happen to be resilient, with the ability to forget and move on much quicker than adults can."

"So, you think this is Sabrina pushing you away for her own reasons?"

"Maybe," I lied. Without a doubt she pushed me away. Because that prick cheated on her, I wholeheartedly believed that she clung to the first legitimate excuse to add distance to protect her heart.

"Maybe you should talk face to face?"

"I've said all I needed to. She knows how I feel." Cassie's raised brows meant she didn't agree. "Don't look at me like that. I told her I loved her, Cass. I've never said that to a woman I wasn't related to." I scrubbed my jaw with my hand. "I think she needs time, we both do. Talking face to face or over a phone, isn't going to change what happened."

"I'm sorry, Luca. I didn't know you loved her," she said with a soothing tone and warm eyes. "That's not entirely true. I had a suspicion, but wasn't sure you had admitted it to yourself let alone her."

"Well, my declaration didn't change the outcome of what happened."

Cassie put her fork down and paused while staring at my face. "Can I ask you one more question about Sabrina, and then I'll drop it?" On my nod, she said, "What would you do if she changed her mind?"

Without any hesitation, I responded, "I'd take her back in a heartbeat. But based on our last conversation, I don't see that happening. If it weren't for Mikey, she never would have called me."

Staying true to her word, she took another bite of her meal and chewed. "When are you flying to L.A.?"

"Monday. I'll be there all week, but I may stick around a bit longer, since my brother has a photo shoot that week."

"You *and* your brother in L.A.? Should I be prepared to send bail money?"

"The only reason you'd have to bail me out was if I killed him." Cassie knew how different Dante and I were, and spending an extended amount of time together could be a huge mistake. But, having said that, I also knew

Dante would provide the perfect distraction.

I finally took the first bite of my dinner and turned the tables. "Tell me about this Carson dude."

"Thomas," she corrected. "Carson is his last name."

"And?"

That was all it took for my friend to bring me up to speed on the guy she had gone on a few dates with. It felt good to think of something else other than Sabrina. Based on the way Cassie smiled throughout, I was glad she seemed happy... one of us should be.

Sabrina

EVERY CLIP, SNIP, AND CURL felt robotic. Client after client, I would don a happy face and listen to their latest trials and tribulations as most hairstylists did. The salon primped many June brides and I was thankful to see this month nearing its end.

After I adjusted the veil on my client, and wished her well, I decided to take a break. I grabbed my phone from my back pocket and checked my text messages. My parents took Mikey to a museum, so I knew I wouldn't have heard from them, but there was a missed call from Cassie.

Sliding the green icon to the right, I called her back.

"Hi, Sabrina."

As always, her chipper voice made me smile. "Hi, Cassie. I'm sorry I haven't called you back."

"That's okay. How are you and your little first grader?" She sighed. "I'm going to miss having him in class."

"We're good, thank you. How are you? Is everything okay?"

"That's what I wanted to talk to you about. I know it's short notice, but I'm at the café around the corner from the salon. Can you meet me for lunch or do you have a busy schedule?"

Worry started to settle in and I felt like a horrible friend. "I have time for lunch. I'll head over now."

"Perfect. See you soon."

Becky's laughter filled the salon as she straightened a woman's hair. "Hey Beck, I'm going to head to lunch to meet Cassie. I'll be back before my two o'clock."

Her lips twitched before turning into a grin. "Sounds good. Have fun."

Surprised to see Cassie beat me there, she looked up and smiled when she saw me approach the table. I slung my purse on the back of the chair and sat down. "Hi, thank you for calling today."

"I've been wanting to talk to you ever since the last day of school. I can't believe almost three weeks have passed. Time flies."

Flies? This has been the longest twenty days of my life. Mustering a smile to match hers, I agreed. "It sure does."

The waitress came by and after a quick skim of the menus, we placed our orders.

Cassie straightened her posture. "There's something I wanted to talk to you about. I know you're pressed for time, so I'm just going to cut to the chase."

"Is everything okay?"

"No, actually it isn't. My best friend's heart is broken." I opened my mouth but she held up an index finger just as I imagined she did in class. "I know it's none of my business, but I'm making it mine. I saw Luca last Saturday." The nerve endings in my face prickled. "Before you get angrier at him, he didn't tell me everything that happened, only that he felt horrible for disappointing you and Mikey… oh, and that he told you he loved you. What happened, Sabrina? The two of you are perfect for each other."

"Life happened. You know how difficult this past year had been for Mikey. Seeing him revert back to the scared, sad, little boy broke my heart. To be honest, it also scared me. Luca meant the world to him."

"What about you? What does he mean to you? And yes, I used present tense because I believe you still care for him."

The waitress set down our meals and walked away. "I do care for him and about him. None of this is fair, Cassie. Do you think I wanted to end things with him? Do you think I wanted my son to wonder why his *best friend* doesn't come around anymore? Because that's how he thinks of Luca." I pushed my salad aside. "Do you think I wanted to break anyone's heart? Don't you think I miss him too? I do. Every day I hope that he's okay, that he doesn't forget us, that he'll find happiness." She stared at me. "But this isn't just about me, and you know that."

Her hand was suddenly on mine. "I do know that. I also know you've had to deal with more than your share of heartbreak, and I'm so sorry about that. I also know you want to protect Mikey, but do you really think keeping Luca out of his life is accomplishing that? You just said Mikey misses him. Luca's here. He's alive and he loves you *and* your son. Do you really want to throw all of that away? You said you want him to find happiness, but do you really? Would you be okay seeing him with someone else?" Tears welled in my eyes. "I didn't think so."

We sat silently for a few minutes. Deep down in my soul, I knew I loved Luca. Remembering all of the words he said to Mikey before he left swam in my head.

"I don't know what to do."

She sat back in her chair. "Jude and Brae are having a party in the Hamptons to celebrate the Fourth of July. She wanted me to extend an invitation to you since she figured, Luca might have forgotten." When my eyebrows rose she added, "Yes, this was before the breakup but who cares. It's still valid."

I remember him telling me about the Hamptons a few weeks ago. "Thank you, but I can't go."

Cassie exhaled, picked up her phone and started tapping something in. My heart stopped thinking she was texting Luca but then my phone chimed. When I read it, she sent me a text with an address.

"The ball is in your court now. I think you're making a big mistake letting go of something and someone so wonderful."

The rest of our meal was awkward and tense, and like a coward I was relieved when the waitress came by with our tab. Before I could get it, Cassie snatched it off the table. "It's on me." We both stood and she hugged me. "Think about what I said, okay?"

I nodded. I had a feeling that would be all I *could* think about.

Chapter 30

Sabrina

UPSTATE NEW YORK WAS BEAUTIFUL this time of year. The serene feel of the suburbs had a calming effect on me. Mikey loved his grandparents' yard and I knew he missed being able to run around on grass anytime he wanted to. But, for the next week, that was just what he would be able to do.

"Don't forget to call me." I pulled him into a tight squeeze. "I'm going to miss my baby."

"Mommy, I'm not a baby anymore." He squirmed out of my hold. "I'm going to be six years old in two weeks."

I huffed at my brave little trooper. "You'll always be my baby... even when you're fifty. Now, give me a kiss goodbye and promise you'll be good this week."

His little lips met my cheek with a smack. "I will be. I'll send you pictures of the fireworks tomorrow."

After one last hug and a quick impersonal wave to my in-laws, I started my way back to the city.

Driving down one of the two-lane roads, I decided to visit a place I hadn't been to since the funeral. Once I parked my car, I took a deep breath and knew I had to take care of unfinished business.

The granite stones, with names and years etched on them, greeted me as I made my way to the one with my last name on it. Dillon's grave was easy to locate because it was marked with an American flag. Flowers that couldn't have been more than a day or so old sat on the marble base. Tucked in between the colorful petals was a small paper heart with two names written in a feminine script. Bile rose in my throat, until I tamped it down with determination. Seeing she visited him recently, and probably did so often, served me well and reminded me of the purpose for my visit.

Blades of grass prickled my knees as I knelt down. The summer breeze lifted the skirt of my sundress as I stared at the gray letters and traced the carving with my fingers.

"Hi, Dillon. I bet you're surprised to see me here— I'm surprised myself. Our son graduated Kindergarten a few weeks ago. He still misses you." I cleared my throat. "He's doing well though. We moved to Manhattan and he loves it there. He has a lot of friends and even joined a soccer team. You should have seen him in his last game, he scored the winning goal.

"I've been thinking about you a lot lately. My thoughts haven't all been pleasant." I shrugged. "I'm sorry about that, but you left me with unanswered questions. I met your mistress, and all I want to know is why, Dillon? Why did you cheat on me… on us? I'm so angry with you and with myself for not seeing it coming." I swiped a tear away. "I met someone and he loves me. He adores our son and Mikey feels the same way about him. But because of you being a deceitful coward and not loving us back, I let him go. When *you* are the one I should have let go of."

Words lodged in my throat. A wave of understanding

coursed through my veins and straight into my heart. I looked down at his name, brushed my legs off and said the words, I had yet to say to him. "Goodbye, Dillon."

Four hours later, I was greeted by tall buildings and traffic. Rather than get off at my exit, my car continued toward the Long Island Expressway.

I pulled my car behind his black Jaguar in the circular stone-paved driveway. The beating in my chest went from a quick trot to a full on gallop. I stared at the gray clapboard-sided house in awe.

Voices carried from the back of the home to where I stood in the driveway. Not having the nerve to walk around the large house, I grabbed my phone and sent a text.

Me: Hi. I need to see you.

Three dots danced.

Luca: I'm in the Hamptons with friends. Is everything okay?

Me: No, everything is far from okay.

My phone started vibrating, his name appeared. In a swift motion, I answered. "Hi."

"Sabrina, what's the matter?"

I heard his voice in stereo and when I pivoted to my right, Luca's concerned face came into view. My heart stilled at the sight of him. Black board shorts hung low on his hips accentuating his muscular torso. On each inhale and exhale, my eyes watched his bare chest rise and fall. My hesitance to respond caused him to stop, shock replaced concern when he saw me.

Realizing he was no longer moving toward me, my arm went slack. Before I could chicken out, run back to my car and drive off, I took strong strides toward him until I was about a foot away. The salty ocean air suddenly felt heavy and thick.

"Hi, Luca." Every part of me wanted to hug him, but his stiff posture scared me into thinking I was too late. All the damage my words had done were too much.

"Why are you here?"

Dread, coupled with remorse flooded me before I said, "I needed to talk to you and didn't want to wait or say it over the phone. I'm sorry to interrupt your time with your friends, but if you can give me five minutes, then I can go." He nodded once. "Can we sit?"

Luca sat next to me on the porch step leaving a gap between us. "What's on your mind, Sabrina?"

"You are." I angled my body toward his. "I've come to a few realizations over the past couple of weeks. What I said to you in my apartment wasn't the entire truth. At the time, I thought it was. But, I've come to realize that you were right. What happened wasn't all because of Mikey, it was because of me too." Looking into his soulful eyes gave me the courage to go on. "Before I came here today, I went to the cemetery. Not to leave flowers, not to cry, but to say goodbye."

"I'm sorry."

I shook my head. "Don't be. I'm the one who is so very sorry." Reaching forward, I placed my hand on his arm. "I love you, Luca. I hope one day, you can forgive me for pushing you out of our lives because I was scared."

My heart pounded as a few long painful seconds passed without a response. He raked a hand through his hair while shaking his head. "You love me?" he asked, not bothering to hide his bitterness.

With determination, I nodded. "Completely and irrevocably."

At my admission, he stood and began pacing back and forth. The way he held his hips, the stiffness in his spine, and the tenseness in his muscles could only mean I was too late. Insecurities kept me immobile, but I needed to know his thoughts. "Please say something."

Fury altered the lines on his face. "Are you kidding me right now?" I watched his body language alter between anger to frustration. He gripped the back of his head, my eyes catching the way his abs flexed from the motion. "Sabrina, you weren't the only one that put your heart on the line. You were scared, well now, *I'm* scared. It was so easy for you to walk away and not give me the opportunity to make things right with you… and with Mikey. I know he's your son, but I love him too and it wasn't fair to either of us. You told me he hated me and that hurt me more than you can imagine. How would you feel if you were in my shoes?"

"Lost."

"Exactly!" he exclaimed, throwing his hands in the air. "I understand what you were feeling that night, but weeks went by. I kept thinking, believing that you would call me. But you didn't."

On shaky legs, I stood and walked over to him. "You're right. Everything you just said I deserve to hear. I did think of you every day, but my heart refused to let me move on and my mind refused to let me believe I could have what I always dreamt of."

"I *never* once gave you the impression that I wasn't capable to give you what you wanted. It turned into my dream, too. You took it upon yourself to halt what we could have been."

"I'm sorry. I came to tell you what I couldn't before. If you don't think you can pick up where we left off and try again, I understand. Please know, anytime you want to see or speak to Mikey you have my blessing. I'm sorry I interrupted." The stretch of pavement that I had to travel to get back to my car seemed a mile long. A slow tear trickled before a few more followed.

"Sabrina?" Cassie's voice sounded behind me. With a quick swipe over my cheeks, I turned and smiled as best I could. As Cassie walked toward me, it was then she saw Luca standing near the porch where I left him. "What's going on?" she asked, placing a comforting hand on my arm.

"I came to talk to him, and now that I have, I'm leaving."

"Why?"

Luca finally moved, and as he approached said, "Cassie, please can you give us a minute?"

Cassie nodded at him robotically. "Sure, but it's getting late and Sabrina shouldn't be driving all that way alone. Luca don't let her leave."

Luca

ONE STEP LATER, CASSIE TURNED back and said, "Remember what you told me. Don't be a fool." She then retreated to where our friends were at the back of the house.

The words I had admitted to Cassie rumbled through

my mind. At the time, I did feel I would take her back in a heartbeat. Things were different for me now. Each day that passed caused the hurt she left me with to fester, making it harder to understand why we were apart, *making* me more resentful.

And absence hadn't helped my resentment, but with her standing before me, beautiful as ever while handing me her heart, made it impossible for me to resist going to her, wanting her. The bottom line was I found two people who completed me. Sabrina and Mikey changed my life, and how could I go back to what I was before them? Basically, as I stood there fighting with myself, it came down to a life with or without them.

The thought of being without them triggered terror to tremble through me. Sabrina taking one step backward, one step further away prompted me to react. "Don't go," I said just above a whisper.

Sadness became obvious in her shimmering eyes. "I think you need time, Luca."

"I've had time… and I *think* I need you." She stood stone still, staring straight through to my soul. I closed the distance between us until our bodies practically touched. "I'm still trying to move past the hurt I felt these past few weeks. Yet, I know watching you drive away right now would hurt so much more."

"Luca, I never meant to hurt you."

I placed my hands on her face. "I know." In that moment I knew nothing could stop my lips from lowering to touch hers. As our kiss progressed, I also knew that now that she came to me on her own accord I wouldn't let anything come between us again.

I gripped the back of her neck, turning our tender kiss into a searing one. Our lips met with such urgency, as if they hadn't touched in years rather than weeks. The familiarity of the softness of her mouth on mine solidified we were meant to be together.

"I love you so much, Sabrina. These past few weeks have been hell for me, but I knew you needed space. It killed me to stay away, and I only did because I'd do anything for you."

Tears leaked from the corners of her eyes as mine misted over. "I'm so sorry."

"No more apologies. I'm going to make mistakes, we both are. From here on out, we will work through them together." I rested my forehead against hers. "Thank you for coming back to me."

"Thank you for waiting."

"Deep down, I know I would've waited forever for you."

Sabrina and I took a walk, talked some more, and reconnected like no time had passed. Almost an hour later, we strolled into the backyard of the home, hand in hand. When we came into view, all eyes were on us. Cassie sprung up out of her chaise lounge with a huge ass smile on her face. Meanwhile, Jude and Kyle tipped their beer bottles in our direction.

"Everyone, look who showed up." I squeezed her hand.

She lifted her free one. "Hi, I'm sorry to intrude."

Cassie ran over and engulfed my girl in a hug, forcing me to release my hold on her. "I'm so glad you stayed."

That's when it dawned on me... how did Sabrina know where to find me? "Did you do this?" I asked my bikini-clad friend.

Cassie nodded. "Possibly." She swatted my arm. "All I did was inform her where you'd be, the rest was Sabrina." Her eyes shifted between us, joy evident on her sweet face. "You two are perfect for each other."

I took her back into my arms and nodded in agreement. "We are." Her smile was electric, and back was the spark I missed in her eyes. Brae followed by Vanessa were next to embrace us. As they chatted with Sabrina, I pulled Cassie into a hug. "Thank you for everything."

"Come see the house," Brae said, taking Sabrina's free hand.

I reached out and gently gripped Sabrina's arm. "No way. I just got her back. Go play with your man."

"He's right, Brae. They need to get it on." Vanessa turned her attention to Sabrina. "I'm glad you're here. This one…" She jabbed me in the arm with her finger. "Has been moping around. Kyle had to throw him in the pool earlier just to wake his ass up."

Sabrina laughed, "That had to be a sight to see."

"Hey!" I nudged her with my shoulder. "Be careful, you could be next."

Fear flashed in her beautiful eyes. "No can do. I don't have my suit."

"We should get your bag out of your car. Give me the keys, I'll grab it." I stuck my hand out but she didn't move.

"I don't have a bag. After I dropped Mikey off at his grandparents' house, my car just sort of drove itself here."

"That's right. Mikey is there all week."

"She curled her bottom lip between her teeth before adding, "Yes... all week.""

Our eyes connected and held. "We'll be back," I announced. Leaving everyone behind us, I tugged Sabrina toward the house, and it was a miracle I didn't give her whiplash. Her feet scurried to keep up with my pace, and once we hit the staircase, I scooped her up into my arms and ran up the stairs, taking two at a time until we made it to my bedroom.

No sooner did the door close behind us that I had her pinned up against it. I yanked her dress over her head, exposing her bare chest and a scrap of lace between her legs.

"Jesus Christ." A fierce growl rumbled up my throat. "God, you're gorgeous."

I sucked on the pulse in her neck before lowering my greedy mouth to her breasts. One by one I licked each nipple, then gave each a gentle bite before trailing my tongue between them and up the slender column on her neck.

"I'll make this up to you later, but first I need to bury myself in you."

Her hands tugged at the white drawstring of my bathing suit before shoving it down my legs. I kicked them to the side, reached forward and snapped the lace covering what I wanted until they came apart in my hand. Without delay, my hand cupped her intimately before I slid a finger inside of her and then removed it to lick it clean.

"I don't have any other panties with me," she said between heavy breaths.

"I don't care." I took her mouth, plunging my tongue in to tangle with hers.

She gripped my wrist and pleaded, "Luca, please. I want you."

"Fuck." In one swift motion, I hoisted her up, forcing her legs to wrap around my waist. Burying my hand in her hair, I eased into her and moved my hips without pause. "You feel incredible. I've missed you so much."

The sound of our bodies coming together, combined with her tight heat encasing me, ensured I wasn't going to last. "Kiss me," she panted and I obliged. Our mouths fused just like our bodies—fast, hot and unbridled. Passion flowed between us, with each grunt, groan, and cry.

"I'm so close, Luca." I increased my pace because I was right there with her. "I'm going to…"

Her legs tightened around my waist, her body shook, and I came like I never had before. She dropped her head to my shoulder. "I love you, Sabrina."

"I love you, too."

Five minutes later, when our breathing returned to a normal pace, I carried her to the bathroom so we could shower before returning to our friends. It took every ounce of restraint not to make love to her once more, but if we didn't get a move on, I was afraid Kyle would be pounding on the door.

I towel dried her hair, and went to get her dress where we left it. Handing it to her, she said, "Besides not having underwear, I don't have any other clothes here either." She pointed to her ripped thong that still remained where it fell earlier. "I suppose I'll be going commando."

"Shit." I reached into my suitcase and pulled out a pair of my boxer briefs. "Wear these. We can run to the store in the morning."

She stared at me as if I had two heads. "You want me

to wear these… under my floral sundress?"

"That's right, you're not going without. I lost my head before. It gets breezy by the water and no one is seeing what's mine."

A pink hue tinged her cheeks. Without argument, she slid on my boxers, folded the waist down and cuffed them on her thighs. She caught her reflection in the full-length mirror and checked herself out. "Hmm… these are kind of cute. What do you think?"

"I think you're fucking stunning and you could be wearing a sack and look like a beauty queen. Put your dress on before we don't make it back downstairs."

"Would that be so bad?" she asked coyly.

"What's gotten into you?" I laughed and watched her body disappear under the cotton fabric.

"You. You've gotten into me."

I looped my arms around her, linking my fingers on the small of her back. "And I plan on staying there."

"Good, I wouldn't want it any other way."

Our lips met in a tender kiss. "Neither would I."

Chapter 31

Luca

I CAME OUT OF THE ensuite bathroom to find Sabrina sitting on the bed, staring at the view. "Are you okay?" I asked, causing her to turn. The smile on her face meant she was more than okay.

She walked toward me and right into my arms. Automatically, my hands found the curve of her ass as I pressed my body against hers. I slipped my hands beneath the short skirt of her dress and smiled that she once again had on a pair of my boxers. "You're addicted," I said, squeezing her ass cheeks to prove my point.

"They're comfortable. I don't think I'll ever go back to wearing thongs again."

"The hell you won't. I happen to like your ass in a sexy thong." After one more squeeze, I added, "But thongs are for my eyes only, and these are good for when you have on insanely short skirts."

"Deal." She twisted her head to take in our surroundings. On a sigh, she looked up with a content smile. "I love it here, and loved spending these past few days with you. If I lived here, I'd never want to leave."

"Well, lucky for us the owner is my best friend," I said with a wink.

"I can't believe he bought this for Brae's twenty-eighth birthday."

"I can. He's an impulsive fucker. I'm just surprised he lied to all of us, and her, about it being a rental when he owned it all along. I can only imagine what she'll get at thirty. A small country?"

She giggled and planted a chaste kiss on my jaw. "The fireworks over the water were spectacular. I don't think I've ever seen anything like that before… just stunning. Mikey would've loved it."

"We can bring him here next year."

"That would be great. I better finish packing… the few articles of clothing you bought me," she said with a smirk before pulling out of my arms.

"You didn't need more than that." Which was true, since whenever we were behind closed doors we were both sans clothes.

But, in spite of my need to have her bare skin against mine as much as possible, she did need garments to wear when with my friends. As promised, I took her into town the next day after she arrived, and picked out: panties, a bikini, a cover up, a pair of shorts and T-shirt, and the sexy black sundress she currently had on.

She zipped up the cheesy "Life's a Beach" souvenir tote bag I insisted on to mark our weekend together. I then threw my own things into my duffle bag and zipped it up. "Ready?"

A few minutes later, we walked out onto the deck where Jude, Brae, Kyle, Vanessa, and Cassie were well into eating their breakfast. "I guess we took longer than

I thought," I leaned in and whispered.

Sabrina offered a salacious smile as she remembered what it was that had us running late. "Worth it, though."

"Well, look who decided to join us," Kyle groaned when we appeared.

"Good morning, everyone," Sabrina said, her cheeks tinged pink.

"Or afternoon," Jude pointed out.

"Not quite." I pulled a chair out for Sabrina and sat next to her. Ignoring the five sets of eyes that were trained on us, I asked, "Coffee, sweetheart?"

"Yes, please."

No one spoke, until Jude said, "Benedetto, I have a proposition for you."

I groaned at my friend/boss, dreading what he was about to propose. Brae beamed at her husband. "We've been chatting, and we think it'd be great if you guys stayed and enjoyed the house for a few more days... alone."

Sabrina's gaze cut to mine as Brae continued. "We know you don't have to pick up Mikey until Friday."

"But..."

"And I spoke to Becky about covering your appointments this week," Cassie interrupted.

"But..."

"And I'll be driving Luca's car back to the city," Kyle then added.

There was nothing left to mention, since they thought of everything. I scanned her face to try and read her thoughts. "What do you think?"

She regarded every one of our friends one by one. "I think you have the best set of friends in the world," she said with a smile.

"Let's not get carried away." I threw my arm around her shoulders, failing to hide the excitement I felt over spending alone time with the woman I loved. "But they have their moments."

Jude flipped me off as Kyle said, "Ingrate. And I was going to leave you guys some new toys to play with. Now you can go buy your own."

The girls giggled before Jude added, "Just don't break anything."

"Speaking of… the counter in the laundry room creaks, and that banister," Kyle said, pointing behind where we all sat, "is very loose."

"And splintery…" Vanessa added.

Jude gawked at them, his mouth hanging open in a comical way. "It's my house, and I haven't had sex on this deck yet."

"Oh well," Kyle said with a shrug of his shoulders.

Vanessa leaned into him and whispered loudly, "Maybe we shouldn't tell him about the porch swing."

"Jesus Christ, Cleary," Jude mumbled, glaring at Kyle.

I turned to Sabrina and said directly into her ear, "We're going to be very busy the next few days."

Sabrina

WE WERE A FEW HOURS into our drive toward my in-laws to get Mikey. Luca drove my little CRV with the same sexy confidence he drove his Jaguar. But the terror in his eyes when Kyle peeled out of the driveway in his baby a few days earlier spoke volumes.

"*Don't over shift her,*" he had said as Kyle grinned, enjoying every moment of Luca's anxiety.

"*Don't you worry about my driving skills.*" Kyle ran a hand over the dashboard lovingly. "*She and I understand each other.*"

Vanessa glared at Kyle. "*Will she understand when you're sleeping with her tonight and not me?*"

It hadn't taken long for Luca to get over it and concentrate on me. The past three days had been absolute heaven on earth. Sure, I missed my son dearly, but having a romantic getaway in a gorgeous home on the beach with my handsome boyfriend deemed to be a great distraction.

Luca's gaze focused on the road, his thumb tapping the top of the steering wheel in tune to the music. Remembering what he had done before we left the house made me laugh. "Do you think Jude will be mad?"

A broad smile appeared on his face. "Do you mean about the sticky notes?"

"Yes, the notes."

Just picturing the yellow squares caused my laughing to increase. Luca had told me that when he was in college with Kyle and Jude, they were pranksters. Not so much Luca, but the other two were on a mission of sorts to one-up each other. I knew the story of Jude and Brae and how Kyle played a hand in that, but the other sorted tales had my jaw slacken more than once.

Before we left today, Luca thought it would be fun to label all the places we christened with a note. The outdoor shower, the kitchen island, the leather chair in the family room, the hot tub, pool, the chaise lounge on the patio, and he left one with an arrow pointing to the ocean. He went as far as taping the outdoor notes down with heavy duty packing tape to protect them from the elements.

Luca shrugged, "Mad? No. Jealous? Yes."

"You all are like little boys." Then a thought occurred to me which caused me to gasp.

"What?" Luca slowed the car as we approached a red light.

"Please whatever you do, do not teach Mikey any of your tricks. Don't even talk about them in front of him. I don't want to have to check the sugar container for salt."

He let out a chuckle. "Pfft. That's too easy."

"Luca!"

"Babe, I hate to break it to you, he will figure all of that out on his own. Just remember to check for plastic wrap over your toilet bowl, that's always a fun one."

I crinkled my nose. "That's gross."

"But, funny."

By the time we made it to my in-laws place, we had laughed so much my stomach ached. When I saw their driveway come into view, I pointed. "Turn there." I was excited to see my son. "Mikey is going to be so surprised you're here."

"You didn't tell him?" He killed the ignition on my SUV. "I can wait in the car."

"Not a chance." I opened my door and grinned back at him. "Now, let's go make a little boy smile."

Hand in hand we walked around the back of the house, where I knew they'd be. The sound of my son laughing elicited a smile. Luca afforded me with a smile of his own. "Someone is having fun."

"Yeah, he loves it here."

He quirked a brow at the reluctance lacing my words. "Isn't that a good thing?"

"Of course. It's me who dreads coming here." I squeezed his hand and shrugged.

"Sweetheart, just say the word and we're out of here."

It was simple things like that that made me fall in love with him more and more. "I love you," I said as a thank you before opening the gate leading to the backyard.

The creak of the hinge brought attention to us. My in-laws sat on Adirondack chairs sipping iced tea, while my son stopped in his tracks with a bubble blower gun held midair.

"Mommy! Luca!" He dropped the toy and sprinted our way. I squatted right before he reached us, taking him into my arms in a crushing hug.

"I missed you so much, baby." Kissing his warm cheek over and over, he giggled and squirmed allowing me my sappy greeting.

"Let me go," he said between huffs and chuckles. No sooner had I released him when he propelled his body at Luca.

"Hey, buddy. How are you?"

"I'm great! But I missed you so much!" Luca ruffled his hair with a smile. "Are you Mommy's boyfriend again?" Luca's eyes cut to mine for direction, while mine cut to my in-laws.

"Hello, Sabrina," my father-in-law saved us both from responding at the moment. He moved closer and gave me a stiff hug.

My mother-in-law stood where she stopped and smiled stiffly. "Sabrina," she said with a nod of her head.

"Hello Brian, Kellie. This is Luca Benedetto…" I paused, drew in a breath, and added with a genuine smile, "My boyfriend. Luca, Brian and Kellie Callahan."

Brian offered a hand to Luca with a smile. "It's very nice to meet you. We've heard so much about you this week."

Luca extended his hand to Kellie next, and the way she accepted only his fingertips, to give him a quick limp handshake, spoke volumes. Of course, the tight grin she had given me was still firmly planted on her face. Screw that, and what she thought. Her son hurt me, and the act was what she refused to acknowledge, and instead focused on the outcome…another grandchild.

"Thank so much," Luca responded. He put his hand on Mikey's shoulder before adding, "I hope all good."

"I told Grandpa how good you are at soccer, and then showed him all the moves you taught me."

"He's very talented," Brian said with a smile. "And passionate about his favorite sport."

Luca and Brian continued the small talk as my mother-in-law elevated the tension level in the backyard to stifling proportions.

"How was your week?" I asked her, in an attempt to be the bigger person.

"It was good."

Silence.

"Um… did he give you any trouble?"

"Nope. He was very well behaved. He's a Callahan." My insides simmered, but I forced a smile and nodded. "You're nice and tan. Did you enjoy your time off?"

"Yes, I did." I stepped closer to Luca and took his hand with purpose. "We did." If she could spit nails, she would.

"Come sit, relax," my father-in-law said. "I'm sure you guys had a long ride up." They had no idea we had come from the Hamptons, nor would I offer that information. My last statement was enough to instigate my ire. "How about a cold glass of iced tea?"

Luca and I exchanged a silent understanding. "Thank you, that sounds nice but we really need to be going."

At my admission, Kellie said, "I'll go grab his bag for you." With that, she retreated toward the house, not bothering to invite us in.

Brian offered an awkward smile once his wife went through the door. "Well, you'll have to visit again so we can get to know you."

"I'd like that," Luca admitted, when all I thought to myself was—yeah, not happening anytime soon.

It took five minutes for goodbyes, and the moment Luca reversed out of the drive, I released a huge sigh of relief.

Mikey chattered in the back about every activity that filled his little vacation. Meanwhile, Luca took my hand in his, brought it to his lips, and kissed it affectionately.

We were driving away from my past, and I looked forward to every minute of *our* future.

Chapter 32

Luca

THE THREE OF US FELL into a very comfortable routine the past few weeks. It took some time for us to build the nerve and come out as a couple to Mikey. Of course, he referenced that I was his mother's boyfriend, but waking up in their apartment would bring that reality to a new level... especially for an almost six-year-old.

That first morning after I stayed over, he came barreling into her room like a bull in a china shop. Sabrina and I had discussed whether it were better for Mikey to see me up and dressed or still in bed. I opted for the first option, worried the latter would confuse him. However, she felt it was a necessary step, and would open a much needed conversation.

Once again, she was right. His brow puckered as he stared at me for a moment, processing why I was in his mom's bed. *"Luca stayed here last night?"* he asked.

"Yes, baby. Is that okay?"

The confusion on his face morphed into a wide-eyed gawk. *"Why didn't you tell me? That's not fair, he should have slept in my room. We could've pretended we were camping out!"*

Sabrina curled her lips over her teeth as I released a chuckle. *"We'll have a camping sleepover soon, buddy."*

"Cool." He bounced his way over, hopped in bed between us, and said, *"Luca, do you like SpongeBob? Mom hates it, but I think it's so funny."* Our eyes met over his head in a silent—*whew*.

And that's how it went with each obstacle we faced. We both knew questions would be asked, in a five-year-old's way. Together, we responded honestly. The topics Sabrina dreaded never came up like she worried they would. Mikey would reference his father in a way that meant he understood it was okay to talk about memories, yet knew new ones were not replacing them but instead enhancing them.

As far as my relationship with Sabrina, it could be described in one word... amazing. I'd known we were well matched, compatible, but not until we became official in every way did it really click how perfect we were together. During alone time, I shared I couldn't wait for her to meet my family, we talked about things we wanted to do alone and with Mikey, and we made *plans*. That was the best part.

The day I took her to my office was a proud day for me. Her eyes widened as she took in the posh yet comfortable atmosphere Jude created at Soren Enterprises. Ever since I missed Mikey's graduation, I had thought of bringing her there.

She ran her hand along the edge of my mahogany desk as she walked around it. The city looked pristine from my window. Beams of sunlight bounced off the adjacent building's windows almost creating a prism effect. *"Wow, Luca, this is beautiful."*

"Thank you. We've worked very hard to get here. To think this all started back in our Frat house."

Sabrina sat in my high-back leather desk chair. *"Oh my God."* She sighed. *"This is heavenly. I can't imagine what it would be like to work sitting on a cloud. The closest thing I have is the memory foam in my sneakers."*

It's when she let out another sigh followed by a moan, that I needed to put a stop to it or I would be locking my office door. *"You're killing m*e." She smiled, stood, and looped her arms around my neck. *"Are you done torturing me and ready for the rest of the office tour?"*

She nodded. *"Yes, sorry."* Her eyes cut to the leather sofa on the opposite side of my office. When she turned to me, her eyes turned sultry, and she smirked.

Taking her hand in mine, I said, *"Okay, let's go."* She laughed at me, prompting me to ask, *"What?"*

"It's just nice to know I have that effect on you."

"Babe, if I didn't have a meeting in forty-five minutes, I'd show you what kind of effect you have on me. And don't think I won't show you later."

Thanks to parts of her past, doubt would creep in… but there would be no way I'd ever give her reason to question my love for her, or Mikey. For instance, I'd go to the ends of the earth to give a little boy the best birthday he ever had.

One last fiddle with the "Happy Birthday Mikey" banner centered it perfectly between the two clusters of helium soccer balls. After taking a few steps backward, I nodded to myself in approval.

"Honey, it's perfect," Sabrina said, wrapping her arms around my waist. On its own accord, my arm circled her shoulders to draw her even closer.

"Now it is. I want everything perfect for him," I admitted, kissing the top of her head.

"It's beyond perfect. He's going to love this." At my

request, Sabrina and I arrived to the Sport Zone an hour before party time to ensure everything was set up just as I wanted it. Pizza was coming during the scrimmage we would play, the soccer ball shaped ice cream cake waited in the freezer, and cellophane-wrapped soccer balls, monogrammed for each guest, lined the room as party favors.

Twelve boys, including Mikey, were about to have the best soccer-themed birthday party they'd ever been to.

Sabrina reached for my left arm, twisting my wrist to see the time. "They should be here any minute." Also on my request, I suggested that her parents hang back at her apartment with Mikey and bring him over closer to party time to surprise him.

Scanning the party room to be sure I didn't forget anything, voices outside the door meant our guest of honor had arrived.

"Wow!" he yelled the moment he walked through the door.

"Where's grandma and grandpa?" his mother asked.

"We're here." They stepped through after Mikey. "He left us in the dust," Sebastian said on a chuckle.

As Sabrina greeted her parents, Mikey's gaze bounced from the banner to the table set with soccer plates to the gift table already holding two boxes in soccer ball wrapping paper. "Can I open them?"

"Stop!" Sabrina's command halted his full-on sprint toward the presents. "After the party, you can open your gifts." I internally laughed at how she had predicted this exact scenario. One box held an array of new soccer gear, from shin guards to cleats to a new athletic cup... it was never too soon to protect the jewels. The other box held a soccer ball signed by David Beckham in a lucite case.

Sabrina knew that would cause a ruckus with the rest of the six-year-olds coming.

"Aw, man." On cue, his brown eyes cut to my face.

"Sorry, buddy. Mom's right."

"Fine." The side of his mouth lifted in a sulking pout. Having me around so much once we got him home from his grandparents caused my little friend to always try and use me as an ally against his mother's rules. You would've thought by now he got the message I was Team Sabrina every time. "Hey, you're friends will be here soon, how about we go out to the field area and warm up?"

And just like that, the presents were forgotten.

Sabrina

THE SMILE ON MIKEY'S FACE had been infectious. As promised, Luca invited us over for dinner and a campout, New York style. This was a big deal in more ways than one. Not only for my son, who was finally having a sleepover with his best friend, but even more so with me.

Side by side we wheeled our overnight bags through the lobby... mine a traditional bag on wheels and Mikey's a Ninja Turtle bag on wheels his friend Jared gave him for his birthday.

I smiled at the Concierge on duty. "Hello, Lester."

"Hello, Ms. Sabrina," he said in response.

"We're having a sleepover," Mikey announced.

"Well, that sounds like a great time. Have fun, little man."

"Oh, I will," my son quipped confidently. The elevator doors opened, and as we stepped in Mikey waved before the doors slid shut. He then studied the panel and asked, "What floor?"

"Number twelve."

He reached for the correct number, pressing it with a rigid finger. "Mommy, this is a big building, way bigger than ours."

"Yes, it is. Can you tell me how many floors there are?"

"Eighteen!"

"That's right. Good job."

The doors slid open with a ding, only for us to hear it followed by a loud, "Roar!" Luca stood, fingers bent like claws and teeth showing. But a giggle wasn't the response he was going for. "I didn't scare you?"

"Nope."

"Not at all?" Luca prompted.

"Nope."

"I'll just have to try harder next time." Luca bent his head to place a quick kiss on my cheek. "Hello, beautiful."

"Hi."

"So, maybe the reason you're not scary to me," Mikey voiced out loud, "is because I'm used to you." This little game they had going started a few days ago.

"Maybe you're right." Luca smiled at me and winked. At his door, he stopped and waited for Mikey's undivided attention. "You ready for a super fun campout?"

"Yes!"

"Okay, let the sleepover begin." With a grand gesture, Luca opened the door to his dark apartment, except for twinkle lights he strung from wall to wall across the ceiling. Mikey and I gasped at the exact same time. His Ninja Turtle rolling bag landed on its side with a thump.

"Stars!" The coffee table that usually sat in his living was moved to a corner, and in its place was a royal blue nylon tent complete with a fake campfire made out of orange and red construction paper rising from a pile of logs. "Wow!" Mikey's eyes were as wide as saucers, and all I could think to myself was how much this man enjoyed spoiling my son. I couldn't even be upset about that because it was the most endearing thing I'd ever experienced.

"Miss Brooks helped me make the campfire. But later I'll light the fireplace and we'll make S'mores."

"I love S'mores!" My son hadn't used his inside voice yet. The balcony caught his attention, and he pointed toward a telescope with his mouth agape.

"Cool right?" Luca asked. "A little birdie told me you always try to spot the Big Dipper. Tonight we'll search for all the stars."

"Mommy said friends are like stars in the sky."

"Your mom is very smart."

Mikey nodded. "This is the best sleepover ever!" My son charged toward the tent, hurtling his body through the opening and landing on the air mattress that was set up inside. As he jabbered on and on, Luca pulled me into his arms with a smile.

"You're unreal, you do know that, right?"

"Yup."

Mikey extended his arms to the side and ran in a circle around the tent making the sound of an airplane motor. Luca and I stared at him. My son wasn't used to running room in an apartment. When he almost crashed into a table with a ceramic vase on it, I needed to put a stop to it. "Michael Dillon, this is not a playground. Inside voice and actions, please."

Luca chuckled every time I used Mikey's full name. He was almost as bad as my son—I now had two boys to deal with.

Mikey's lips quirked to the side "Sorry."

Luca changed the topic. It was apparent he didn't like to see Mikey get scolded. "How about I show you the rest of the apartment?"

Without haste, Mikey headed toward the hallway leading to the bedrooms. Luca pointed out the bathroom which didn't interest Mikey, the master bedroom, again, not much interest, but when he opened the last door, Mikey said, "Wow!"

The room was a little boy's dream; a twin bed, covered in a red comforter with navy blue accent pillows, and one in the shape of a soccer ball, a poster of a couple of soccer players, a carpet that doubled as a racetrack for the box of Matchbox cars waiting for my son, and some of the same toys as he had at home.

"What's that?" Mikey pointed to a netlike container. "The opening is on the top. How do I kick the ball in there?" His little eyes narrowed. "I suppose I could head it."

Luca shook his head. "That's a hamper for your dirty clothes. If you'd like to kick those in there, that would be fine, but that's it, okay?"

"Yup!" He rubbed his tummy. "Are we going to eat soon?"

Back in the kitchen, three balls of dough sat resting on the counter. Also laid out was a container of homemade sauce, pepperoni, sausage, a variety of vegetables, and mozzarella cheese.

We had both decided it'd be fun to make our own individual pizzas even though I knew Mikey would want whatever Luca had. The three of us stood in the kitchen. Luca and Mikey wore their *Kiss the Cook* aprons, and I wore one Luca had bought for me that said, *Caution: Hot Stuff.* And we made the best pizzas we ever had.

When the sun went down, we put our pajamas on, flattened out our sleeping bags, and sat around the faux fire, eating S'mores.

"We need a campfire story!" Mikey exclaimed. "Luca, will you tell it?"

Luca's brows furrowed. Then a smile spread across his face. Leaning in, he said in a soft voice, "Once upon a time, a man got hit in the head with a soccer ball…"

Mikey laughed. "Yay! I love this story!"

"Me too, buddy. Me, too."

Epilogue

Luca

TONIGHT WE WERE HEADED TO Vanessa's thirtieth birthday party. Sabrina must have tried on three different outfits until she settled on a little black dress paired with a killer pair of *come fuck me* heels that she promised to keep on later when we were home alone.

"Babe, you look beautiful."

She ran her hand down her sleek hair. "I hope so. Have you talked to Dante?"

"Last I knew his flight was on time. He'll meet us at the party." My brother, much to my mother's pleasure, was moving to the city. I think she felt that maybe us being together in the same place was one step closer to us coming home. Of course, that was wishful thinking on her part.

"I feel so bad he's coming straight from the airport."

When Kyle planned this party, I told him Dante would be in town and didn't hesitate to invite him. Anytime my brother would come and visit me, Dante fell right in line with my friends as if he had known them for years. And the ladies... many times we'd go to a party and I wouldn't see Dante until the next morning.

"Nah, he'll be fine, he just about lives out of airports. Plus, if we don't get moving, he just might beat us there." Sabrina glared at me. "What?" I kissed the top of her head. "I'm just kidding." *Not really.* "Before we go, there's something I want to talk to you about."

"You sound so serious."

I pressed the pad of my thumb over the crease between her brows. "I am. I just found out I have to go to L.A. next week."

"Okay. For how long?"

"Just a few days, but I'd like you and Mikey to come with me." The wheels were spinning as she contemplated my request. "Do you think you can reschedule your clients for the week?"

"Probably, it's a light week since many take a vacation at the end of August." In spite of her admission, unease altered her features.

"What's the matter?"

"I just want you to be sure. Traveling with a six-year-old isn't a picnic."

"Well, with what I have planned all week, he'll be too exhausted to act up. Disneyland, box seats at the Galaxy charity benefit game, Knott's Berry Farm Amusement Park... the works."

Her expression slowly morphed into one filled with emotion. In the parting of her lips, the shimmering of unshed tears in her beautiful eyes, I wondered what ran through her mind. When I watched her delicate neck work a swallow, I pinched her chin between my thumb and forefinger. "Hey, talk to me. If you don't think it's a good idea we can do it another time."

She shook her head and brought a hand up to palm

my jaw. "It's not that. I just…" We gazed at each other for a long moment. I waited, allowing her the time to work through what she needed to say. "You overwhelm me, Luca. I am *overwhelmed* with my feelings for you."

A surge of joy shot right through me, and I revealed as much through the smile on my face. "I feel the same way, Sabrina. And I plan to enjoy every *overwhelming* minute. I plan to take you and Mikey to Italy and meet my family. I want to escape with you to remote locations while my mother spoils Mikey. My list of places we will be traveling to is very long." Without preamble, I buried my fingers into her hair and pulled her closer. My kiss was thorough, moving from sweet and soft to crazed and needy. She gripped my wrists, her fingertips pressing into my skin in a desperate way.

After it was clear we either needed to take it to my bed or end it, the only thing that had me doing the latter was knowing Kyle would kick my ass if we didn't show… and I knew if I got her naked in the next five minutes, we would *not* be showing.

"We need to go, now."

She nodded, her eyes wide and alive with lust as she tried to calm her breath. "I agree."

Seconds later, hand in hand, we walked out of my building into the hot humid August night. As usual, cars filled the streets, and after an annoying amount of time, we pulled into the lot at Cleary Labs. Kyle decided to have Vanessa's party at his place of business so he could control every detail, the OCD bastard.

After I handed the attendant my keys, Sabrina grabbed the gift we bought Vanessa and let out a deep breath.

"Sweetheart, relax. Why are you so nervous? These

are your friends, too."

"Not them, your brother. What if he doesn't like me?"

"You've talked to my brother via video chat. He already loves you. Just remember when you see him in person, which Benedetto you're with. I wouldn't want to kick my brother's ass the first night he's in town." I winked and my girl smiled. Little did she know I wasn't kidding.

Her fingers flexed between mine. "No worries there... I'm all yours."

"Bet your fine ass you are."

The party was booming, Kyle had thought of everything. Purple and white balloons and streamers adorned the lab, along with a happy birthday sign draped along the far wall. All the tables were decorated with candles and party favors marked each place setting. There was a small tended bar in the corner and waitresses passed around trays of hors d'oeuvres.

Kyle, Vanessa, Jude and Brae had cocktails in hand and were laughing. Meanwhile, others that I didn't know, but I assumed were Kyle's employees, mingled about.

My friends, who had turned into lovesick puppies, brought a smile to my face—especially since I was now in the same category. Thinking back to our crazy college days, I never would've guessed that any one of us, not to mention *all* of us, would fall in love.

I thought for sure Jude would be marked as a confirmed bachelor, yet he was the first to fall. Kyle, although he had a brilliant mind, wasn't too smart when it came to the opposite sex. And me, well, I never thought I'd be so lucky for a woman like Sabrina to love me. Yet, there we all were, happy and utterly entranced by the three best women in the city.

It was a shame Desiree couldn't be at the party. Kyle told me he offered to buy her an airline ticket back to the states, but unfortunately, she was tied up in a court case.

"There you are!" Brae beamed.

"Hey guys." After obligatory hugs and kisses, I turned to Vanessa. "Happy birthday." "This is for you," Sabrina said handing her the square box wrapped in pink paper.

"Thank you for coming, you didn't need to bring me a gift." Her eyes scanned the area behind us. "I thought your brother was coming? I can't wait to meet him."

"He'll be here soon. Where's Cassie?"

Brae glanced at her Gucci watch that Jude bought her as an, *I missed you,* gift when he was away on business. The man needed an intervention. He was verging on Oprah's level of gift giving. "She should have been here by now. I hope she's okay."

"Sparky," Jude said coming up from behind and roping his arms around her waist. "She'll be fine. I'm sure she's stuck in traffic."

Sabrina was in awe of our surroundings. "This is unbelievable. What an incredible place to work."

Kyle grinned when he heard Sabrina's compliment. "Would you like a tour? Actually, I have a couple boxes of product for you to bring to the salon."

"Really?" My girl's face lit up. "Thank you and yes, I'd love a tour."

"I'll take her." I put my hand on the small of her back.

Vanessa sidled up to Kyle. "Sweetie, let Luca give her the tour." She winked at me. "Just so you know, stay clear of the table in the fourth floor conference room… it isn't very stable."

Sabrina's cheeks flamed. Kyle smacked Vanessa's ass.

"Whose fault is that? One sniff of the new fall scent and she was all over me like a wetsuit on a surfer."

She laughed. "Whatever, you loved riding my wave."

On that note, I took Sabrina by the hand and lead her out of the room. "Don't mind them."

Sabrina snickered. "I'm surprised it wasn't worse. Do you think they think we're going to have sex in one of the rooms?"

"I think, yes."

One by one I showed Sabrina all the different labs the building housed. Each one impressed her more than the last. The air was filled with various scents, but they all seemed to come together in a way that soothed.

When we came upon a small conference room, Sabrina closed the door. She popped up on her toes and began to pepper my skin with kisses. Did they pump an aphrodisiac into the vents? "So," she said in a sultry tone. "Since they *think* we're having sex…"

"Are you saying you want to have sex with me right now?" She sucked her bottom lip between her teeth. "Be careful what you admit to, Miss Ricci. I left my apartment with a raging hard-on, and I know for a fact my dick wasn't happy I ignored it." I pulled her firmly against my hips proving I was already game. "Ti amo."

The apples of her cheeks deepened in hue with her blushing. "Okay, bad idea especially if you're going to speak Italian. We'll wait until we get home."

I couldn't help but laugh. "I agree."

After completing the tour, we made our way back down to the party. Music played, forcing the guests to chatter louder than before. Sabrina and I helped ourselves to a glass of wine when a blonde blur flew into the room. "Oh. My. God!" All eyes went to a disheveled

Cassie.

Brae scurried toward her. "Are you okay?"

"No. I just got into an accident with an obnoxious Uber driver and an even more obnoxious tourist. No, obnoxious is too kind for that... that... jackass."

Vanessa and Brae flanked each side of their friend, scanning her body for injuries. "Sweetie, are you okay?" Vanessa repeated Brae's question while frisking her.

"Yes, my car isn't though. I can't believe this." As she went on about what went down that caused her delay, my phone buzzed in my pocket.

On my screen was a text from Dante.

> **Running late. Wacko hit my Uber. Just filling out paperwork. Will be there soon.**

Sabrina picked up on the _oh, fuck_ look I sported.

"What's wrong?"

I flipped my phone so she could read Dante's text. And in less than three seconds, she sported the same _oh, fuck_ look that I had. "Should you warn her?"

"No. This one needs to play out on its own."

In a matter of minutes, things were about to get crazy. All I could do was hope my brother survived the wrath of Cassie Brooks.

The End

You can get to know each of these hot book boyfriends in:

Finding Mr. Wrong, Jude Soren's story.
Taming Mr. Flirt, Kyle Cleary's story.
Scoring Mr. Romeo, Luca Benedetto's story.
Craving Mr. Kinky, Dante Benedetto's story.

Details for each book can be found on the author's websites.

www.ammadden.com
www.joanneschwehmbooks.com

Keep reading for a preview of Taming Mr. Flirt

Taming
MR. FLIRT

USA TODAY BESTSELLING AUTHOR
A.M. MADDEN
JOANNE SCHWEHM

CHAPTER 1

Kyle

THE CROWING OF AN IRATE cock in the distance caused a spontaneous snort laugh to escape my mouth. My best friend Jude had a hate/hate relationship with that cock, and the fact that rooster chose to keep crowing every five minutes couldn't be more hilarious. I warned my friend when he told us they planned to get married on his future in-laws' farm that it would be a bad idea. Did he listen? No.

Another squawk, another snort, and when Jude shook his head I couldn't be sure if the rooster caused it, or me. The way the minister cleared his throat, and the bride-to-be, Brae, glared at me over Jude's shoulder, supplied all the confirmation I needed.

I didn't dare look behind me at my other best friend, Luca. If he were on the verge of losing it as well, Jude would kick our asses. A flip of the coin won me the coveted best man responsibility. Jude couldn't decide between Luca and I. When I won the toss, the asshole groom said, *"Best two out of three?"*

Jude Soren had no faith I could play the part of best man, and proving him right I had to force every muscle in my body into lockdown mode to keep from laughing again. When I met Vanessa's eyes, the sight of her lips curling over her teeth to keep from losing her shit had my body convulsing. Clearly, the maid of honor had the same sense of humor as I did.

I felt like a kid again when I'd get a fit of hysteria in church. But instead of my mom pinching my arm, a solid punch to the middle of my back by Luca made matters worse.

The squeak that escaped my lips caused the bride and groom to stare at me, as did the minister and Brae's bridal party. "Sorry," I mumbled while looking down. I could also feel the eyes of every guest attending this wedding on me, including Jude's family who flew in from Sweden.

The warm Indian summer day made for a perfect wedding day, but it also caused me to break out into a sweat. It felt like we'd been standing in that tent for days, and not minutes. Because of the unprecedented warm temperatures for October, the inside of the tent felt like a sauna. The combination of flowers and about a hundred different scents of perfume and cologne were giving me a headache... an unfortunate occupational hazard.

It felt like an eternity passed after the happy couple said their vows. The minister recited a good portion of prayers. As he went on and on, absolving us all from our sins, I ran a finger between my shirt collar and my damp skin.

Dammit, when will this end?

I wanted out of that tent, and I'd love a feisty brunette to be the one to settle me down. My eyes caught Vanessa's eyeroll as the minister droned on and on. Christ, he could talk. Her audible sigh almost initiated another snort laugh. She made an even worse maid of honor than me a best man. Since Brae also couldn't pick one out of her three best friends, Vanessa won her role today by drawing the longest straw.

For the record, Vanessa should have been a supermodel. Her long brown tresses fell like silk over her shoulders. The way her green eyes sparked to life when she spoke could have any man forgetting his own fucking name. But her tall, lean body could make a man beg. The thought of her long legs wrapped around my waist had me acting like a male dog chasing a female dog in heat.

Personality wise, the chick couldn't be more opposite of Brae and her friends. She loved partying, dancing, and having a good time... my kind of woman. She also had a thing for nicknames. She dubbed Jude, *Mr. Wrong,* the day we met at the game show where I pranked him into participating, and until now the name stuck.

We'd been out a few times with the lovebirds. Vanessa nicknamed me *Mr. Flirt,* which suited me fine since that was all I'd done from the moment I laid eyes on her.

A few passionate moments passed between us on the dance floor when we all hung out at a bar called Dispatch. Another time we made out in the engine room on the yacht where Jude and Brae had their engagement party. Every one of our encounters, four to be exact, had been steamy foreplay... that was until last night.

During the rehearsal dinner, Miss Vanessa Monroe blew my cock, and my mind, in the coatroom. I couldn't wait to see her today and hoped to take the flirting to the next level. The next level in my mind meant being horizontal, if and when the damn ceremony would fucking end already.

I should've been happy and elated for Jude. After all, those two pledging eternal devotion today wouldn't be happening if not for me. Long story short, I pranked him and then he wanted to kill me. My little stunt sent him to a deserted tropical beach for six weeks with a complete stranger. Within a year, Jude went from plotting my death to planning his wedding to Brae.

I couldn't relate to the way Jude stood beside me while staring at his bride, like his very existence depended on her. I'd known Jude Soren my entire adult life, and this man making goo-goo eyes was an imposter.

Sure, Brae was a stunning brunette and just his type. But I couldn't help but wonder if she drugged him while living on that secluded beach. He left a cocky prick and came back a sap in love.

Of course, I was happy for my best friend who *claimed* he found the love of his life. Did I believe he did? Fuck, no. With almost eight billion people on earth, how could one person be destined as a soul mate?

The scientist in me argued that mathematically finding love with one person didn't make sense. I believed in love, but to love just one? Again, fuck no. Things like curiosity, creativity, statistical thinking, and *logic* meant something better was at the next discovery.

Discovering new things was the reason for my existence.

In my job, that next discovery translated to a beaker filled with an exotic combination of liquids ready to be made into an intoxicating scent. In my personal life, that next discovery could slam into me at every turn. I met beautiful women all the damn time, and I was supposed to choose one forever?

Yeah, no.

There were too many decisions in this world, whether it be in the cosmetics creation process or in choosing my next lay.

Applause brought me back to the Hallmark movie we were forced to endure. Party time. As the only groomsman, Luca offered his arm to Brae's two bridesmaids, Cassie and Desiree. I followed behind with Vanessa.

The short black dresses they each wore complemented their bodies. Where Cassie was blonde, small, and petite with some impressive curves, Desiree was brunette, taller, and slimmer, similar to Vanessa.

I admired the two women walking ahead of me, with Luca sandwiched between them, before looking down at the hottie on my arm. "Damn, Brae has some beautiful friends."

"Why, thank you," Vanessa chirped beside me. I couldn't help but smile at her. Most other females would have taken offense to my declaration.

Leaning toward the gorgeous woman whose hand rested in the crook of my arm, I took an exaggerated whiff. "Miss Dior?"

Her head snapped toward mine. "Why did you just sniff me?"

Before I could explain, the happy newlyweds were getting ready to greet family and friends. Vanessa released me and stretched her arms out to Brae. When she leaned over, I appreciated her long toned legs. The short black dress hugged her assets, and by assets I meant her perfect tits and great ass.

With the women in some sort of female huddle giggling, I held my hand out to the groom. "Well, you did it, Soren. Again, you're welcome."

"I already thanked you a million times," Jude said as he shook my hand. "You're fired by the way."

"No, I'm not. Any best man would have snorted."

"I wouldn't have," Luca quipped.

"Fuck you." I turned back to Jude and asked, "This is the thanks I get? I should have been best man without a coin toss. You met her because of me."

"Yeah, yeah, you're responsible for getting us together. I take all the credit for making her mine." He looked at Brae who looked right back at him with a smile. "Today, that gorgeous woman is my wife. So, I thank you for being the jackass who forged my name on a contract. Try not to be a jackass during the toast."

"Ingrate."

Luca clapped my back. "Let's get a drink. Looks like there are some single women at the bar."

Speaking of women, I needed to get Miss Dior alone. As if she heard my thoughts, Vanessa looked at me with a mischievous glint in her eyes. From my calculations, we had about an hour before we were due to deliver our toasts. That was more than enough time.

The women all looked at me as I sauntered up to them. I kissed Brae on the cheek. "Congratulations, Mrs. Soren. I wish you all the luck in the world with that crazy Swede." After a roll of the eyes, Brae smiled. There was nothing anyone could say to her that would make her smile falter. "Vanessa, can I see you for a minute?"

Our friends looked at us. "We're rehearsing our toasts. We wouldn't want to disappoint anyone."

Before anyone of them could comment, I took her hand and led her out of the ceremonial tent. When everyone turned right toward the one for the reception, I pulled Vanessa left.

"What toast?" she asked as we reached the barn. "I didn't prepare a toast. I was just going to say, 'Congrats and you have my permission to ditch the rest of your wedding to start consummating as husband and wife.' Not appropriate?"

"That sounds like the perfect toast to me, although Brae may not think so. But speaking of consummating, we have an hour to get nasty ourselves."

"Good plan," she drawled with a salacious grin. I slid open the barn door and our eyes scanned the surroundings. Just as I tugged her inside, Vanessa's nose crinkled. "It stinks in here."

"Trust me, in a few minutes the last thing you'll be thinking about is the scent." I squeezed her hand and pulled her toward the bales of hay.

"Speaking of scents, how did you know what perfume I was wearing?"

"It's what I do."

"What does that mean? Do you hang out in department stores and memorize fragrances? Wait, are you one of those perfume-spritzing guys at Macy's? Please tell me you are." She laughed, but I didn't.

"No, smartass, I'm a chemist. I create fragrances and I can tell you, Miss Dior, although popular, isn't what you should be wearing." Her eyebrows shot up. "Not that you don't smell great, because you do. Believe me, I've wanted to devour you since you devoured me last night."

We both stood staring at the hay strewn all around the barn. "That looks very scratchy," Vanessa said with a frown.

"Allow me." I removed my monkey-suit jacket and spread it over a mound of hay that was closest to us. A quick glance toward the door ensured we were out of sight if someone were to walk in. "Better?" With an enthusiastic nod, Vanessa lowered herself on my jacket, rested on her bent elbows, and stared up at me. I looked down at her and considered all the things I could do to her with my tongue. "That dress looks amazing on you, but I bet having it pushed up around your waist would make it look even better. I can't wait to see if there's a thong under it or lace panties. I'm a thong guy."

"You talk a lot. Are you just going to flirt with me or are we going to put this hay to good use? You owe me an orgasm."

"Oh, you'll get one. Trust me." My dick was in agreement as it came to life in my pants. Poor thing had struggled throughout the entire ceremony. With each look and smile Vanessa gave me, my cock responded. There were a few times I had to glance at Brae's great aunt Myrtle just to calm him down. But now, there was no calming down in his future.

There wasn't anything romantic about this encounter, then again she didn't seem to be into that bullshit. Neither was I, and that was what made our connection perfect. Hovering over Vanessa, supported only by my left arm, I skimmed my right hand up her leg.

Warmth filled my palm with each stroke of her soft skin. Once my fingers reached the hem of her dress, I pushed it up right where I wanted it. She raised her ass a bit to allow the fabric to gather up around her waist. Fuck me, she was naked under her dress. "Okay, this is my new favorite," I said, cupping her bare skin. "Do you always go without panties?"

"Depends on my mood."

"Thank fuck I didn't know that during the ceremony or I never would have made it through." She giggled at my admission, but I was dead serious.

Shifting my body, I settled my head in between her legs. "Spread." Vanessa dropped her bent knees to either side. Her bare pussy glistened with anticipation. Jesus Christ, she was going to make this quicker than it already needed to be.

Taking a moment to appreciate the beauty in front of me, I stared at her. "You're fucking gorgeous." My thumbs spread her open. Vanessa moaned and lifted her hips. "Just a minute, beautiful, I'll get you there. I want to play for a bit." And that's just what I did when I teased her with my tongue.

Her chest still covered by her dress rose and fell with each deep breath she took. When I slid one finger in, she moaned—when I added another, her hips bucked as I finger fucked her. "You like that?" She nodded and before I continued, I removed my fingers from her tight channel and put them in my mouth. "Delicious."

"Oh, God. Kyle… I need… you… inside… me. Now." Vanessa's words came in halted, short commands. Before I knew it, she yanked on the end of my bow tie and pulled until it slid off my neck.

I stood to remove my pants, first retrieving a condom out of my wallet. Her green eyes resembled lasers as they zoned in on the motion of me rolling it over my cock. With a devious smirk on my face, I again positioned myself between her legs, but this time with the tip of my dick pressed against her entrance. "For the record, this is going to be a quick hard fuck."

"I'm good with that," she purred. "But first…" She wrapped the bow tie around the base of my cock with a devilish grin.

"What are you doing?"

"Impromptu cock ring." Damn this woman was perfect. Tying the end in a bow, she added, "Okay, I'm ready now." On her consent, I leaned down and kissed her at the same moment I thrust into her.

Fuck me.

Her heat encased my cock tighter than the condom and bow tie I had on. Our tongues mimicked the movements of our hips. Everything about this woman was perfection. Rocking our way to chase an orgasm, I slowed down.

"Don't stop, I'm almost there, please." Cupping her face with my hands, I lowered my lips back to hers. Stiff hay scratched my knees, and if it weren't for my jacket beneath her I imagined it would also be marking her ass—something I'd like to do myself one day. "I'll get you there, don't you worry." We sped up our movements. She crossed her ankles on my lower back, causing the heels of her shoes to dig into my ass. Her pussy pulsed around me, milking every ounce of my climax. Our mouths devoured each other's as we swallowed one another's groans.

"Fuck me, that was fantastic," I said through labored breaths.

"Isn't that what I just did?" She looked up at me with her gorgeous green eyes and grinned.

"Yes, and we will be doing that again before the cake is served." As soon as I pulled out of her we heard voices. "Shit. Pull your dress down." I slid off the condom, tied it off, and put it in my suit coat pocket. My fingers tried and failed at working the knot on my bow tie. "Where the fuck did you learn how to tie a knot like this? Girl Scouts?"

"No, the Boy Scouts." Vanessa laughed.

"Why are you laughing? This isn't funny." The voices grew louder and panic set in. "I need to put the bow tie back around my neck where it belongs."

"Your dick is out and you're worried about the bow tie?" She shimmied her dress down and with steady dexterity removed the bow tie from around my cock. Her fingers brushing against him almost set things in motion again. With one deft movement, the noose was removed, and my dick was freed.

Fuck. I dusted off strands of hay stuck to my legs before rushing to put myself back together. When I inspected Vanessa to be sure she looked as she did when we walked in, it was my turn to laugh. "You might want to get the straw out of your hair."

She raked her fingers through the long dark strands only to make matters worse. "Holy shit. How much is in here? It's like a goddamn nest!"

Just as I was assisting her in the straw removal, Jude cleared his throat behind us. "Cleary."

Uh oh. He used my last name. Vanessa and I turned to find Jude and Brae. "Soren."

Brae stood with her mouth in the shape of an "O" and Jude glared at me with eyes narrowed into slits. "What are you doing in here?"

"Well, nothing now." The sound of me raising my zipper echoed in the barn. Vanessa snickered when I added, "A minute ago we were fucking. Why are you in here?"

"Same reason, but we're entitled... it's our wedding day." His irritated voice made us laugh.

"And we're entitled to celebrate our best friends' wedding day."

"And as maid of honor and best man, you should conduct yourselves with a touch more class." Brae added her two cents.

"My wife is right. Shouldn't you two be out there

ensuring our guests are having a good time instead of Kyle's cock?"

Vanessa clucked her tongue against the roof of her mouth. "Oh, calm your jets Jude-alicious." Jude furrowed his brow and all I could do was stare at her.

"What did you just call him?"

"It's my nickname for Jude," Brae chided. "She stole it."

Vanessa turned to me. "Since I can't call him Mr. Wrong any longer, then Jude-alicious it is."

"I can't wait to see what I graduate to if this clown is whatever you just called him."

Vanessa shook her head. "You are and will always be Mr. Flirt. Now let's get out of here and let these two consummate their marriage."

I clapped Jude on the back. "Have fun and watch out for that hay. It's brutal on the knees."

At that, Vanessa plucked a few more pieces out of her hair and quipped, "And your bare ass if you don't use his jacket as a buffer."

Brae looked up at Jude who tossed his arm around his wife. "Bedroom?"

She nodded with a firm, "Yes."

"Don't take too long, or you'll miss our speeches," I reminded them.

With my hand on the small of Vanessa's back, I walked her out of the barn and into the tent where the reception was held.

She smiled at me. "That was fun."

"Getting caught or screwing?"

Her tongue wet her lips. "Both. Although, getting caught in public is a complete turn-on, I was referring to the sex."

Who was this woman? The thought of fucking her in public made my dick go hard once again. Grabbing her hand, I grumbled, "I need a drink."

What I needed was to calm the fuck down before I threw her over my shoulder and cut out of the wedding way too soon. Jude would definitely kick my ass, but once the reception was over, all bets were off.

Acknowledgments

Scoring Mr. Romeo was as fun to write as the first two books we collaborated on, Finding Mr. Wrong and Taming Mr. Flirt. Once again, we laughed, cried, and swooned... and we can't wait to do it again for a fourth time. We hope we don't forget anyone, and if we do, please know it wasn't intentional.

First, we'd like to thank the readers. We all love to read and talk about the books and characters we love, and we're so thankful for your support.

To our beta readers, in spite of the natural disasters that hit us hard, you guys came through and we really appreciate it. Your feedback, comments, suggestions, and more importantly, your honesty, were incredibly helpful. Thank you from the bottom of our hearts.

Thank you to our very handsome cover model, Steven Brewis, who was a perfect Luca Benedetto, and David Wagner for providing that amazing shot we used for our cover.

Sommer Stein at Perfect Pear Creative Covers, your talents are unsurpassed. You did it again. We are as in love with this cover as the others you have created for you. We are so happy to have you on our team.

To Nina Grinstead and the team at Social Butterfly, PR. Thank you for helping us spread the word and prepare all the amazing readers for Scoring Mr. Romeo's release.

To all the bloggers, thank you for all the time you

spend supporting authors and reading our stories. You take time out of your personal lives, and we are very thankful.

Nichole Strauss, Insight Editing Services, thank you for helping prepare our book for release.

Tami at Integrity Formatting, you're always a pleasure to work with. Thank you for making our words look pretty. You're the best!

Brower Literary Management, specifically, Kimberly Brower and Jess Dallow, no matter how ridiculous our questions, you ladies are quick to respond and are always efficient. We are honored to be part of the Brower family.

To our families. Thank you for putting up with our long nights, takeout dinners and all the craziness that ensued while we wrote Scoring Mr. Romeo. Without your love and support, we wouldn't have been able to write about the most romantic book boyfriend for others to fall in love with.

A & J
xo

About A.M. Madden & Joanne Schwehm

A.M. Madden

A.M. MADDEN is a USA Today bestselling author, as well as 2016 eLit Gold Medalist for Best Romance Ebook, and 2016 Ippy Award Silver Medalist for Best Romance Ebook.

A.M. is a wife, a mother, an avid reader of romance novels, and now an author.

"It's all about the HEA."

A.M. Madden is the author of the popular Back-Up Series, as well as several other contemporary romances. She is also a published author with Loveswept/Random House.

Her debut novel was Back-up, the first in The Back-Up Series. In Back-Up, A.M.'s main character Jack Lair caused readers to swoon. They call themselves #LairLovers, and have been faithful supporters to Jack, as well to the rest of his band, Devil's Lair.

A.M. truly believes that true love knows no bounds. In her books, she aspires to create fun, sexy, realistic romances that will stay with you after the last page has been turned. She strives to create characters that the reader can relate to and feel as if they know personally.

A self-proclaimed hopeless romantic, she loves getting lost in a good book. She also uses every free moment of her time writing, while spending quality time with her three handsome men. A.M. is a Gemini and an Italian Jersey girl, but despite her Zodiac sign, nationality, or home state, she is very easy going. She loves the beach, loves to laugh, and loves the idea of love.

A.M. Madden, Independent Romance Author.

Sign up for A.M. Madden's newsletter at www.ammadden.com to get up to date information on new releases, cover reveals, and exclusive excerpts.

Contact A.M.

Website www.ammadden.com

Facebook www.facebook.com/pages/AM-Madden-Author/584346794950765

Twitter @ammadden1

Instagram @ammadden1

Goodreads
www.goodreads.com/author/show/7203641.A_M_Madden

Email am.madden@aol.com

A.M.'s Mad Reader Group
www.facebook.com/groups/893157480742443/

Joanne Schwehm

JOANNE SCHWEHM is a mother and wife and loves spending time with her family. She's an avid sports watcher and enjoys the occasional round of golf.

Joanne loves to write and read romance. She believes everyone should have romance in their lives and hopes her books bring joy and happiness to readers who enjoy modern day fairy tales and breathless moments.

She is an independent romance author and has written

several contemporary romance novels, including The Prescott Series, Ryker, A Heart's Forgiveness, The Critic and The Chance series which she has recently sold the screenplay right to and will be adapted into a movie.

Joanne looks forward to sharing more love stories in her future novels.

Contact Joanne

Website: www.joanneschwehmbooks.com

Facebook: www.facebook.com/joanneschwehm

FB Group Page:
www.facebook.com/groups/joanneschwehmsreaders/

Twitter: www.twitter.com/JSchwehmBooks

Pinterest: www.pinterest.com/nyy2fan/

Instagram: www.instagram.com/jschwehmbooks/

Spotify: www.open.spotify.com/user/1293937868

YouTube:
www.youtube.com/user/JoanneSchwehmBooks

Goodreads Reading Group:
www.goodreads.com/group/show/156533-joanne-schwehm-s-romantic-reading-friends

Newsletter: www.eepurl.com/cgUvSf

To the Reader

Thank you so much for purchasing and reading this ebook. Please support all Indie authors and leave a review at point of purchase as well as your favorite review forum. Indie authors depend on reviews and book recommendations to help potential readers decide to take the time to read their story. We would greatly appreciate it.

xoxo,

A.M. Madden & Joanne Schwehm

Join the MadJo Romance Reader group on Facebook.
www.ow.ly/ZE0W30cR5if